EXIT
WOUNDS

ALSO AVAILABLE FROM TITAN BOOKS

New Fears

New Fears 2

Phantoms: Haunting Tales from the Masters of the Genre

Dark Cities: All-New Masterpieces of Urban Terror

Dead Letters: An Anthology of the Undelivered,
the Missing, the Returned…

Wastelands: Stories of the Apocalypse

Wastelands 2: More Stories of the Apocalypse

Associates of Sherlock Holmes

Further Associates of Sherlock Holmes

NINETEEN TALES OF MYSTERY
FROM THE MODERN MASTERS OF CRIME

EXIT
WOUNDS

EDITED BY PAUL B. KANE & MARIE O'REGAN

TITAN BOOKS

Exit Wounds
Print edition ISBN: 9781785659188
E-book edition ISBN: 9781785659195

Published by Titan Books
A division of Titan Publishing Group Ltd
144 Southwark Street, London SE1 0UP

First edition: May 2019
2 4 6 8 10 9 7 5 3 1

TABLE OF CONTENTS

INTRODUCTION
By Paul B. Kane & Marie O'Regan

We have both been fans of the crime genre for as far back as we can remember.

Our tastes have always been wide-ranging, as broad as the genre itself. From the mysteries of Agatha Christie to Colin Dexter's Morse, from the hard-boiled detective stories of Raymond Chandler to the serial killer tales of Thomas Harris and Jeff Lindsay – over the years we've lapped them all up. Needless to say, they've also influenced our own work, from novels like *The Gemini Factor* to collections such as *Nailbiters* and *In Times of Want* …

And over the course of our careers in fiction, we've also been fortunate enough to meet a lot of our crime-writing heroes, whether it's at conventions – some of which we've even run ourselves – or online, either through social media or just on email. This got us thinking, over a drink in a pub (drinking and thinking, just like all the best detectives), what if we were to try and put together an anthology of stories by some of our favourite crime writers, something we would love to read ourselves? After all, we've racked up a fair amount of experience between us compiling anthologies such as *Hellbound Hearts*, *A Carnivàle of*

Horror, *Phantoms* and *Beyond Rue Morgue* (also by Titan and of interest to crime fans because it gathers together new stories featuring Poe's detective Dupin).

But what should the focus be this time? As already mentioned, there's such a wide scope to crime fiction; from psychological to procedural, from the armchair detective to hit-men and assassins, the genre takes them all in. There's one thing you tend to find in a crime story, however, and that's an exit of some kind. Sometimes it's a death, an event that kicks everything off … or even ends it. Or it could be a case of someone going missing, leaving a family not knowing what happened. Or simply somebody skipping out on a marriage, or a deal, or even a country. Or it might be that a character has reached the point of no return and sees no option but to end it all themselves.

And, of course, an inevitable consequence of that exit or absence – whether it comes at the end or the beginning of a tale – is likely to be a wound of some sort. It doesn't have to be physical, it can be emotional (sometimes those kinds of wounds are even worse). Put both of these ideas together and you have … *Exit Wounds*, the book you are holding in your hands and which we're incredibly proud of.

Inside these pages you'll find many varied tales of both exits and wounds, the topics left as wide open as possible for authors to deliver their very best work. And do we have some treats in store for you! From how the main character in Jeffery Deaver's "The Bully" deals with the titular threat, to an overbearing mother in Fiona Cummins' "Dead Weight"; from a certain famous painting in John Connolly's "On the Anatomization of an Unknown Man (1637) by Frans Mier" to a journalist's hunt for a story in Sarah Hilary's "The Pitcher" and the depravities of love in Martyn Waites' "Disciplined".

Dennis Lehane, meanwhile, offers a cautionary tale about modern life in "The Consumers", Alex Gray's haunting "Voices Through the Wall" will give you pause for thought, as will Christopher Fowler's affecting "Lebensraum", and Lee Child's jumping-off point is the sale of a house in "Wet With Rain". We present Dean Koontz's first ever published story here in the form of the shocking "Kittens", mix mythology and crime in A.K. Benedict's "Take My Hand", and serve up a slice of good ol'-fashioned Texas noir in Joe R. Lansdale's "Booty and the Beast".

There's a double helping of crime favourite Mark Billingham in the form of "Like a Glass Jaw" and "Dancing Towards the Blade", plus a hard-hitting novelette from Paul Finch, "The New Lad", and a subtly chilling look at suburban life in Louise Jensen's "The Recipe". All this and appearances from Val McDermid's beloved characters Tony Hill and Carol Jordan in "Happy Holidays", bounty hunter Lori Anderson (her first adventure, actually) in Steph Broadribb's "Fool You Twice", and Scottish detective Inspector McLean in James Oswald's "Dressed to Kill". All in all, a line-up that should please fans of crime in all its forms.

But now, it's time for you to read; to be wounded by some real professionals.

And for us, the editors, to exit …

Paul B. Kane & Marie O'Regan
Derbyshire, 2018

THE
BULLY

JEFFERY DEAVER

He's here.

Hell.

I'm in the back of the Eagle Tavern, which at six thirty isn't yet highly populated, and what customers there are aren't three sheets to the wind. Mostly now it's an after-work crowd and these imbibers will be driving on home after only a wine or beer or two. Later, the place will be bustling and Ubers and cabs and designateds will get the seriously impaired home for bed tuckee-in. That's the kind of neighborhood this is.

I've been watching some of the action, just curious, but the minute I saw him, all my other thoughts vanished.

He's getting a drink and talking to Sharee the bartender, a sweet African American girl not much over the legal drinking age. My impression is he wants to reach out his meaty paw and close his fingers around her arm or shoulder – her butt being inaccessible from where he stands. But as tough as he is, it seems she's a notch tougher, being a bartender, and she's not having any of his bullshit. He wears a shabby navy sport coat and tan slacks with explosive wrinkles radiating out from the crotch. His gray shirt clings tightly to a barrel chest.

For a moment – since he's focused on Sharee – I think maybe I've got it wrong. He works around the corner, so maybe it's just a coincidence he's here.

But then his round head, covered with a shaggy blond pelt, turns slowly toward me and tips that creepy smile my way. He's not surprised in the least to see me. It means that, oh yeah, he knew I was in the Eagle. Maybe he got off work and happened to see Larry and me stop by for a fast one. Or, also possible and more troubling, he followed me here.

My jaw tightens and heat swells around my face, which often happens whenever I see him. This is so unfair. I'm a twenty-six-year-old successful web designer, a good brother, a good boyfriend, a genial host at parties I throw for my clients and friends, a donor to NPR and animal rescue outfits. Objectively? I'm too old and too nice to have a bully.

But I've ended up with one. And what a bully he is: Stan Whitcomb, all six foot, three inches and two hundred and fifty pounds of him.

Being of diminished height and having had a horrifically embarrassing parent, I experienced bullying as a kid, plenty of it. I learned young that there're people who become convinced it's their mission to ruin your life for no better reason than that they think you did something they didn't like, or there's something about you – you're fat, you stutter, you're short (!) – that rankles them.

At the shadowy high-top, I sip my Diet Coke and debate next steps. I look around for Larry and spot him in the back room, by the digital jukebox. He's struck up a conversation with a slim blonde in a cowgirl getup. I spend a fair amount of time with Larry – we met because of the Ambrose Avenue tornado. He was the insurance investigator who assessed the aftermath of the contest between a hundred-year-old oak tree and my garage (two months after I'd moved in, *two!*). And we started to hang out some after the claim was settled.

Larry's trim, with dark hair and a great tan, since he's outdoors most of the day. He's not talkative and comes off a bit distant. My theory is it's because he's always sizing people up, a habit developed because there're some who don't think ripping off insurance companies is a crime; somehow their deep pockets make fake claims all right. So he comes off as standoffish and shy – though for some reason I tend to think of him as "bashful." I'm not sure there's a difference between those two, but the latter word seems to fit better.

This makes Larry's search for a girlfriend an uphill battle. Witness now: I can see he's struggling to make conversation with the cowgirl. She's none too receptive. He's trying hard, grinning – not a natural expression for Larry – and probably telling jokes she doesn't want to hear, and that he can't tell well. Also, it's possible there's another thought in the back of her head: the recent unsolved murders, women about her age in Auburn Hills, the town next to Mammoth Falls. The killer still being at large has put a crimp in the county dating scene. When I met Sarah and asked her out, she said sure but added – subtly – that, since I was new to town, she'd gladly be in charge of the itinerary. I realized later she set it up so that we were never alone that first night out. I called her on it later and she stammered for a moment, then broke into a blushing grin and admitted the truth. It's been a private joke between us ever since.

Finally Larry's cowgirl gives him one of those nice-talking-with-you-even-though-I-don't-mean-it smiles. She feeds her own dollar into the jukebox, punches some numbers and walks back to her friends. Larry looks after her. His face isn't defeated. Just blank. I feel bad for him but this is good news for me. Now that the bully, Whitcomb, has showed up, I want to get the hell out of here. If Larry had hooked up with Blondie, it would've meant staying for a while.

Now, at last, out of the corner of my eye I see Whitcomb push away from the bar and I know where he's headed. Just then Larry too starts my way but, fast, I pull my phone from my pocket and glance at the screen, pretending I've gotten a call – you can't hear ringtones because the cowgirl picked a loud Bruno Mars song. It's not exactly being honest with Larry but I haven't told him about the bully and want to keep it that way.

I hold up a wait-a-minute finger and lift the unit to my ear. Larry nods and moves to the pool table, watching a couple of ladies play. They nod in response to his greeting but then strike identical expressions: We're ignoring you; why try?

Then the low voice rattles in my ear. "You're not making a call."

Whitcomb.

"Because, Little Hank, it's your locked home screen. Anybody can see that. You're faking."

The "Little" is an obvious insult. The "Hank" part is because when we met the first time I said I preferred "Henry." And, of course, he's been calling me Hank ever since.

I sigh.

"That's kinda pathetic, wouldn'tchya say? That crap with the phone. Hopin' to avoid me. Like I'll think, 'Oh, the big man's talking to some phone sex whore, so Stan won't bother him.'"

I'd be amused that he's misinterpreted the ploy if I wasn't so upset.

"I just … I was going to make a call."

"Really? *Hm*."

"What do you want, Stan?"

"I like that we're on a first-name basis, Hank." He sips more of his liquor. "Oh, there's nothing I want. Just came by to say hi. Who's your girlfriend?"

For an instant I think he means Sarah, but then he adds, "That you sashayed in here with."

Larry.

"Nobody. A friend. Come on, I don't want any trouble."

"Trouble? Trouble? You saying I'm trouble, Hank?"

Stan is a foot taller than I am. For some reason that damn grin makes him seem taller.

"I'm just having a drink here. Minding my own business is all." I look away. There are some people glancing toward us now. Those watching mano-a-mano shit like this are like sharks noting blood.

"What're you drinking?" He picks the glass up and sniffs. He laughs and sets it onto the high-top. The implication is that I'm not man enough for real liquor. Which he doesn't bother to say out loud.

Of course, fighting isn't an option. I'm not in bad shape. I bike everywhere – I ride fifty, a hundred miles on the weekends – and work out on the machines at a nearby health club. But I can easily imagine what would happen if I took a swing. Disaster. Still, the scene calls for me to push back in *some* way. "Why don't you crawl back under your rock?"

He roars with a laugh. But then, in a clock click, his eyes narrow, just like I knew they would. He leans close and I back up, as far as I can. He rages, "Listen, prick, you're mine. You know you are." Whitcomb doesn't touch me. He knows he can't – I've complained to the Sheriff's Department about him and they've issued a warning. But that doesn't mean he couldn't snap and pound me to a pulp, taking the consequences later. He's not normal. There's something wrong in his mind.

I smell his sweat and garlic and whiskey, and it makes me want to puke. I almost think I will, and wonder what he'll do to me if I mess up his boots. Naturally, he wears boots. With pointy toes. They look like weapons.

"Hey," a voice mutters. "Leave the guy alone. He wasn't doing anything to you." Here's a stocky, broad-shouldered man, a construction worker or truck driver, in a plaid shirt and jeans. Big, bearded. He was on his way to the john and I guess he just didn't like the looks of what was happening. In the testosterone dimension, whatever I'd done to Stan didn't justify an uneven fight like this.

I give him a look: No, don't do it, buddy.

In a half a second Whitcomb spins around and is right in the guy's face. "You're talking to me why?" And what's really chilling is the calm tone. It would be less scary if he was shouting.

Neither of them moves for a brief moment, then the guy says, "I'm just saying."

Whitcomb does not respond but I can sense his whole body tense. Vibrating, like a machine at high rpms. The worker probably outweighs Stan by twenty-five pounds but I know in my heart Stan would put him down, TKO, if not a real knockout, in minutes.

The worker walks on, not bothering to try to save face. Sometimes you just give up.

Whitcomb turns back, and, like I expected, he's looking at me as if the encounter was my fault.

"Stan, look—"

"Oh, I'll be looking. I'll be looking for *you*, Little Hank. It's my new hobby."

He turns and strides toward the door, tossing a crumpled bill on the bar before stepping through outside into the cool April evening.

With a shaking hand I finish my soda.

I gesture to Larry, who's missed the whole thing, it seems. I nod toward the door. He says a word of goodbye, I assume, to the two girls at the pool table. They ignore him even more than a moment ago, if there are degrees of ignoring.

We leave the Eagle and walk into the parking lot. The asphalt is still speckled with sand from last winter's muscular snows and glass from the occasional break-in. Our footsteps are gritty and harsh. I look around for Whitcomb. No, he's gone. Then I glance toward Larry, to try again to catch a clue as to whether or not he noted the bully. But I think not; it looks like he's into his own thoughts. He can be moody. I wonder sometimes if he's this way because all day long he investigates accidents – houses burning, people dying in car crashes, and, oh, yeah, garages squashed during tornadoes. Though it's also possible he's always been moody and he went into claims adjustment so he can spend his working hours outside, away from co-workers. Nature/nurture.

We're different, Larry and me, but his company is easy. We go out for dinner a couple times a week, watch games – baseball more than football, soccer some. We've double-dated, though he's never brought the same girl twice; they're always pretty and quiet and strike me as insecure. We both like working for ourselves. And we're both later-in-life orphans. His parents had health problems, unrelated, but they passed away around the same time. Mine? One I lost to drinking. The other to being with a drunk – a missed centerline and an oncoming tractor trailer.

Larry's been a good guy to know. He doesn't hesitate to do you solids. I'll call him up and ask to borrow his car or to look for a dropped Fitbit near a bike trail when I'm stuck on Skype. And I pick up his mail and feed his goldfish when he's out of town on a claim investigation; I'm his designated driver when he decides to have more than one or two.

We climb into our respective vehicles and caravan to the Heron Inn, one of the fancier places in town. Sarah's a part-time hostess here. She's pretty in a librarian sort of way. I mean, a librarian from old-time movies, black-and-white ones like my father used to watch hour after hour after hour, Mom being upstairs. She dresses conservative – high collars and longer skirts – and her hair is often held in place with pins. Glass, though they're a rather unlibrarian red or blue. She's tall – three inches over me – and voluptuous, and her hours at the gym are evident in her sculpted arms, thighs and tummy.

Larry and I park and walk inside and see Sarah at the hostess podium. Her eyes light up, and I'm sure mine do too.

"Hey, honey," she says.

I wink – I'm a winking kind of guy – and kiss her on the cheek. Larry shakes her hand. It's a funny, broad gesture, forearm pumping up and down, as if they've just concluded a business deal. His awkwardness rises once more, as he scans her long black skirt, white blouse and pearl necklace, then looks away.

Bashful …

Sarah Preston is blonde, slim and twenty-nine. Her passion is painting, sticking mostly to large-format acrylic abstracts. We met at a gallery in a redeveloped part of Mammoth Falls – the old warehouse district, which is less gentrified than artsy-fied (my word). I'm no connoisseur but I enjoy the creative arts and it's fun to go to the galleries on Saturdays or Sundays and see what I can see. She and several other artists were having a show at the Fromer Gallery, one of my favorites, and I noticed her standing by herself, trying not to be embarrassed that nobody was looking at her work. I liked what I saw – the paintings and the painter. I complimented her work, saying that several reminded me of Willem de Kooning's, which they did. That delighted her. I stayed until the show was over and the gallery was closing. I said to myself, *go for it*, and asked her out. The guess-he's-not-a-killer date the next night was a lot of fun. We've seen each other a couple of times a week since then.

She seats a couple, and Larry and I wander into the chrome and mahogany bar and I have another Diet Coke. He has a vodka and tonic. It's a slow night and Sarah joins us for a bit. Larry buys her a sparkling water. She thinks it's charming. She calls him gallant, and he gives a faint laugh as this seems to put him at ease. He tells her about a video game he's been playing, one of the online ones. I'm a geek by profession but I'm not into games, especially the first-person shooters that Larry likes. Sarah, I can tell, has no clue what he's talking about but she's polite and nods. I wonder if Larry talks about gaming when he tries to pick a girl up. I should tell him that's probably not a great idea, unless, of course, you're at Comicon and the girl you're hitting on has purple anime hair and is wearing a Sailor Moon outfit.

Then Larry blurts, "Oh, that painting of yours? *Old Woman at the Harvest?*"

After I told him about her website, he would've looked her up. It sounds like he's been waiting to drop into the conversation something he learned.

"You know it?" she asks, surprised.

"Yeah," he says, gazing down at the bar. "I liked it. And I liked that sculpture too. *Raven on the Beach.*"

"'Shore,'" she corrects.

He blushes and says, "Right. 'Shore.'"

"Well, thank you, Larry." She taps her glass against his. She tells him that working with clay doesn't come naturally to her but she enjoyed the experiment. "It was a lark."

Larry doesn't get the pun – the bird thing – and Sarah nips the laugh fast, so he doesn't feel stupid. I struggle not to smile either.

At eight, Sarah goes off shift and the three of us walk to the parking lot. I, of course, automatically scan the surroundings. Not that I expected Stan Whitcomb to follow me here, but apparently I can't make assumptions like that anymore.

I'll be looking for you, Little Hank. It's my new hobby …

Larry says goodnight and starts to shake Sarah's hand but

she pulls him in for a kiss on the cheek, which surprises him. I think he might've gasped. He drives off and Sarah gets in my SUV – she carpooled to work, knowing we'd see each other tonight. And we head over to a new seafood place on Grand. It's called Squids. Not the best name in the world. Not the best food either. They overcook the lobster and undercook the asparagus. But it doesn't matter; we have fun talking and, since I'm driving, she has two big glasses of Chardonnay, which she loves.

I spend the night at her house and when I awake in the morning, I shower and dress quietly, leaving her in bed asleep, because in her case neither profession – art or food service – are pre-noon endeavors.

Unlike Sarah, I'm most productive in the mornings, and today I have to put the filigree, I call it, on two websites. They're for clients who are my favorite kind: they have absolutely no knowledge of how to write code, so they leave all the technical stuff to me, and they have very, very large budgets.

But that will have to wait.

Because I have another errand.

The County Sheriff's Department.

It's nine when I walk into the functional government buildings – decked-out green-flecked walls, yellowing acoustic tile and scuffed linoleum. The main difference between here and, say, City Hall, is this receptionist – a uniformed officer – sits behind bullet-proof glass.

Lots of crazies in this world.

I get a little heebie-jeebie in the place, uneasy. The times I've been here before I haven't been treated very well, like they didn't believe me or take me seriously. But I control it and wearily explain to the sergeant or whatever her rank might be that I'm here to complain once again about Stan Whitcomb. She wearily jots notes, makes a call and nods to a bench. I sit. On the wall opposite are reward posters, including two seeking information about the young women – the ones stabbed to death in neighboring Auburn Hills. I wonder why the posters are here. It's not like the deputies are going to say, "Goddamn, that's right; I forgot all about those murders." Nor would announcements here, in a dim civil servant corridor, reach a horde of good citizens, alerting them to be on the lookout for suspects.

After a five-minute wait, I end up at the desk of a uniformed minion and complain about the bullying.

"Bullying?"

In my earlier complaints – two of them – I don't think I used that word before.

"Stan Whitcomb's in my face all the time."

"What's 'all the time'?"

"A couple of times a week."

The young deputy – he looks to be about eighteen, though he's probably my age – jots notes. "This was in the Eagle, sir? Had either of you been drinking?"

"He had. I hadn't."

"Did he physically touch you?"

What other way would there be to touch someone?

"No. But he's in my face. I mean, inches away."

"Were you at any time unable to leave the premises?"

I hesitate. "No."

"Has he threatened you?"

"Not ... not explicitly. But there's this tone he has."

"Tone."

The deputy sits back.

I know what he's thinking: that the office deals with real bullies: domestic abusers, child beaters, cops who're racist and shoot unarmed civilians, kids who intimidate classmates into attempting suicide.

Somebody being "in your face" doesn't exactly rise to that level of offense.

"Look, Officer ... Deputy. This shouldn't be happening to me. I haven't done anything. I'm not guilty of anything. He's got it into his head that I'm the devil incarnate. He's making my life miserable." My voice has risen – in pitch and volume.

"OK. I'll give my supervisor this information."

His clipped delivery tells me that the conversation is over.

"Thanks for your time." I don't try too hard to control the sarcasm, but he gives no indication that he notices. Maybe he doesn't get it, maybe he's just numb to irritated citizens.

Well, I've done all I can do. I head home to get the projects finished. After, I'll hit the bike trail. I was planning on twenty miles. But as I drive past the Eagle Tavern I get mad again and I decide I'll go for fifty.

Two days later, early Sunday morning, I'm sitting in my dimly lit, carefully ordered office. I haven't seen Stan Whitcomb since the Eagle and I'm absently wondering if my complaint had some effect.

Third time's the charm, which my father used to say all the time.

I hear the double chime from upstairs and I walk to the first floor. I open the door to find two somber people in suits – a man and a woman, both in their forties. The man is holding out an ID card. County Sheriff. Detective Terrence Stone. He's slim and tall. He identifies himself by name. The woman is a detective too. Emily Fillmore. She has dry, blonde hair and has applied thick make-up over bumpy skin.

"Henry Larson?"

"Yes?" I'm frowning. "What's this about?"

"Do you know a Sarah Preston?"

"I— Is she all right?"

"You do know her?"

My eyes widen. "What's going on?"

"Do you, sir?" Detective Stone persists, but gently.

"We've been dating."

I have to repeat this so they can hear. I swallow hard.

"Mr Larson," Detective Fillmore says, her voice a bit stiffer than his. "I'm sorry to have to tell you this but Ms Preston's been killed."

I don't say anything for a moment. Then: "No, there's been a mistake. I saw her yesterday. We had lunch before her shift at work … I— No!"

Detective Stone says, "It happened last night."

I look down. "But, no. I spoke to her, I don't know … Seven thirty. After she got off work."

"Yes, we saw your call on her phone – this happened about nine thirty," Detective Fillmore explains.

"*This* happened? *This? What?*"

But before they can answer I'm spiraling to the floor, both of the detectives lunging, breaking the fall before my head cracks on the tile.

They get me more or less vertical and walk me to my living-room couch.

"No, no, no." I lower my head into my hands and the tears flow. Fillmore has tissues in her purse and she unwraps the pack and plucks one from it. I take it and wipe my eyes and nose. "What happened?" I whisper. "Was it a robbery? Was she—"

They look at each other. Detective Stone asks, "Do you know a Lawrence Keddle?"

"Larry? He's a friend. Sure. What— What is this?"

"Did he know Ms Preston as well?" From Detective Fillmore.

"Yes. They met through me."

"Did either of them say anything to you about him going over to her house last night?"

"Larry? To Sarah's? No."

"Would he have known what time she'd be home?"

"Not really …" But then I tell them that he knew where she worked and could've found out her schedule. Now, my voice grows harsh. "Tell me what this is all about."

Detective Stone says, "It appears that Mr Keddle went to see Ms Preston last night. She let him in. When she did he stabbed her but—"

"*What?*"

"Ms Preston fought back and got the knife away. She stabbed him several times and called 911 but, unfortunately, she expired before help got there. Mr Keddle died too."

"Oh, Jesus, no." I wipe at the tears.

Fillmore says, "Mr Larson, a crime scene unit went to Mr Keddle's house. In his basement we found evidence linking him to the Auburn Hills murders. The two women who were stabbed to death. Some articles of clothing … Some other things too." This is delivered with a softer, more reverent tone.

Meaning, I suppose, the body parts removed from the victims after they died.

"We had a DNA sample of the likely killer from the second murder but there was no match in the database. Our lab tested Mr Keddle's DNA and it was his."

I close my eyes briefly, breathing hard.

"Sir, can I get you some water?" Fillmore asks.

I hold up a hand.

"Do you have family in the area?" she continues.

I don't respond. I simply stare at the floor, a stain in the shape of an hourglass on the old carpet in the entryway. I'd never noticed it before.

"Sir?" Detective Stone asks.

I blink and look up. "Family? I— My brother's in Holcomb."

"I think it'd be a good idea if he came over. Or you stayed with him. Are you OK to drive?"

"Yes, sure," I whisper. "Oh, Sarah's parents?" I say this with some hysteria in my voice. "They're in Freeport."

"There're two detectives speaking to them now."

I'm nodding. More tears, more tissues.

"I'll call them. I should call them."

"We'll want to interview you some more about Mr Keddle. Just a few questions."

"Sure, yes." In a faint voice I say, "He was always quiet. I didn't think anything of it. A little distant. But— Jesus." My voice catches. "My fault."

"What's that, sir?" Detective Stone asks.

"This is my fault! He met her through me."

"You can't play the blame game," Detective Fillmore says. "The first thing we learn in this business."

I don't respond.

They rise. Detective Stone says, "Give your brother a call, Mr Larson."

"I will, yes. I'll do it now."

The following Wednesday I'm in the sheriff's office once more.

No minions this time. I'm speaking to the sheriff himself. He's a beefy guy, whose round belly swells drummingly over his taxed belt. He wears a brown uniform just like any other deputy, though he has more gingerbread on his chest and sleeve.

His name is Farrell, according to the name badge, and there's an S in front of that, which I suppose stands for his first name, not "Sheriff." He's crew cut and tanned, and he'll need a new wedding ring soon, if he keeps gaining weight. His wedding picture, on the desk, suggests the expansion has been recent and fast.

"First, Mr Larson, I'm so sorry for your loss. I understand Ms Preston was your girlfriend."

I nod, and press a tissue into my red eyes.

"Now, this is, as you can imagine, a bit awkward. I wanted to tell you what our assessment of the situation is."

Assessment.

Situation.

Another nod.

"I know that a few weeks ago you were, obviously, considered a person of interest in the Auburn Hills killings. Suzanne Humboldt and Karen Miller."

"OK." Now my eyes, which are indeed red, are cold and boring directly into his.

"We've been through this before, explained it to you, but I have to tell you again that at first we did have some reason to look into your whereabouts the nights they were killed. That's why we asked you in for those interviews."

Heebie-jeebie …

There was indeed some justification for what they'd done. It turned out that I used my ATM card about a mile from where the first victim was abducted. Every man who'd used a cash machine or credit or debit card within that mile also ended up on the lead investigator's watch list for suspects. The list was huge but he interviewed every single one of them, and personally reviewed CCTVs in and around where Suzanne Humboldt lived and the bars and restaurants she hung out in. My face was identified in one of the bars.

Naturally, the authorities would do whatever they could to stop a serial killer.

They found no other evidence and took me off the list – without an apology.

The sheriff grimaces. "After Ms Preston's death, we reviewed the earlier CCTV footage again. Yes, you were in one tape. But so was Lawrence Keddle."

"He was a friend. We hung out a couple times a week."

"And we saw him in other footage, too, in places where Suzanne and Karen were. He was apparently checking them out as targets. And we've gone back and looked at things more closely. We've found footage from the gas station on the corner near Suzanne's house two days before she was killed. And we found Parks Department footage near the grove where Ms Miller was killed. He was looking for something he must've dropped as he fled the scene the night of her murder." His lips tighten, then he adds, "And we got video from an ATM near the Heron Inn. He parked there one night this past week, near where he could see Ms Preston leave."

I look down for a moment and dab tears.

"So, sir, we dropped the ball on this one." The sheriff's office phone rings and he answers, then listens. "OK. Send him in."

The door opens and the lead investigator in the Auburn Hills killings walks in.

Detective Stan Whitcomb.

The big man is grim-faced. He walks up to me and I stand. I glare and he, clearing his throat, looks away. "Sir, I've heard what happened. I want to apologize. I was wrong to dog you the way I did. You were cleared as a person of interest but I ignored that." He inhaled deeply. "See, sometimes I get an idea and it won't let go of me. I can't see the forests in the trees."

The expression's wrong but I don't say anything.

"It's an instinct. I think somebody's guilty, I can't get that thought out of my mind."

"But sometimes the people you think are guilty aren't."

"That is correct." He glances toward the sheriff, looking on coolly, and then says to me, "You're not the first person this's happened to. I've agreed to talk to somebody about it. How I behave, I mean. A counselor the Sheriff's Office works with. I have an appointment. I should've done it sooner. You complained to the department, and they talked to me a couple of times."

Three.

"But that only made me madder. And I wanted to get you, make your life miserable."

I snap, "If you hadn't been so focused on me, you might've kept looking for the real killer and stopped Larry before he killed Sarah."

He swallows. "That is a likelihood, Mr Larson."

No longer "Little Hank."

He continues, "I'll wear this one for a long time."

I look from Whitcomb to the sheriff. "You know, I talked to a lawyer about this. He tells me I could have a case."

The other two return my gaze with emotionless expressions but I'm sure if you dug down, you'd find two very nervous law enforcers.

"I might have gone forward with that, too. But, you know, that apology? That'll be enough for me. I appreciate it."

My bully digests this with surprise. He offers his hand. It won't be a bone crusher, I know instinctively, and it isn't. His huge paw encircles mine gently and we shake.

* * *

Back home, I pull my mountain bike from the rack in the garage, don my helmet and pedal onto the quiet street where I live. Soon I'm on the bike path that runs along the Albemarle Valley river. The afternoon is overcast and cool, and I have the path to myself.

I'm on autopilot, as I often am when riding; it's at times like this that I do my best thinking.

When I have a web design assignment, I spend days planning, planning, planning. This is critical; one can never spend too much time getting organized before the work begins. Mistakes are unacceptable to me.

When at last I'm comfortable that every eventuality has been taken into account, I execute the plan. And then I assess. I call that the post-completion phase, which is not a very artful term, since if a project is complete, nothing should come after it, right? But I've found that my clients like that portion of the PowerPoint; they seem to think I'm giving them special added service.

And now, too, it's time to assess how my present project has gone.

This post-completion analysis will have to be particularly diligent.

Since my life hangs in the balance; this state has the death penalty.

First, I think about Stan Whitcomb's face when he offered his apology in the sheriff's office. Was it the face of a man who truly believed his heart-set belief was wrong?

I think so.

Which is quite a coup for me, since he was, of course, one

hundred percent correct about me and the murder of Suzie and, later, Karen.

A fluke of circumstance – that ATM glitch – put me on the list of persons of interest, and at my first interview Whitcomb decided I was guilty. An investigation didn't turn up anything else and the other detectives running the case moved on.

But not Whitcomb.

I was his boy.

I found him intolerable, intimidating. But one man's bully is another man's bulldog, and his persistence in investigating me, pushing me, hoping to make me crack or make a blunder, was understandable … even laudable to an observer.

And he might very well have succeeded.

But now, replaying the apology, I do believe he's convinced I'm innocent.

So, post-completion item one: the bully? Check.

But he's not the only one running the case, of course. Should I be concerned about the other investigators?

I certainly have been careful. I don't satisfy my addiction willy-nilly, an expression of my beloved father's. Murder, of course, is a task, like anything else, and requires a disciplined approach – if you want to get away. Judging by the stupidity of some murderers, I sometimes feel that I'm in the minority. Maybe there are those who don't care about ending up in prison for the rest of their lives. Not me. With my stature, I don't think I'd be treated very well. Besides, I enjoy my job; web design is quite creative and rewarding. I really do enjoy art galleries, like the one where I met Sarah.

And my bicycles. Oh, I live for riding.

As I pump my way up a seven-degree hill, I'm wondering if I have in fact tricked them all.

Nowadays, you simply *have* to have the forensic stuff down cold. Goes without saying. Gloves, booties, caps (and even then, always mousse your hair up nice and sticky – *all* your hair, *everywhere*, so not a single strand finds its way to the crime scene). Don't park near CCTVs or walk past them. Change clothes often, use disguises. And pitch every garment and shoe in dumpsters bound for landfills. Burning's efficient but, my, how smoke where smoke should not be makes people curious.

Then bleach, bleach, and more bleach.

Car washes are your friend.

But if you own a TV you know how to do all that. Anybody who gets nailed on forensics isn't worthy of being a killer.

You need to do more. Like moving from town to town often. After three victims in Ridgefield, Connecticut, I went to Toledo. Only one victim there but still I thought it best to pack up and head to lovely Mammoth Falls.

And you must always have a Larry.

That is, a sacrificial lamb.

When I'm scoping out the victims, I never go alone. I always bring along somebody I've befriended – to be my fall guy. Because there will always be witnesses and CCTVs and random selfies that catch your image, so I make sure that they also capture the buddy. I borrow his car, as I did Larry's, and drive it past security cams near the victim's house – wearing hat and sunglasses – or park it outside places like the Heron Inn, evidence of stalking Sarah.

I lift a hair or something else DNA-rich from the fall guy

and plant it at the murder. Always DNA, never fingerprints, since very few people are in the CODIS database and many, many people have been printed.

It's tedious work, setting up a stooge. But so is writing code in C++. So is composing symphonies. Do it right, or don't do it at all, my father told me.

Here in Mammoth, after the suicidal oak tree incident, when I met Larry, I decided he'd be my insurance. (I smile at the word, since that was, of course, his job. A pun that he probably wouldn't've gotten.)

When I was checking out the particulars of Suzanne, whom I'd decided would be the first victim of the man who became the Auburn Hills Killer, Larry was with me, at the same bar she staggered out of.

I even said to him, "Is that girl OK?" Nodding to the door. And, bless him, he went to look. Some witnesses, a camera or two, I'm sure, saw him do so.

He said, "She's got an Uber."

"Good for her," I offered.

"Nearly tripped getting in."

"Poor thing," I said. But I didn't mean it. That's the answer, by the way. I'm convinced that I was born drunk, thank you, Mom. And while I can easily control any urge to drink alcohol, I cannot control the need to scratch the itch to get even. I was very close to my father and have never gotten over the belief that I'm sure he died with two instantaneous thoughts in his doomed mind: that his wife, behind the wheel of the family sedan, had snuck copious vodka into her Starbucks cup; and that the airbags were going to do zero good against a Peterbilt tractor trailer. A shrink could explain the warm satisfaction I get when I go to work on one of those sad, sad drunk girls, but the fact is that shrinks exist to do one thing: to cure. And a cure is the last thing I want.

So Larry was with me as I checked out Suzie, and he was with me as I checked out Karen, who was even more of a lush than her predecessor. He also was kind enough to do me the favor of looking for that nonexistent Fitbit near where I'd slashed Suzie to twitchy silence, just to get another image of his face: on the Parks Department CCTV.

While I always do this – plan, plan, plan – until now, I've never had to actually rely on a fall guy.

But until now I've never run up against a bully like Stan Whitcomb.

Because of him, the Larry Plan had to go into effect.

Which required one more player. The fall guy has to die and the least suspicious way to arrange that is for him to murder his last victim, who in turn dispatches him.

I picked Sarah Preston for this role. And, being charming and funny and not bad in the bedroom, I must admit, I started seeing her. She was perfect: pretty and sexy – the sort Larry would be drawn to. And in good shape, which proved important to the plot.

The day they were to die, I called Larry and asked him to meet Sarah and me at her house for dinner. He was surprised, but pleased, and muttered that it'd be cool. Later, I left my phone at home and biked, not drove, over to Sarah's – *always* watch that GPS stuff.

Sarah and I were sipping wine and diet soda when the

doorbell rang. She frowned and I said I'd get it. I pulled on the gloves on my way to the door to let Larry in.

Neither of them were expecting the knife work, so they both went down fast. Larry was more horrified than Sarah was, I think. She seemed bewildered, though not for long. I set up the scenario to fit the MO of the other murders. In this case, though, it seemed that Sarah slipped out of the zip tie and fought back, grabbing the knife and slashing Larry's throat.

I used a few precious minutes – the time of death can be calculated very accurately nowadays – to plant some hairs and tissue from the first two murders in Larry's trunk. A bit of dirt from the murder scenes as well.

I eliminated evidence of my presence that night, though not everything (we *were* dating). Then I used Sarah's bloody finger to dial 9-1-1 from her landline and let the receiver fall. I bolted, heading to Larry's house. I had his key – from the goldfish favor – and planted some more souvenirs from the other murders in his basement, as well as an SD camera card of pictures I'd taken clandestinely of Suzie and Karen and Sarah at the hotel. They were reencoded – no metadata from the camera I'd used was present. The police would also find on Larry's computer visits to Sarah's website and those of galleries she'd shown her work at – as I'd suggested he should do.

Then I biked back home to await the call or the visit. I was surprised it took so long for them to show up. When they did I was ready for the performance to begin, complete with props – Tabasco on my fingertips for my eyes. I tried hard not to overact.

Now, speeding along a flat stretch on the bike path, I run through everything once more. Recalling where every bit of evidence was planted or disposed of. Where I was at every moment before, during and after the murders. I see no flags, no glitches. Yes, I think it'll work. There will be a few questions in the minds of the investigators. Always are. But I've learned that the police vastly prefer to go with the most obvious explanation and close the case.

Occam's razor.

Another pun, another smile.

I hit the ten-mile mark and turn my bike around to head for home.

Yes, feeling comforted that I've done all I can. But, in truth, there's a little hollowness I'm feeling.

Thinking of Sarah.

Because now that she's slashed to death the Auburn Hills Killer, I can hardly go on hunting here anymore. That makes me just a little sad. I've developed quite a liking for Mammoth Falls.

Picturesque. Quaint. And home to such wonderful bike trails.

———✳———

DEAD WEIGHT

FIONA CUMMINS

"You're not going to eat that, are you?"

Lula Piper paused, the forkful of cake halfway towards her mouth. She had not heard her mother come in from work and now there would be a Discussion. The taste of bitterness elbowed out the sweet kick of chocolate, but she forced herself to laugh.

"What else do you think I'm going to do with it?"

Her mother's answer was to whisk away her plate and replace it with a selection of chopped carrots and cucumber from the fridge.

"A moment on the lips, a lifetime on the hips," her mother said, scraping sponge and buttercream into the food bin. She smoothed her skirt over her own narrow hips. Mrs Piper did not eat. Eating was for the weak.

Lula counted the squares on the red-and-white chequered tablecloth. Sixty-four horizontal, two hundred and six vertical. The folds of her stomach pushed against the kitchen table, her thighs spilling over the sides of the chair. She often counted the squares. It was a way to quell the shame that seemed to rise in her every time she sat down to eat. Breakfast, lunch, dinner. She was fifteen years, five weeks and four days old. Sixteen .thousand meals, give or take. Sixteen thousand cycles of loathing. Even during the birthday parties that marked out so many primary school weekends, her mother would swoop down and police the contents of her paper plate, tipping handfuls of crisps back into bowls, collecting up chocolate biscuits, and the most traitorous offence of all, confiscating party bags. Even ten years on, the injustice still burned inside her.

Mrs Piper sat on the kitchen stool opposite Lula and took a delicate nibble of carrot. "Dress fitting next week," she said, adopting a tone of faux brightness that Lula found unbearable.

Lula did not answer. She did not like Uncle Malcolm. She did not want to travel to Leeds for a wedding. And most of all, she did not want to be a bridesmaid.

"Do you think you've lost some weight, dear?" Lula's mother looked her up and down, frowning.

"I'm not sure."

"Perhaps a pound or two?"

"Well, my skirt does feel a bit looser."

This conversation was as familiar to Lula as breathing. Over the years, it had become a ritual. She murmured something mollifying in the gaps of conversation, her mother would smile hopefully and the dance would continue.

"Keep at it, dear. Peach is not an easy colour to wear. You don't want to look like a stuffed sausage."

Lula excused herself and went upstairs to finish her homework.

On the way to the dressmaker's Lula chose to sit in the back of the car. She ate a packet of crisps and a Kit-Kat during the journey, although Mrs Piper had no idea because she hated driving, knuckles white against the steering wheel, eyes screwed up in concentration.

Lula had learned to silently retrieve a single crisp from its plastic bag and suck it until all the salt had dissolved on her tongue and the potato was wet and claggy. It took her fifteen minutes to eat a packet of cheese and onion in this way, but she didn't mind, because the journey was almost forty minutes. As for the Kit-Kat, she broke it into pieces and held each one in her mouth until the chocolate and wafer had melted.

Mrs Andrews, the dressmaker, was a plump-cheeked and friendly woman, although the pins she held between her lips while tacking up hems gave her the appearance of a metallic-mouthed film villain.

She directed Lula to a changing room. The peach bridesmaid dress was waiting for her on a hanger. It had spaghetti straps and a nipped-in waist with a side zip that finished just below her armpit. Behind the curtain, Lula could hear her mother and Mrs Andrews chatting about the weather.

The girl kicked off her jeans and pulled the dress over her head. A month ago it had slid easily over her breasts and the satin had been smooth against her stomach. Now, the fabric strained and groaned beneath her flesh and the zipper's teeth would not meet.

"How do we look, then?" Mrs Andrews came bustling into the changing room. The "oh" escaped her mouth like air from a deflating balloon. "What happened, dear?"

Lula remembered the empty crisp packets beneath her bed, the chocolate wrappers and biscuit crumbs, and thought it best not to answer that question. She wasn't greedy. It was simply that these kinds of foods seemed to fill the empty space inside her in a way that vegetables could not.

Mrs Andrews was talking to herself. "We'll have to let out the sides and the waist, I think. When's the wedding? Two weeks from now. I can just squeeze it in, but the timing will be tight."

"Everything all right?" Mrs Piper poked her head through the curtains.

"We'll have to let it out. Might cost you a bit more," said Mrs Andrews, less plump-cheeked friendliness and more businesslike. "You'll have to collect it the day before you leave. If it doesn't fit then, there's not much I can do."

"It will fit," said Mrs Piper through pressed-together lips.

The car journey home passed in a tirade of accusation and personal insults. *Lula lacked self-control. She would never find a husband. She was a disgusting pig, an embarrassment.*

Lula, who had heard all of this before, counted the cars that drove past them. Twenty-three red. Fourteen green. Sixty-four black.

It was long past teatime when they walked through the front door. Knowing her mother as she did, Lula was reluctant to ask about food, but her stomach growled in protest. Mrs Piper did not react, however, but poured herself a cup of black coffee. Lula hovered in the kitchen doorway. Her mother stirred in sweetener irritably, her brow furrowing when she looked up and saw her daughter standing there.

"What is it?"

Hesitant. Conciliatory. "I was wondering – um, what's for supper, Mum?"

Her mother banged a saucepan against the hob.

"Vegetable soup."

Lula sat down at the kitchen table. She hated vegetable soup, but there was nothing else on offer, not even bread, and she knew better than to ask. Asking meant *nothing* to eat.

Mrs Piper sipped her coffee and watched as Lula wolfed down the anaemic liquid and its unidentifiable lumps, which barely filled her up. Mother and daughter did not speak, and the silence stretched between them, widening the cracks.

When Lula had cleaned her teeth and changed into her pyjamas, she returned to the kitchen to kiss her mother goodnight. Padlocks had appeared on the cupboard doors.

She pressed her lips to Mrs Piper's dry cheek.

"'Night, Mother. I'll try harder tomorrow, I promise."

It was gone three a.m. when the pain in Lula's stomach woke her. Her insides were roiling around and she convinced herself she was suffering from appendicitis. She rushed to the toilet, the seat cool against the backs of her thighs, sweat stippling her forehead.

The relief was instant but short-lived.

Lula sat there for so long that by the time she crawled back into bed, the edge of the toilet seat had left an imprint on her skin.

Her sleep was fitful, the dawn chorus an unwelcome lullaby. As it was the weekend, there was no need to get up for school.

Around mid morning, she was aware of her mother putting a mug of tea on her bedside table. She sipped it gratefully.

"How are you feeling, dear?"

"A bit better, thanks."

By lunchtime, Lula was back in the bathroom, where she spent most of the afternoon and early evening. By the time the dusk had darkened into night, she felt as hollow inside as a shell.

Lula's illness lasted for more than a week. She missed the auditions for the school play and an important maths test and a trip to the Natural History Museum.

But her mother proved a tender and devoted carer. She kept up a regular supply of drinks and soups.

On the tenth day – three days before they were due to catch the train to Leeds for Uncle Malcolm's wedding – Lula began to feel better. Her mother prepared her some lightly steamed broccoli and a piece of fish. Lula, wan and exhausted, smiled her thanks.

The day before the wedding, Lula stood on the scales. She had lost eleven pounds. At the dressmaker's, her bridesmaid dress was too loose. It swung around her waist and gaped under her arms. Mrs Andrews was dismayed because there was no time to fix it, but Mrs Piper was delighted.

"It's too big for you now," she said proudly.

They parked the car at the train station. Mrs Piper's mobile phone rang. "It's Malcolm," she mouthed. She handed her handbag to Lula. "Go and find a luggage trolley. You'll need a pound."

Lula found the trolleys near a concession stand that sold muffins. Since she had been ill, her appetite had diminished and she looked at them without interest. She rummaged in her mother's purse and pulled out a shiny coin. As she put the purse back, she noticed a small, unfamiliar box at the bottom of the bag. Curious, she turned it over to read the back.

Extra strength. Dependable overnight relief.

Lula opened the box of laxatives. The blister strip was empty except for two tablets. A scribbled piece of paper had been stuffed in the box. *Eight tablets crushed. Add to drinks or food. Keep an eye on dosage.* Her mother's neat handwriting.

Her stomach plunged. She knew exactly what this meant.

Lula dropped the packet back into her mother's handbag, withdrew the purse again and took out the crisp five-pound note she had noticed earlier. At the concession stand, she bought a chocolate muffin and a piece of carrot cake. She was cramming the muffin into her mouth as she pushed the trolley back to the car. Her mother, who was still on the phone, flapped her hand at Lula, but the girl ignored her. Tiny chocolatey crumbs were falling down the front of her T-shirt, but she didn't care. She started on the carrot cake, the icing thick and teeth-stickingly sweet.

"Lula, what are you doing?" Her mother squeaked out her outrage. "Don't spoil it now, darling. You'll get spots and you don't want to put all that weight back on, do you?"

Lula ignored her and refused to speak for the entirety of the train journey.

* * *

At the hotel, Lula managed to avoid her mother. There was a drinks reception and a rehearsal and little bridesmaids and pageboys to play with. Uncle Malcolm and her soon-to-be-aunt Christine had arranged for waiters to circulate with canapés, and Lula took three at a time from each of the trays. She licked her fingers and watched her mother watching her. She drank lemonade and orange juice, and ordered peanuts from the bar. At bedtime, she helped herself to the complimentary biscuits from the tea tray in their twin room, dropped crumbs on her sheets and rolled over in her single bed and faced the wall when her mother tried to talk to her.

In the darkness, she listened as her mother's breathing evened into sleep and the hate she felt surprised her.

The day of the wedding was a glorious spring gift, tied up with sunshine and the smell of freshly cut grass.

The hairdresser swept Lula's hair into a bun, apart from a few loose tendrils that fell around her face. The make-up artist used a soft green to bring out her eyes. The dress swished around her legs, which looked longer than usual because of her heels.

Lula felt beautiful.

Christine, dressed in a vintage lace wedding dress, smiled at her and squeezed her hand. "You look wonderful." The young bridesmaids crowded around her, their small hands plucking at her dress. "You're very pretty," said one of them shyly. Lula sipped the half-glass of prosecco that Christine had poured her, and excitement fizzed in her.

But when Mrs Piper entered the room where they were

getting ready, all fuchsia fascinator and matching suit, she glanced at her daughter and her mouth twisted into a bitter lemon shape.

"Do you know how many calories are in alcohol?" she whispered, taking the glass from Lula's hand. "And I think you might need to loosen your bra. I can see a bulge under the satin. Not very flattering, dear."

Mrs Piper's words pricked the bubble of her joy until it became something flat and tasteless.

Lula balanced a plate on her knee. It was filled with French bread and sausage rolls and crisps. The music was Frank Sinatra and Dean Martin, and she tapped her foot, entranced by the way that Uncle Malcolm looked at Christine as they whirled around the dance floor.

A boy sat down next to her. He was about her own age and he was wearing a shirt and tie, his hair sticking up. He smiled.

"I'm Ted."

"Lula."

"Chrissie's my godmother."

The conversation between them faltered. Ted shifted awkwardly, running a finger along the inside of his collar. Lula stared at her plate, her mind blank.

He leaned into her, a gentle nudge. "That looks good."

She looked up quickly, to check if he was poking fun at her. But he was smiling and it seemed so genuine that she found herself smiling back. She offered the plate to him. "Have a sausage roll."

They ate in silence for a bit, and then Ted said, brushing the pastry off his trousers, "Would you like to dance?"

Lula had never danced with a boy before. Matt Cranleigh had asked her at the school disco but Jemima Norris, with her flicky hair and fake eyelashes, had told everyone it was for a bet because Lula was the fattest girl in the year. She had promised herself she would never fall for that again.

But Ted was gently taking her plate from her and holding out his hand, and she found herself walking onto the dance floor with him.

The lights had dimmed, and he rested his hand in the small of her back, the fingers of his other hand closed around hers, and he was warm, and she was dizzy from the champagne toast, and she thought this might be the most perfect moment of her whole life.

They swayed together, and he leaned towards her, his breath tickling her ear.

"You're so—"

But Lula never got the chance to hear what he was going to say, because her mother was on the dance floor, and she was pulling her away from him, her firm grip pinching the skin on Lula's arm.

"You are making a show of yourself." Her sibilant whisper and narrowed eyes made Lula think of a snake. Mrs Piper sniffed her daughter's breath. "Have you been drinking alcohol again?"

Despite the fact it was not even ten, and there were fireworks and bacon sandwiches due at midnight, Mrs Piper insisted on taking Lula back to their hotel room.

"If you cannot behave, you will be punished."

Lula, head bowed, humiliated, could not bear to look at the boy, standing alone on the dance floor, who had been so kind.

Lula sat in the dark in her pyjamas and watched the fireworks from the bedroom window. Each explosion was like a gunshot.

As soon as she heard her mother's key in the lock, she hid under the covers and pretended to be asleep. The room filled with the smell of wine and bitterness. Her mother was muttering to herself, criticising the food, the bride's dress, the uncomfortable mattress. Lula listened as she changed into a nightie and switched off the bedside lamp. Pins and needles pricked her arm, and eventually, Lula was so uncomfortable she had to move. The bedsprings squeaked.

"Are you awake, dear?"

Lula held her breath. She did not want to speak to her mother ever again. But Mrs Piper had the bit between her teeth and spoke again in the darkness.

"Lula, I know you're awake. What did you think of today? Did you like Christine's dress? Too tight—"

Lula let her breath go, and something loosened inside her. Her mother was still speaking and her voice was like nails against a blackboard. "—and I'm sorry, darling, but peach isn't your colour at all. You looked so washed out. Satin's such a difficult fabric to wear. I hope the photographs don't pick out every lump and bump—"

Lula shut her eyes and tried to drown out her mother, but it was impossible.

"—and I thought it was so nice of that young man to ask you to dance, even though I didn't approve. I expect Christine asked him to ask you because she felt a bit sorry for you sitting all by yourself—"

Lula couldn't bear it, the incessant chatter, the slow chiselling away at her confidence. Hardly aware of what she was doing, she rose from her bed. She wanted her mother to stop talking, to shut up. To allow Lula to enjoy the unfamiliar memory of a boy's hand on her back.

She picked up the pillow. "Shut up, Mother," she said. She placed it across her mother's face, intending nothing more than to silence the cruel words that tumbled from her. Mrs Piper writhed beneath it, trying to break free. Lula leaned forward, fighting to hold her mother still, attempting to quieten her for long enough to stop talking and understand that words were like stones, painful when carelessly tossed about. But still she bucked and shifted, and so Lula pressed herself down into the pillow, and laid across her mother until she stilled and stopped talking.

Blissful silence.

Lula returned to her own bed and slept like a log.

For breakfast, Lula had cereal, eggs, bacon, sausages and beans, and two muffins from the baked goods selection of the buffet. No one frowned at her or told her how much she should or shouldn't eat. Ted was sitting at another table. When she rose to refill her glass with orange juice, he left his own seat and stood behind her. She could feel the heat radiating from his body.

As he walked past her table, he dropped a paper napkin by her plate, his phone number printed into its folds.

When she had finished her breakfast, Lula collected her belongings from the hotel bedroom. Her mother had still not stirred, her hand hanging over the side of the mattress. It was unprecedented that she should stay in bed so late. Lula removed the pillow from her blue lips. Then she shut the door behind her and didn't look back.

An hour later, Ted was waiting for her by the bus stop. The boy gave her a lopsided grin and took her case from her without asking. "Milkshake? Coffee?"

They sat on silver chairs outside a café, their knees touching, and made plans to meet again.

The day was waking up, the Sunday morning sky flat and blue, the road still empty of cars. Lula breathed in deeply, fingered the train ticket in her pocket and smiled up at Ted. An unfamiliar sensation gripped her.

Freedom.

———✳———

LIKE A
GLASS JAW

MARK BILLINGHAM

You can call it "unlucky" if you want. I heard one of the coppers say that when he was talking to one of the doctors. Not that it'll make any difference when it comes to charges or whatever. I mean, it's *unlucky* if you're caught trying to steal a car, but it doesn't mean they won't nick you, does it?

'Course, there's *loads* of doctors around now, but back then, when all of this kicked off, there was just the one …

"You used to box a bit, didn't you?" he said.

"Long time ago," I said.

He'd been banging on about exercise, said it would help to get the old ticker pumping a bit. Get my cholesterol down and shift a bit of weight, which wasn't exactly helping matters, let's be honest.

"Shouldn't be too difficult to get back in the swing of it," he said.

I got Maggie's husband to give me a hand fetching my old gear out of the loft. We scraped the muck off the skipping rope and hung the heavy bag up in the garage. I thought I would be able to ease myself back into it, you know? Stop when it hurt and build up slowly. Trouble was it hurt all the time, and I just got angry that I'd let myself go to pot so badly; that I'd smoked so many fags and put so much booze away down the years.

"There's a class," Maggie said. "One night a week, down

our local leisure centre." Once my eldest gets a bee in her bonnet, that's it for everyone. It was her that had nagged me into going to the doctor's in the first place.

"Class?"

"Just general fitness, you know. Come on, it's only an hour and there's a bit of a drink afterwards."

"Hmmm." I rolled my eyes, and that was it. That's how easily a misunderstanding happens and you get yourself shafted.

See, I thought she was talking about a few lads jumping about, maybe a quick game of five-a-side and a couple of beers afterwards. When I walked out of that changing room in my baggy shorts and an old West Ham shirt, I felt like I'd been majorly stitched up. There was Maggie, beaming at me, and a dozen or so other women, all of them limbering up in front of these little plastic steps.

A sodding *step* class. Jesus H …

And not just women, either. There were a couple of men there to witness the humiliation, which always makes it worse, right? A skinny young bloke in a tight top who I thought was probably gay and a fit-looking sort who I guessed was there to pull something a bit older and desperate. Looking around, trying my hardest to manage a smile, I could see that most of the women were definitely in that category. I swear to God, you wouldn't have looked twice at any of them.

Except for Zoe.

You just get on the thing, then off again; up and down, one foot or both of them, in time to the music. You can get back down the same way you went up, or you can turn and come down on the other side, but basically … you climb on and off a plastic step.

I swear to God, that's it.

Maybe, that first time, I should have just gone straight back in that changing room. Maggie had that look on her face though, and I thought walking out would be even more embarrassing than staying.

So, I decided to do it just the once, and actually, it wasn't as bad as I expected. It was harder than it looked, mind you, make no mistake about *that*. I was knackered after ten minutes, but what with there being so many women in the class, I didn't feel like I had to compete with anyone, you know what I mean?

Ruth, the woman in charge, seemed genuinely pleased when I showed up again the second week and the week after that. She teased me a bit, and I took the mickey because she had one of those microphone things on her ear like that singer with the pointy bra. They were *all* quite nice, to be honest. I'd pretend to flirt a bit with one or two of the women, and even Craig seemed all right, to begin with.

The pair of us ended up next to each other more often than not, on the end of the line, behind Zoe. Him barely out of breath after half an hour; me, blowing like I was about to keel over. The two of us looking one way only, while she moved, easy and sweet, in front of us. One time, he took his eyes off her backside and glanced across at me. The cheeky sod winked, and I felt the blood rising to my neck.

* * *

It was mostly Diet Coke and fizzy water in the pub afterwards, but I wasn't having any of that and Zoe drank beer from the off. She said the rest of them obviously reckoned their bodies were temples or something.

"My body's more of a slaughterhouse these days," I said.

She laughed, low and dirty, and it still amazes me really, to think of it coming out of a mouth like hers. A face like that. It felt fantastic to make her laugh. We shared a big packet of crisps and I asked her why she came. "I mean, it's not like you need to lose weight or anything."

"You're sweet." She leaned her shoulder into mine and took another swig from her bottle. "I'm lazy," she said. "I need to make myself get out and do things. Anyway, it's a laugh, don't you reckon?"

I did reckon, and I told her.

"I work in a stupid office," she said. "The people are all right, I suppose, but I don't want to see them after work or whatever. I think it's good to meet people who aren't anything like you are. People with different lives, you know?"

She had a voice it was easy to listen to. She wasn't posh, but there wasn't really an accent either. Just soft and simple, you know?

"What about you?" she asked.

I told her I was basically there to keep Maggie happy, and get some of the old fitness back. I mentioned that I used to box a bit and she said she could see it. That it was in the way I carried myself.

I had to hide my face in my glass, and I'd all but downed the rest of the pint by the time the blush had gone away.

"Someone needed a drink," she said.

I went up to get us refills, and exchanged nods with Craig, who was standing in the open doorway with a fag on. I was deeply bloody envious and I might well have ponced one if Maggie hadn't been around.

"Enjoying yourself?" he said. He tossed his fag end away and came back inside. He looked across at Zoe, then turned to me. His face said, *Dream on, mate*. It said, *Yeah, she's lovely, but look at* me *and look at* you.

Or he might just have been waiting for me to get him a drink. Oh Christ, who knows?

Things really started to go pear-shaped a few weeks later, when Zoe turned up looking like she did and Craig didn't turn up at all. It was like I suddenly knew all sorts of things at once. I knew they'd got together, that everyone else had probably sussed it a damn sight faster than me, and I knew exactly what had happened to her face.

In class, I stamped on and off that bloody step like I could do it all day. Ruth said how well I was doing and when Zoe smiled at me, encouraging, I had to look away.

Afterwards, she didn't turn towards the pub with the rest of us, and when I saw she was heading for the car park, I went after her. I tried to get a laugh when I caught her up; made out like I was knackered, you know, from chasing after her, but she didn't really go for it. "Not fancy it tonight, then?" I said. "Not even a swift half?"

She was digging for car keys in her bag and keeping her

head down. "I've got an early start in the morning," she said.

I nodded, told her that one wasn't going to hurt.

She caught me looking, not that I was trying particularly hard not to. It was like a plum that someone had stepped on around her cheek, and the ragged edges of it were the colour of a tea stain. There was a half-moon of blood in her eye.

"I didn't know there was a cupboard open and I turned round into it," she said. "Stupid."

"It's all right," I said.

"What is?"

"Have one quick drink," I said. "Who am I going to share my salt and vinegar crisps with if you don't?"

It was as though she suddenly noticed that my hand was on her wrist, and she looked down and took half a step back. "I'll see you next week."

"Look after yourself." It came out as a whisper. I didn't really know what else to say.

She didn't turn up at all the following week.

Craig looked confused when I walked round the corner and grinned at him. It was halfway through the morning, and he'd come out the back entrance of the bank for a crafty smoke.

"All right, mate?"

"Ticking along," I said. "You?"

He looked at me for a few seconds. Took a drag and shook his head. "How d'you know where I worked?"

"Zoe must have said, last time she came to the class, you know?"

Something in his expression that I couldn't read, but I didn't much care.

"Shame she stopped coming, really. We were all saying how she made the rest of us work a bit harder, trying to keep up."

"She just lost interest, I think. Me an' all, to be honest." Then a look that seemed to say they were getting their exercise in other ways, and one back from me that tried and failed to wipe it off his face.

It was warm and he was in shirtsleeves. I was sweating underneath my jacket so I slipped it off, threw it across my arm.

"Are you feeling OK? You've gone a bit red."

I stared at the pattern on his poxy tie. "I'm fine."

He flicked his fag end away. "Listen, I've got to get back to work …"

"How's Zoe's face?"

That took the smile away quick enough. Put that confused look back again, like he didn't know his arse from his elbow.

"It's fine now," he said. "She's all gorgeous again."

"Not seen many shiners worse than that one. Cupboard door, she said."

"Yeah, she forgot it was open and turned round fast, you know?"

I was just looking at him by now.

"What?"

I knew I still had *that*. You never lose the look.

"What's your problem?"

Breathing heavily, a wheeze in it. For real some of it, like the red face, but I'd laid it on thick, just to get his guard down.

"I think maybe you ought to go home now," he said.

I bent over, suddenly; dropped the jacket like I might be in some trouble. He stepped across to pick it up, which was when I swung a good hard right at his fat, flappy mouth.

It wasn't the best punch I ever threw, but it did the job and I was watching the blood running down his shirt front as he swung me round and pushed me against the wall.

"What's your game, you silly old bastard?"

I put my boot into his shin nice and hard. I tried to bring my knee up, but the pain in his leg must have fired him right up, because suddenly his fists were flying at me. It was no more than a few seconds. Just flailing really, like kids, but blimey, I'd forgotten how much it hurts. Every blow made the sick rise up. I felt something catch me and rip behind the ear; a ring maybe. Stung like hell.

When the gaps between the punches got a bit longer, I knew it was my chance to get a dig or two in, just to keep my end up, you know? The last one snapped his head back and he was already falling when the background went blurry and his face started to swim in front of me. I dropped my fists to clutch at my arm and heard something crack when he hit the deck, right before I went over myself. But trust me, it was the pain in my chest that put me down, and not him.

Not him.

Some people can take a punch. I learned that the hard way a long time ago. Then there's the unlucky ones that can dish it out, that *like* dishing it out, but struggle a touch when they're on the receiving end.

The ones with glass jaws.

I said as much to the two coppers at the end of the bed, when I found out he still hadn't come round. A glass jaw or a thin skull, it's much the same thing.

Blimey, the quacks are *at* me again …

Poking and prodding. Talking over me, like I'm deaf as well as everything else.

It's not … pain exactly.

It's warm and wet and spreading through my arms and legs like I'm sinking into a bath or something. They've got those things you see on the TV out again, like a pair of irons on my chest. Like they're going to iron out my wrinkles.

Now they're going blurry either side of me, same as that scumbag did when I was sorting him out. The sound's gone funny too, and I've just got time to decide that some people don't deserve to be missed and to wonder if the coppers are going to be annoyed or relieved, and then all I can see is her face.

Clear as you like …

That stain around her eye and the purple bruise. And then the music starts and I'm standing there; a silly old bugger in baggy shorts, sweating in front of that stupid plastic thing.

And it's time to step up.

ON *THE* ANATOMIZATION OF AN UNKNOWN MAN (1637) BY FRANS MIER

JOHN CONNOLLY

I

The painting titled *The Anatomization of an Unknown Man* is one of the more obscure works by the minor Dutch painter, Frans Mier. It is an unusual piece, although its subject may be said to be typical of our time: the opening up of a body by what is, one initially assumes, a surgeon or anatomist, the light from a suspended lamp falling over the naked body of the anonymous man, his scalp peeled back to reveal his skull, his innards exposed as the anatomist's blade hangs suspended, ready to explore further the intricacies of his workings, the central physical component of the universe's rich complexity.

I was not long ago in England, and witnessed there the hanging of one Elizabeth Evans – Canberry Bess, they called her – a notorious murderer and cutpurse, who was taken with her partner, one Thomas Shearwood. Counterey Tom was hanged and then gibbeted at Gray's Inn fields, but it was the fate of Elizabeth Evans to be dissected after her death at the Barber-Surgeons' Hall, for the body of a woman is of more interest to the surgeons than that of a man, and harder to come by. She wept and screamed as she was brought to the gallows, and cried out for a Christian burial, for the terror of the Hall was greater to her than that of the noose itself.

Eventually, the hangman silenced her with a rag, for she was disturbing the crowd, and an end was put to her.

Something of her fear had communicated itself to the onlookers, though, and a commotion commenced at the base of the gallows. Although the surgeons wore the guise of commoners, yet the crowd knew them for what they were, and a shout arose that the woman had suffered enough under the Law, and should have no further barbarities visited upon her, although I fear their concern was less for the dignity of her repose than the knowledge that the mob was to be deprived of the display of her carcass in chains at St Pancras, and the slow exposure of her bones at King's Cross. Still, the surgeons had their way for, when the noose had done its work, she was cut down and stripped of her apparel, then laid naked in a chest and thrown into a cart. From there, she was carried to the Hall near unto Cripplegate. For a penny, I was permitted, with others, to watch as the surgeons went about their work, and a revelation it was to me.

But I digress. I merely speak of it to stress that Mier's painting cannot be understood in isolation. It is a record of our time, and should be seen in the context of the work of Valverde and Estienne, of Spigelius and Berrettini and Berengarius, those other great illustrators of the inner mysteries of our corporeal form.

Yet look closer and it becomes clear that the subject of Mier's painting is not as it first appears. The unknown man's face is contorted in its final agony, but there is no visible sign of strangulation, and his neck is unmarked. If he is a malefactor taken from the gallows, then by what means was his life ended? Although the light is dim, it is clear that his hands have been tied to the anatomist's table by means of stout rope. Only the right hand is visible, admittedly, but one would hardly secure that and not the other. On his wrist are gashes where he has struggled against his bonds, and blood pours from the table to the floor in great quantities. The dead do not bleed in this way.

And if this is truly a surgeon, then why does he not wear the attire of a learned man? Why does he labor alone in some dank place, and not in a hall or theater? Where are his peers? Why are there no other men of science, no assistants, no curious onlookers enjoying their penny's worth? This, it would appear, is secret work.

Look: there, in the corner, behind the anatomist, face tilted to stare down at the dissected man. Is that not the head and upper body of a woman? Her left hand is raised to her mouth, and her eyes are wide with grief and horror, but here too a rope is visible. She is also restrained, although not so firmly as the anatomist's victim. Yes, perhaps "victim" is the word, for the only conclusion to be drawn is that the man on the table is suffering under the knife. This is no corpse from the gallows, and this is not a dissection.

This is something much worse.

II

The question of attribution is always difficult in such circumstances. It resembles, one supposes, the investigation into the commission of a crime. There are clues left behind by the murderer, and it is the work of an astute and careful observer to connect such evidence to the man responsible. The use of a single source of light, shining from right to left, is typical of Mier. So, too, is the elongation of the faces, so that they resemble wraiths more than people, as though their journey into the next life has already begun. The hands, by contrast, are clumsily rendered, those of the anatomist excepted. It may be that they are the efforts of others, for Mier would not be alone among artists in allowing his students to complete his paintings. But then, it could also be the case that it is Mier's intention to draw our gaze to the anatomist's hands. There is a grace, a subtlety to the scientist's calling, and Mier is perhaps suggesting that these are skilled fingers holding the blade.

To Mier, this is an artist at work.

III

I admit that I have never seen the painting in question. I have only a vision of it in my mind based upon my knowledge of such matters. But why should that concern us? Is not imagining the first step towards bringing something into being? One must envisage it, and then one can begin to make it a reality. All great art commences with a vision, and perhaps it may be that this vision is closer to God than that which is ultimately created by the artist's brush. There will always be human flaws in the execution. Only in the mind can the artist achieve true perfection.

IV

It is possible that the painting called *The Anatomization of an Unknown Man* may not exist.

V

What is the identity of the woman? Why would someone force her to watch as a man is torn apart, and compel her to listen to his screams as the blade takes him slowly, exquisitely apart? Surgeons and scientists do not torture in this way.

VI

So, if we are not gazing upon a surgeon at work, then, for want of another word, perhaps we are looking at a murderer. He is older than the others in the picture, although not so ancient that his beard has turned grey. The woman, meanwhile, is beautiful; let there be no doubt of that. Mier was not a sentimental man, and would not have portrayed her as other than she was. The victim, too, is closer in age to the woman than the man. We can see it in his face, and in the once youthful perfection of his now ruined body.

Yes, it may be that he has the look of a Spaniard about him.

* * *

VII

I admit that Frans Mier may not exist.

VIII

With this knowledge, gleaned from close examination of the work in question, let us now construct a narrative. The man with the knife is not a surgeon, although he might wish to be, but he has a curiosity about the nature of the human form that has led him to observe closely the actions of the anatomists. The woman? Let us say: his wife, lovely yet unfaithful, fickle in her affections, weary of the ageing body that shares her bed and hungry for firmer flesh.

And the man on the table, then, is, or was, her lover. What if we were to suppose that the husband has discovered his wife's infidelity? Perhaps the young man is his apprentice, one whom he has trusted and loved as a substitute for the child that has never blessed his marriage. Realizing the nature of his betrayal, the master lures his apprentice to the cellar, where the table is waiting. No, wait: he drugs him with tainted wine, for the apprentice is younger and stronger than he, and the master is unsure of his ability to overpower him. When the apprentice regains consciousness, woken by the screams of the woman trapped with him, he is powerless to move. He adds his voice to hers, but the walls are thick, and the cellar deep. There is no one to hear.

A figure advances, the lamp catches the sharp blade, and the grim work begins.

IX

So: this is our version of the truth, our answer to the question of attribution. I, Nicolaes Deyman, did kill my apprentice Mantegna. I anatomized him in my cellar, slowly taking him apart as though, like the physicians of old, I might be able to find some as yet unsuspected fifth humor within him, the black and malignant thing responsible for his betrayal. I did force my wife, my beloved Judith, to watch as I removed skin from flesh, and flesh from bone. When her lover was dead, I strangled her with a rope, and I wept as I did so.

I accept the wisdom and justice of the court's verdict: that my name should be struck from all titles and records and never uttered again; that I should be taken from this place and hanged in secret and then, while still breathing, that I should be handed over to the anatomists and carried to their great temple of learning, there to be taken apart while my heart beats so that the slow manner of my dying might contribute to the greater sum of human knowledge, and thereby make some recompense for my crimes.

I ask only this: that an artist, a man of some small talent, might be permitted to observe and record all that transpires so the painting called *The Anatomization of an Unknown Man* might at last come into existence. After all, I have begun the work for him. I have imagined it. I have described it. I have given him his subject, and willed it into being.

For I, too, am an artist, in my way.

THE PITCHER

SARAH HILARY

It took a day and a half to find the bloody place. You'd think tracking down *la tasca*, an authentic Spanish tavern on the west coast of England, would be a piece of cake, but trust me. A day and a half. The rental car guzzled petrol; I had to refuel twice en route from London, tackling the last leg on foot having parked, after a fashion, in a hedgerow rotten with blackberries. My sandals were thick with dust by the time I reached the whitewashed shack with its red roof, a jaunty blue sign bearing the unlikely name of TIMANFAYA.

He wasn't what I'd expected, either. I'd thought a suntan, at the very least. Black curls and a devilish smile; *swarthy* was uppermost in my mind. After the expense of the rental, I was cursing my editor for proposing the trip and my divorce for making a necessity of it. And then there he was behind the bar, an unremarkable chap in a brown linen shirt open at the neck, sunglasses like black bottle tops. When later he removed the glasses, his eyes were the same: little black bottle tops.

"What can I get for you, sir?" I'd wanted a Spanish accent but instead heard a West Country burr. "Sangria?"

"First one on the house?" I suggested with what ex-editors have called my customary insolence. "For a weary traveller who fought through thorns to find you?" Lifting an arm and leg to show off my battle wounds, which were nothing to the scratches on the car I'd buried nose deep in brambles half a mile up the road, but impressive nonetheless.

He looked me over. "Why not?"

A free drink, how often does that happen? I watched as he mixed the sangria in a tall glass pitcher, squeezing the lemon in his fist and chunking in ice, swirling with a long spoon until the inside was a merry dance of fiery orange and blood-red. He poured a generous measure and slid it across the counter. "*Salud!*"

I took the glass, "You're a gentleman," tilting it in his direction before sipping. What my ex-wife refers to as my "dainty habit of getting shit-faced".

"You've come a long way," he remarked, returning the brandy bottle to its shelf.

For a second I thought he was familiar with my less dainty habits – could it be he used to work in JoJo's or Boules, a recent arrival in this dusty hellhole? – but of course he was referring to my physical journey rather than anything arduous in the rehabilitation line.

"All the long way from London."

"Ah." He picked a lemon pip from the counter, wiping a cloth in its wake. "London." That burr again, lending a wurzel twang to the *ah*.

"You know London?" I asked the question to be friendly, and since my editor expected a story. Until (or unless) I enlightened her, I was supping sangria with a Spaniard. "Foreigners Thriving in Unfriendly Post-Brexit Britain", trimmed to fit a red top headline. The Matalan Matador? Ah, well. If it could be greased along with a free drink or two, perhaps the job wouldn't be so very hellish.

"Never been," mine host replied. "Never wanted to."

"Wise man." I took another sip. "Especially in this heat."

"It is a little close." He pointed at the ceiling fan.

"Unlike bloody London!" I laughed.

He laughed. We laughed together. My glass was shrinking fast. Funny how sips will do that.

"So, Timanfaya … That's an exotic name for this neck of the woods." I swirled what was left of my drink. "Spanish, I take it?"

"Canarian. From Lanzarote." He rolled his tongue around the island name, sounding for the first time as if he might be the real deal. "A place of volcanoes. They erupted six years without stopping, destroyed everything in their path."

"Sounds like my ex-wife!"

He didn't laugh this time, but he did something better. Refilled my glass from the pitcher before returning it to my elbow, a curl of orange peel bobbing like a tiny surfboard on the rosy tide. After which he bent below the bar – I heard the suck of a refrigerator door – straightening to slide a little gleaming dish of olives in my direction.

"Very civil of you," I said, wishing to be clear this wasn't a billable item.

"We can be civil." He shrugged. "Why not?" He polished the counter with his blue cloth. "You've come a long way. I'm stuck out here alone. It's nice to have a little company."

"Precisely!" I saluted with my replenished glass. "Good man."

The pitcher was prickled with condensation, ice melting so fast it moved under its own momentum, muttering against the glass. Outside, the sun was packed like butter about the white walls, slathered across the red roof. The shade inside was soupy, sticking my shirt and shorts to my skin, the ceiling fan for show rather than function. I swivelled to take a look at my surroundings, keeping the pitcher in my eye line for fear he'd think I'd lost interest in the liquid refreshment.

The place was small, its corners dim and pinwheeling with the dust that had blown in with me. He kept it clean – wooden tables with scrubbed zinc tops, chairs with neat straw seats, swept terracotta tiles – all achingly authentic. A shelf ran around the room at head height, cluttered with colourful stabs at pottery and glass, an impotent string of dried chilli peppers hanging from a brass hook. I could picture it after dark, candles winking in the corners, the warm cluck of bottles behind the bar, a big plate of paella, its saffron rice studded with purple chorizo. A soft-focus mirror gave the impression of not caring who looked into it. I've a likeable face, I'm told, but untrustworthy. My skin's lined (some say ruined), my smile borders on regret, my teeth were an expensive mistake, but the mirror was gentle with me, reinforcing the sense that here was a place I could happily waste an afternoon or evening. Through a crack in the tiles, a shaft of sunlight fingered the necks of bottles and kissed the lips of glasses. I settled myself more comfortably at the bar. My editor hadn't wanted to send a photographer until I'd scoped the lay of the land. Tight as a camel's hole in a sandstorm but with an eye for a story, I must give her that. There *was* something here. Under the surface gloss so pleasantly provided by the sangria, my old instincts bristled. Yes, there was certainly something. I finished my second glass and eyed the pitcher.

"Please," the barman said. "Help yourself."

I hadn't known hospitality like this since my days – short-lived – with the British Embassy. The glass pitcher was heavier than it looked, needing both my hands to lift and pour without slopping a fresh measure for myself. "You won't join me?"

He shook his head. "Not while I'm working."

Good Christ, I thought, *what a maxim*. Had I lived by it, I'd not have done a day's work in fifty-seven years. Funny old job at the Embassy but by God, the hospitality! I never once had to resort to the mini-bar, no matter how far they flung me. I remember settling for what I thought was a cup of coffee in Minsk only to discover it was laced with vintage Armenian cognac. *Erebuni*, they called it. Kicked like a caffeinated mule. I got into the habit of telling people I knew the ambassador's darkest secrets, which, since he looked like a choirboy guilty of no more than vaping in the vestry, created quite the stir in certain circles. When pressed for details, I'd tap my nose and murmur something enigmatic such as, "To each his alibi."

"The trouble with you, Hal," they started saying, "is you're getting too big for your boots."

"The gilt's coming off the gingerbread, old boy."

Let it come, said I. All in all, not my brightest hour. Still, *persona non grata* has a certain ring to it, or so I'm told. My editor likes to drop my past indiscretions into conversations with truculent press barons or executives at toppling global enterprises who need to know they aren't being sent some snot-nosed infant with an iPhone and not the first idea about how the real world operates. "He had the ambassador's ear," my editor purrs from behind her desk with its assault course of paperweights and pens, a photo cube of poolside faces flanked by palm trees, the last gasp of a pot plant. "They considered him for Abu Dhabi." True enough, although I don't get on with camels as a rule. Or sand for that matter; what's left of my nose wouldn't thank me. So here I am in deepest Devon, trying to prise a story out of a Spaniard who upped sticks to work in this backwater. Pig's Knuckle, Arkansas, or wherever the hell I am.

"You're not from round here," I put it to him. "Surely?"

He moved on to another glass, polishing it roundly. From the way everything shone, he spent most of his time in here polishing. "Only lately."

"I mean, you're Spanish. Or Canarian." I waved a hand expansively. "Not a lot of volcanoes around here."

He nodded, as if to say he didn't want any trouble. I hear that a lot after I've had a couple of drinks: "We don't want any trouble, sir." I propped an elbow to the bar, picking an olive from the dish. Lemon oil, and lots of garlic. It tasted like the day, sour and slippery. "You're a long way from home, must've been hard to start over."

"It suits me." He shrugged. I couldn't see his eyes behind the damn sunglasses.

"You don't miss the landscape? Not that I've anything against Devon, personally." Apart from its bloody roads, and brambles. "But it's hardly Lanzarote."

"It's very different," he agreed, polishing the bottles now, raising a hard gleam from the shelves above the bar.

"Hard to scratch a living." I was flagging and we both knew it.

He served up a distant smile, still polishing. The Matalan

Matador, and here I was the bull, charging at him with my clumsy questions, which he flicked away with a lavish turn of his wrist. Pale wrists, no suntan, just fine black hairs growing very straight. His hands repulsed me for a reason I couldn't name. I turned to take another look around the bar. It was a lovely little spot, a shame it was out on a limb. I couldn't imagine the turnover made it worth the slog, even before Brexit took a blunt axe to any appetite the yokels might once've had for tapas. Cream teas were the order of the day around here. If you wanted exotic, you added sultanas, or put the cream on first.

"Took some guts to give that up for this," I tried.

He flourished the blue cloth, chasing away a solitary fly so stupefied by the heat it wasn't even buzzing. "A long time ago."

I experienced a familiar sense of dislocation, as if I'd missed a step on the stairs and almost fallen flat on my arse. He was placating me, the way people always placate drunks. From here on in, he'd agree with everything I said. I'd end up with no story and no way to pay for the scratched paintwork or the plastic pillows in whichever hellhole awaited me for the night. Travelodge, knowing my luck. No, worse than that – some godforsaken B & B where the landlady insisted on reciting the house rules she'd had framed for every wall in the house: shoes off, no food in the bedrooms, nothing but loo paper down the lavatory in case you'd been thinking of flushing *The Communist Manifesto* down there. I drained my glass and studied its sugary dregs morosely.

"Where I come from," the barman said, "they call it the island of fire and water."

Fire and water. I thought of single malt, tasting the zing of fresh green apples on my tongue, an oakiness in my throat. The sangria was too sweet, sickly, orange rind furring the inside of the pitcher like mould. "I don't suppose ..."

He studied me in the manner of an anthropologist before reaching a long arm for the whisky bottles above the bar. Men like him – I'd known them all my adult life. Men who know just from looking at you, from the smell of your skin, which drink to pour. I'd loved more men like him than I'd ever loved women. Not romantically or sexually, God forbid. I loved them for their perception, the speed with which they serviced my needs. Women like my ex-wife only knew how to nag when it came to my comforts, but men like this understood. By God, the barmen who'd understood me over the years. Like this handsome Spanish devil with his bottle-top glasses, brown linen shirt damp at the neck with clean sweat. My mouth watered as he wiped a glass before pouring a neat double measure of my favourite nectar.

"Fire and water," he murmured, "the name of my island. A place of caves carved by flames, where it's said the Devil still lives. So little rain falls there it is practically a desert. I owned a small vineyard, planted in the black sand behind a wall of white stones ..."

I sipped at the whisky jealously, not wanting his story, not right now. All my attention was on the drink in my hand because that's how it is when you're thirsty. You're selfish, greedy. He kept talking and I kept sipping, tuning him out as he busied himself wiping with his blue cloth at the counter, the pitcher, the dish of olives. A fastidious man, mine host. It struck me how little sound there was out here, not even the drone of bees or flies. You'd have expected that in this heat, flies bumping their bloated bodies into everything, drunk on sunshine. But apart from the solitary specimen he'd flicked away, the bar was quiet. In the dense silence, my sipping sounded like gulping.

My ears pricked up when he said, "My wife hated it there. It was her idea to move away."

"Wives …" I wagged a finger at him from the fist around my glass; I could spare one finger. "They'll be the death of us."

"Yours too?"

I bared my expensive teeth at him. "Mine too."

He studied me from behind those round, black lenses, then set the bottle on the bar. "Excuse me." He flicked his cloth over his shoulder and walked away. "Just for a moment."

He shouldered open a door, disappearing through it into the back of the bar. He knew I could be trusted if I wanted to keep enjoying his hospitality. Blinking at my drink, I crooked an elbow around the glass. I wanted to do the same with the bottle but I was preserving my dignity, one sip at a time. Damn him, though. He'd summed me up the way my ex-wife always said everyone could: "One look at your eyes and they know you're a drunk," which was a lie because my eyes are a nice shade of blue, rather like the cloth he'd carried off with him, or the sign outside this place.

Timanfaya. A land of fire and water.

I knew all about the volcanoes of course, did my research as soon as my editor handed me this job. Knew everything there was to know about Lanzarote and its Timanfaya National Park, where you can take a coach trip at sunset across a lunar landscape left by the lava that flowed for six years, drowning the whole town, vaporising cattle and crops, driving out the people with its bubbling black fire. The tour guide invites you to gaze from the coach window at the sheer drop while anticipating your certain demise, "Say farewell to your loved ones!" At the summit you're expected to climb from the coach and stretch your shaking legs while the wind buffets you like a boxer's punchbag and you try not to get into the photos of the keener tourists. From there you can see the sun slinking ever closer to the horizon, painting the craters red and making the dust dance with glass that once was sand. All a far cry from cream teas.

I swallowed my drink and refilled my glass. If I'm honest, I was on the way to getting jolly tight. Jolly *jolly*, you might say. I'd skipped breakfast and lunch and the hire car came without air-conditioning and then the walk here and the sun – I wasn't in the best shape. There was a ringing in my ears and my fingers buzzed as I scooped an olive from the dish, chewing quickly as I'm not a fan of olives. What I needed was carbs. Bread or potatoes. *Patatas bravas*, that was the thing, those tough little skins crusted with salt … The thought made my mouth water. I finished the whisky, deciding to switch back to sangria, which at least had fruit in it. The whisky would wait. Whisky always does. Funny thing – the pitcher didn't seem to get any lighter no matter how hard I worked to reduce its contents. All the ice had melted, the brandy burning my throat, so I moved behind the bar to search the fridge for fresh ice and perhaps a slice of frittata.

That's when I saw it. The body.

"Excuse me …!" That was my first instinct, to apologise.

He was taking a little nap, my heat-fuddled brain decided. A siesta. It was a warm day and the terracotta tiles were cool. He was lying with his legs at an odd angle but there wasn't a lot of room behind the bar so perhaps that accounted for it. In a pair of faded jeans with a red print or—

"Christ almighty!"

"Sir?" The barman was behind me. He'd changed into a clean white shirt, the sunglasses hooked into the breast pocket, a tan leather holdall hanging from his hand. His eyes—

His eyes were little black bottle tops.

"He's—! Good Christ! You—!"

He turned and walked away, silent as a cat across the tiles. I watched him take the blue cloth from his pocket and use it like a glove to push open the door. He didn't look back, not once.

Of course my prints were all over the pitcher, all over the place. I couldn't answer their questions; it was shock, I didn't seem able to frame a sentence. I had a history, that's what they said, a history of getting violent when I was drunk. It began as belligerence but all too often ended in fisticuffs. It'd happened that way in Minsk, among other places. They listed the places. My ex-wife practically stood on a stool to tell them what a shit I was. As for me, I pleaded for them to find the barman, described his eyes, his accent, the black hairs on his pale wrists. No one believed me.

"A Spaniard living in Pig's Knuckle, Arkansas?" they scoffed. "Pull the other one."

Of course they didn't call it Pig's Knuckle. But I'd no paperwork to make my trip legitimate, nothing linking me to the bloody place other than my fingerprints. No formal commission, just the hope of one. "Ask my editor!" I insisted, but she didn't want any part.

Persona non grata no longer had a ring to it, unless it was a death knell.

"We found your car," they said. "Hidden in the hedge. Why hide it?"

"You were running away, weren't you? Because of what you'd done."

"I'd never seen him before in my life!"

"And yet you killed him. This total stranger, as yet unidentified. A young immigrant, that's what you thought, wasn't it? Didn't serve your drinks fast enough, was that it? You've a record with foreigners, haven't you? We reckon you've been chucked out of bars right around the world."

"That's a ridiculous exaggeration. Ask my editor!"

"Oh we have." A grim species of satisfaction, the second time around. "Believe us."

I was afraid to press the point.

I have tried asking for his name, the young man on the tiled floor, whose skull I'm accused of smashing. I've tried to find out who he was. No one will tell me. It's my suspicion they don't know. They confronted me with his photograph, before and after. There was a ghastly moment when I recognised him, or thought I did. Where had I seen that face before? Smiling, seated beside an aquamarine pool, a fan of palm trees behind his head. I fought to keep the jolt of recognition from my face, certain it would confirm their suspicions. It's only now I'm alone in the cell that I struggle to grab hold of the memory. Her desk, its litter of paperweights, the photo cube of poolside faces – is that where I'd seen him? Why didn't I pay attention? She gave me the commission, knew my weakness, denies all knowledge now. Am I her patsy, is that how this worked? Or am I overthinking it, having failed to put in sufficient thought earlier? I've been sleepwalking, I appreciate that now. I appreciate a great many things, in here. There's not much else to do but think, and so I try and unpick how it happened, where it started. Years ago, I suspect, when I first picked up a bottle and crawled inside to a place where I didn't have to listen or learn, where the world was reduced to a soft wash of echoes. My solicitor looks on me with something akin to pity, my fellow detainees with contempt. I sit facing a brick wall for most of my waking day. At night, I dream of little black bottle tops resting like coins on his dead eyes.

"It was *him* …!"

But there was no him. No one in a white shirt with a tan leather holdall. He vanished. Walked out of the whitewashed shack no one ever visited, with its roof of cracked red tiles and its blue sign swinging in the wind, TIMANFAYA, leaving me with the pitcher that matched the fatal wound to the boy's head, my fingerprints all over it, a single slice of orange rind sinking in its fiery red sea.

DISCIPLINED

MARTYN WAITES

It was swallowing the needle that changed everything. That's when I realised I was serious.

I felt it, all the way down. All the way through. It took a few days. Hurting as it went. Hurting like I'd never felt before. Tearing and damaging. I could feel it. But I thought there'd be more blood in the end. That was a bit disappointing.

I showed it to her afterwards. Proudly, holding it up in my hands with reverence like it was a sacred artefact. She just stared at me, the mask almost slipping, showing the actor not the act.

"What the fuck's that?"

"The needle. Like you told me to do. I did it. And it hurt." I smiled. Brave, soldier-like. "It hurt a lot."

She stared at me again. Questions in her eyes. All about her.

"It's all right," I said. "You've got nothing to worry about. It's what we agreed. I can sign something if you want. Keeps you free of blame. I'm doing this because I want to. And because you said you want to do it to me."

She was back to normal after that. And I loved her for it. And when she spoke, I followed her every word.

It started with Julia. When I lost her. When she died. We say things like "lost" and "passed over" and "passed on", but that's just to avoid what we're really talking about. "At peace." "Resting." "Gone to a better place." No. We don't need them. We just need the one word. It encompasses everything. *Dead.* Julia died. And my life started to go to pieces.

No. I suppose I should start before that. With me. But there's nothing really to tell, I don't think. I've got a steady job. I work in a big corporation at a desk behind a computer. I sit there all day staring at my screen, doing things with numbers. I don't need to tell you what. Don't need to bore you with it. Because that's what I was always doing. Boring people about my job. Telling them in detail what I did. And I couldn't see them losing interest, eyes glazing over, as they say. Because I was so into my story. It took Julia to tell me to stop, to make me realise. She did that a lot with me. She made me a better person. The kind that people liked to be with. Or said they did. And now she's dead. No. All you need to know is that I love what I do. I take random numbers that appear on the screen, a chaos of them, and I tame them. I make them work. I give them discipline. It's all about the discipline.

And I thought that would be it, that would be me for life. I'd do my job, come home. Keep my regimented existence going. My disciplined life. But then I met Julia. She was the kind of person that my kind of person would never be involved with. Never even get looked at. But she did. And so much more than that. She was younger than me for a start. Much younger. And pretty. Really pretty. A ten, if I was the kind of man to measure such things like that. Even more than a ten, but I can't say that because as we know that's numerically impossible. So a ten, then.

And we fell in love. Oh yes, I knew I'd fall in love with her, that was obvious, but I didn't think she'd fall in love with me. She did. And it was wonderful.

All my regimentation, all my discipline, went out the window. She showed me life. She showed me how to live. I did things with her I never thought I would do. Ever. Not just, you know, the sex things. Although we did do things I'd never imagined. Well, I'd imagined them. But I never imagined doing them for real. At least not with someone who also wanted to do them. Someone I didn't have to pay for.

Oh yes. I've done that. Paid for women. I'm not proud of it but then I'm not ashamed either. I had a lonely life before Julia. I admit it. Sometimes I'd have to do things to … you know. But not any more. No. Not any more.

I'm not going to describe her. You don't need to know what she looked like. You can all imagine her as you want to. You just need to know that she was the most beautiful woman who ever lived and ever loved. She had me wrapped round her little finger. I would do anything for her. I did.

We used to play games. Dare each other. Do things against routine, against order. Usually involving sex. That's what Julia really loved. Transgressing, she said. Having sex in public, where people might find us. Having sex outside. Risky sex. Exciting sex. And more. She enjoyed tying me up. Having sex with me. She would call me names when she did it. Names to do with her father who she said was about my age. Sometimes she would slip into a different world when she did it. Hit me. Sometimes hard. I didn't mind it, after a while. I came to enjoy it as much as she did. Afterwards, it was like she would become a different person. Quieter. Almost shy. Ashamed, even. I told her not to be. That I knew she had problems, issues. That I didn't mind her working them out on me if it made her better. That I enjoyed it, being told what to – made what to do.

She would go silent for long periods after that. Just let me hold her.

Those were the best of times. Because what happened was we started out railing against the norm, against the regimented, straitjacketed discipline of the world. Against routine. And we ended up, like you always do, making that into a new routine. A new discipline. And I loved that even more. That became my life. She became my life.

And then she died.

Cancer. Really quick. She didn't know she had it. And by the time she did, by the time she started to hurt, it was too late. She was gone. And I had nothing. Nothing at all left. Just my routine. Just my numbers. My old discipline.

It got dark, then. Really, really dark. I wanted to kill myself. I tried to kill myself. Stood over the sink, crying and screaming, tears streaming down my face, with a knife pressed against my wrist. But I couldn't do it. Couldn't bring myself to find the strength to do it on my own. I threw the knife down, walked away, hating myself for being weak. For being lost without her. And for not having the courage to join her.

My work began to suffer. I would look at the numbers and not be able to make sense of them. They would remain in chaos. I had to do something. Find a way through this, to go on.

And there was something else I missed. The sex with Julia. The physicality. Being told what to do. Holding her afterwards.

I got on the internet. Found some sites easily. Escorts offering what I wanted. Nearby. Reasonable rates, too. I met with one. Told her what I wanted. And she gave it to me. It wasn't the same, not nearly the same. And she wouldn't let me hold her afterwards. In fact I was barely allowed to touch her. But it was better than nothing.

I went back. Again and again. I became her best customer. After a while, I couldn't get enough. And it was helping me in the rest of my life. Helping me at work. I began to find discipline again. I kept going.

But …

I missed Julia. My heart was gone. Outwardly I kept going, inwardly there was nothing.

And that's when I had an idea. And the idea became so all-encompassing, consuming, I could barely sleep. It was all I thought about. All I could think about. I told her.

"I want you to give me things to do. Tasks to perform. Chores."

"What kind of chores?"

"Ones that'll hurt. That you think'll punish me."

That's when she told me to eat the needle.

I don't know if she expected me to actually do it. I don't think she did. Just wanted to punish me for not doing it. But I did. It wasn't easy. Standing there, trying to force it down, override the natural impulse to gag, the body's self-preservation instinct kicking in. But I thought of Julia standing there, beckoning me on, and I did it. Eventually. And it hurt.

Christ, it hurt.

But I did it.

"Give me another," I said.

She did.

When I made my packed lunch the next day I remembered to fill it with unspent wooden matches. I sat at a table on my own in the canteen, getting a real frisson from doing this when other people were present, and ate. God, that hurt too. Really hurt. Wooden spikes and sulphur. Swallowed down with Diet Coke. I didn't sleep at all that night, thought of calling for an ambulance. But I stopped myself. Thought of Julia, looked at her picture. Kept going.

I had to take a couple of days off work after that. It damaged me. Really, really damaged me.

I went back to her. Told her that I had completed her task. She stared at me. Could tell I was still hurting.

"I think we'll leave off for a while," she said. "Until you're feeling a bit better."

"No," I said. "We go on. Give me another."

She did so. Reluctantly. Bleach, this time. Watered down, of course. But bleach all the same. I nearly didn't come back from that one. Luckily I had the dose just right. It didn't kill me. But it hurt me. Hurt like hell.

"Next one," I said.

"No. You're not punishing yourself, you're killing yourself."

I smiled. "Tell me what to do," I said.

"You'll kill yourself."

"That's the idea," I said.

I'm a weak man. I always have been. And I've been dead for most of my life. Doing what I'm told, living an existence of routine and quiet desperation. Well, not desperation. Discipline. And when I had Julia she didn't just show me how to live, she told me how to. And now I don't have her.

But I have someone to tell me how to die.

And this is going to be it, I think. I've got the razor blades in my hand. I'm looking at Julia's picture. And I'm ready to swallow them.

I'm just waiting for her to tell me to do it.

THE CONSUMERS

DENNIS LEHANE

It wasn't that Alan didn't love Nicole. She was possibly the only person he did love, or certainly the only one he trusted. And after he'd beaten her or called her all kinds of unforgiveable things in one of his black rages, he'd drop to his knees to beg her forgiveness. He'd weep like a child abandoned in the Arctic, he'd swear he loved her the way knights loved maidens in old poems, the way people loved each other in war zones or during tsunamis – *crystallized* love, pure and passionate, boundless and a little out of control, but undeniable.

She believed this for a long time – it wasn't just the money that kept her in the marriage; the make-up sex was epic, and Alan was definitely easy on the eyes – but then one day – the day he knocked her out in the kitchen actually – she realized she didn't care about his reasons anymore, she didn't care how much he loved her, she just wanted him dead.

His apology for laying her out in the kitchen was two round trip tickets to Paris for her and a friend. So she took the trip with Lana, her best friend, and told her that she'd decided to have her husband killed. Lana, who thought Alan was an even bigger asshole than Nicole did, said it shouldn't be too much of a problem.

"I know a guy," she said.

"You *know a guy?*" Nicole looked from the Pont Neuf to Lana. "A guy who kills people?"

Lana shrugged.

Turned out the guy had helped Lana's family a few years back. Lana's family owned supermarkets down south, and the guy had preserved the empire by dealing with a labor organizer named Gustavo Inerez. Gustavo left his house to pick up training pants for his two-year-old and never came back. The guy Lana's family had hired called himself Kineavy, no first name given.

Not long after Nicole and Lana returned to Boston, Lana arranged the meeting. Kineavy met Nicole at an outdoor restaurant on Long Wharf. They sat looking out at boats in the harbor on a soft summer day.

"I don't know how to do this," she said.

"You're not supposed to, Mrs Walford. That's why you hire me."

"I meant I don't know how to hire somebody to do it."

Kineavy lit a cigarette, crossed one leg over his knee. "You hire somebody to clean your house?"

"Yes."

"It's like that – you're paying somebody to do what you don't want to do yourself. Still has to get done, though."

"But I'm not asking you to clean my house."

"Aren't you?"

Hard to tell if he was smiling a bit when he said it because he'd been dragging on his cigarette. He wore Maui Jim wraparounds with brown lenses, so she couldn't see his eyes, but he was clearly a good-looking guy, maybe forty, sandy hair, sharp cheekbones and jaw line. He was about six feet tall, looked like he worked out, maybe jogged, but didn't devote his life to it.

"It feels so *odd*," she said. "Like this can't be my life, can it? People don't *really* do these kinds of things, do they?"

"Yet," he said, "they do."

"How did you get into this line of work?"

"A woman kept asking me questions, and one day I snapped."

Now he did smile, but it was the kind of smile you gave people who searched for exact change in the express line at Whole Foods.

"How do I know you're not a cop?"

"You don't really." He exhaled a slim stream of smoke, one of those rare smokers who could still make it look elegant. The last time Nicole had smoked a cigarette the World Trade Center had been standing, but now she had to resist the urge to buy a pack.

"Why do you do this for a living?"

"I don't do it for a living. It doesn't pay enough. But it rounds off the edges."

"Of what?"

"Poverty." He stubbed out his cigarette in the black plastic ashtray. "Why do you want your husband dead?"

"That's private."

"Not from me it's not." He removed his sunglasses and stared across the table. His eyes were the barely blue of new metal. "If you lie, I'll know it. And I'll walk."

"I'll find somebody else."

"Where?" he said. "Under the hitman hyperlink on Craigslist?"

She looked out at the water for a moment because it was hard to say the words without a violent tremble in her lower lip.

She looked back at him, jaw firm. "He beats me."

His eyes and face remained stone still, as if he'd been replaced with a photograph of himself. "Where? You look perfectly fine to me."

That was because Alan didn't hit her hard every time. Most times, he just held tight to her hair while he flicked his fingers off her chin and nose or twisted the flesh over her hip. In the last couple years, though, after the markets collapsed and Alan and men like him were blamed for it in some quarters, he'd often pop the cork on his depthless self-loathing and unload on her. He'd buried a fist in her abdomen on three different occasions, lifted her off the floor by her throat, rammed the heel of his hand into her temple hard enough for her to hear the ring of a distant alarm clock for the rest of the day, and laid her out with a surprise punch to the back of the head. When she came to from that one, she was sprawled on the kitchen floor. He'd left a box of Kleenex and an ice pack by her head to show he was sorry.

Alan was always sorry. Whenever he hit her, it seemed to shock him. His pupils would pop, his mouth would form an "O," he'd look at his hand like he was surprised to find it stinging and still attached to his wrist.

After, he'd fill the bedroom with roses, hire a car to take her to a spa for a day. Then, after this last time, he sent her and Lana to Paris.

She told this to Kineavy. Then she told him some more. "He punched me in the lower back once because I didn't move out of his path to the liquor cart fast enough. Right where the spine meets the ass? You ever try to sit when you're bruised there? He took a broomstick to the backs of my legs another time. But mostly he likes to punch me in the head, where all my hair is."

"You do have a lot of it," Kineavy said.

It was her most striking attribute, even more so than her tits, which were one hundred percent Nicole and had yet to sag, or her ass, which had, truth be told, sprouted some cellulite lately, but not noticeably so for a woman closing in on thirty-six, or even her smile, which could turn the heads of an entire cocktail party if she entered the room wearing it.

Her hair trumped all of it. It was the dark of red wine and fell to her shoulders. When she pulled it back, she looked regal. When she straightened it, she looked dangerous. When she let it fall naturally, with its tousled waves and anarchic curls, she looked like a wet dream sent to douse a five-alarm fire.

She told Kineavy, "He hits me mostly on the head because the hair covers the bruises."

"And you can't just leave him?"

She shook her head and admitted something that shamed her. "Pre-nup."

"And you like living rich."

"Who doesn't?"

Nicole grew up in the second floor apartment of a three-decker on Sydney Street in the Savin Hill, a neighborhood locals called Stab-'n-Kill. Her parents were losers, always getting caught in the petty scams they tried to run on their soon-to-be-ex employers and then on the city and the welfare system and DSS and the Housing Department and just anybody they suspected was dumber than they were. Problem was, you couldn't find a dead fucking houseplant dumber than Jerry and Gerri Golden. Jerry ended up getting stomach cancer while in minimum-security lock-up for check kiting and Gerri used his death to justify climbing into a bottle of Popov for the rest of her life. Last time Nicole checked, she was still alive, if toothless and demented. But the last time Nicole checked had been about ten years ago.

Being poor, she'd decided long ago, wasn't necessarily a bad thing. Plenty of people did it without letting it eat their souls. But it wasn't for her.

"What does your husband do?" Kineavy asked.

"He's an investment banker."

"For which bank?"

"Since the crash? Bank Suffolk."

"Before the crash?"

"He was with Bear Stearns." Finally some movement in Kineavy's face, a flick in his eyes, a shift of his chin. He lit another cigarette and raised one eyebrow ever so slightly as the match found the tobacco. "And people call me a killer."

She thought about it later, how he was right. How there was this weird disconnect at the center of the culture between certain acts of amorality. If you sold your own body or pimped someone who did, stuck up liquor stores, or, God forbid, sold drugs, you were deemed unfit for society. People would try to run you out of the neighborhood. They would bar their children from playing with yours.

But if you subverted federal regulations to sell toxic assets to unsuspecting investors and wiped out hundreds of thousands, if not millions, of jobs and life savings, you were invited to Symphony Hall and luxury boxes at Fenway. Alan had convinced the entire state of Arkansas to invest in bundled sub-primes he knew would fail. When he'd told Nicole this back in '07, she remembered her initial outrage.

"So the derivatives you've been selling, they're bad?"

"A lot of them, yeah."

"The CD, um, whatta you—?"

"Collateralized debt obligations. CDOs, yeah. They pretty much suck, too, at least a good sixty percent of them."

"But they're all insured."

"Well …" He looked around the restaurant. He shook his head slowly. "A lot of them are, sure, but the insurance companies over-promised and underfunded. Bill ever comes due, everyone's fucked."

"And the bill's going to come due?"

"With Arkansas it sure looks like it. They bundled up with some pretty sorry shit."

"So why not just tell the state retirement board?"

He took a long pull from his glass of cab'. "First, because they'd take my license. Second, and more importantly, that state retirement board, babe? They might just dump those stocks, en masse, which would *ensure* that the stocks would collapse and make my gut feeling come true anyway. If I do nothing, though, things might – *might* – turn out alright. So, so we may as well roll the dice like we've been doing the last twenty years anyway and it's turned out OK. So, I mean, there you go."

He looked across the table at her while she processed all this, speechless, and he gave her the sad, helpless smile of a child who wasn't caught playing with matches until after the house caught fire.

"Damned if you do, damned if you don't," Alan said and ordered another bottle of wine.

The retirees lost everything when the markets collapsed in 2008. *Everything*, Alan told her through sobs and whimpers of horror. "One day – fuck, yesterday – old guy worked his whole life as a fucking janitor or pushing paper at City Hall, he looked at a statement said he'd accrued a quarter million to live off for the final twenty years of his life. It's right before his eyes in bold print. But the next day – *today* – he looked and the number was zero. And there's not a thing he can do to get it back. Not one fucking thing."

He wept into his pillow that night, and Nicole left him.

She came back, though. What was she going to do? She'd dropped out of community college when she met Alan. The only prospects she had now, at her age and level of work experience, could be narrowed down to selling french fries or selling blowjobs. Not much in between. And what would she be leaving behind? Trips, like the one to Paris, for starters. The main house in Dover, the city house twenty miles away in Back Bay, the New York apartment, the winter house in Boca, the full-time gardener, maid, and personal chef, the 750si, the DB9, the two-million-dollar renovation of the city house, the one-point-five-mil reno' of the winter house, the country club dues, one country club so exclusive that its name was simply The Country

Club, Jesus, the shopping trips, the new clothes every season.

So she returned to Alan a day after she left him by reminding herself that her duty was not to honor the tragedies surrounding a bunch of people in Arkansas she didn't know. (Or a bunch of people in Boston, New York, Connecticut, Maine, and, well, forty-five other states.) Her duty was to honor her husband and honor her marriage.

That became a harder and harder image to sustain of herself – and her marriage – as 2008 turned into 2009 and then 2010.

Outside of losing his job because his firm went bankrupt, Alan was fine. He'd dumped most of his own stock in the first quarter of '08, and the profit he made paid for the renovation of the Boca place. It also allowed them to buy the place she'd always liked in Maui. They bought a couple of cars on the island, so they wouldn't have to ship them back and forth, and hired two gardeners and a guy to look after the place, which, on one level, could seem extravagant but on another was actually quite benevolent – three people were now employed in a bad economy because of Alan and Nicole Walford.

Alan cried a lot in early '09. Knowing how many people had lost their homes, jobs or retirement savings ate at him. He lost weight and his eyes grew very dull for a while and even when he signed on with Bank Suffolk and hammered out a contract feathered with bonuses, he seemed sad. He told her nothing had changed, nobody had learned anything. No longer was investment philosophy based on the long-term quality of the investment. It was based on how many investments you could sell, toxic or otherwise, and what fees you could charge to do so. In 2010, banking fees at Alan's firm rose twenty-three percent. Advisory fees spiked at forty-one percent.

We're the bad guys, Nicole realized. We're going to hell. If there is a hell.

But what were they supposed to do? Or better yet, what was she supposed to do? Give it back? She wasn't the one shorting stock and selling toxic CDOs and CDSs. And even if she were, the government said it was OK. What Alan and his cohorts had done was, while extremely destructive, perfectly legal, at least until the prosecutors came banging down their door. And that wouldn't be happening. As Alan liked to remind her, the last person to fuck with Wall Street was the governor of New York and look what happened to him.

Besides, she wasn't Alan. She was his wife.

Maybe the service she was doing to society was hiring Kineavy. Maybe, while she'd been telling herself she didn't want to leave the marriage poor, the truth was far kinder – maybe she hired Kineavy so he'd right a wrong society couldn't or wouldn't right themselves.

Seen in that light, maybe she was a hero.

In another meeting, at another part of the waterfront, she gave Kineavy ten thousand dollars. Over the years she'd been able to siphon off a little cash here, a little cash there, from funds Alan would give her for the annual Manhattan shopping spree or the annual girls' weekend in Vegas or Monte Carlo. And now she passed some of it to Kineavy.

"The other ten when I get there."

"Of course." She looked out at the water. A gray day today,

very still and humid, some of the skyline gone smudged in the haze. "When will that be?"

"Saturday." He looked over at her as he stuffed the cash in the inside pocket of his jacket. "None of your servants work then, right?"

She chuckled. "I don't have servants."

"No, what are they?"

"Employees."

"OK. Any of your employees work Saturday?"

"No. Well, I mean, the chef, but he doesn't come in until, I think, two."

"And you usually go out Saturday, go shopping, hang with your girlfriends, stuff like that?"

"Not every Saturday, but it's not uncommon."

"Good. That's what you do this Saturday between ten and two."

"Between ten and two? What're you, the cable company?"

"That's exactly what you're going to tell Alan. On Thursday afternoon, your cable's gonna go out."

"Out?"

He popped his fingers at the air in front of their faces. "*Poof.*"

"Alan'll go crazy. The Sox play the Yankees this weekend, there's Wimbledon, some golf thing, too, I think."

"Right. And the cable guy will be coming to fix it Saturday, between ten and two."

Kineavy stood and she had to look up at him from the bench.

"You make sure your husband's there to answer the door."

* * *

117

At nine Saturday morning, Alan came into the kitchen from the gym. They'd had the gym built last year in the reconverted barn on the other side of the four-car garage. Alan had installed a sixty-inch Sony Bravia in there, and he'd watch movies that pumped him full of American pride as he ran the treadmill – *Red Dawn*, *Rocky IV*, *Rambo III*, *The Blind Side*. Man, he loved *The Blind Side* lately, walked around quoting it like it was the *Bhagavad Gita*. He was covered in sweat, dripping it all over the floor as he pulled a bottle of OJ from the fridge and popped the cap with his thumb, and drank directly from the bottle.

"Cable guy come yet?"

Nicole took an elaborate look at the clock on the wall. Nine O five. "Between ten and two, they said."

"Sometimes they come early." He swigged half the bottle.

"When do they come early?"

"Sometimes."

"Name one."

He shrugged, drank some more orange juice.

Watching him suck down the orange juice she was surprised to remember that she'd loved him this past week. Hated him, too, of course, but there was still love there. He wasn't a terrible guy, Alan. He could be funny and he once flew her brother, Ben, in to surprise her for her thirty-third birthday, because, Lord knows, he could always be depended on for the grand gesture. When he spent two weeks in Shanghai on business right after her third miscarriage, he sent her white roses every day he was gone. She spent the week in bed, and sometimes she'd place one of those white petals on the tip of her nose and close her eyes and pretend she'd have another child some day.

This past week, Alan had been surprisingly attentive, asking her if everything was OK, anything she wanted, was she feeling under the weather, she seemed tense, anything he could do for her?

They fucked twice – once in the bed at the end of the day, but once on the kitchen counter, the same counter he was leaning against now, good and lusty and erotic, Alan talking dirty into her right ear. For a good ten minutes after he'd come, she'd sat on the counter and considered calling the whole thing off.

Now, only an hour (or four) away from ending her husband's life, her heart pounded up through the veins in her neck, the blood roared through her ear canals, and she thought there still might be time to call it off. She could just run upstairs and grab the number of Kineavy's burner cell and end this madness now.

Alan burped. He held up a hand in apology. "Where you going again?"

She'd told him about a hundred times. "There's an art fair in Sherborn."

Drops of sweat fell from his shorts and plopped onto the floor. "Art fair? Bunch of lesbos selling shit they painted in their attics from the back of Subarus?"

"Anyway," she said, "we won't be all day or anything."

He nodded. "Cable guy's coming when?"

She let out a slow breath, looked at the floor.

"I'm just asking. Christ."

She nodded at the floor, her arms folded. She unfolded them

and looked up, gave him a tight smile. "Between ten and two."

He smiled. Alan had a movie-star-wattage smile. Sometimes, if he put his big almond eyes behind it, tilted his chin just so, she could feel her panties evaporate in a hushed puff of flame.

Maybe. Maybe …

"Don't be all day with the lesbians, that's all, OK? Money's like rust – shit doesn't sleep." He winked at her. "Know what I'm saying, sister?"

She nodded.

Alan took another slug of orange juice and some of it spilled into his chest hairs. He dropped the bottle on the counter, cap still off. He pinched her cheek on his way out of the room.

Nah. Fucking time for you to go, Alan.

Kineavy had been very clear about the time line.

She was to stay in the house until 9.45, just to make sure Alan didn't forget he was supposed to stick around for the cable guy because Alan, for all his attention to detail when it came to money, could be absent-minded to the edge of retardation when it came to almost anything else. She was to leave through the front door, leaving it unlocked behind her. Not open, mind you, just unlocked. At some point, while she was out with Lana on a Bloody Mary binge at the bar down the street from the Sherborn Art Fair, Alan would answer the front door and the cable guy would shoot him in the head.

Oh, Alan, she thought. *You weren't a bad guy. You just weren't a good one.*

She heard him coughing upstairs. He was probably sitting

in the bathroom waiting for the water to get hot, even though that took about four seconds in this McMansion. But Alan liked to turn the bathroom into a steam room. She'd come in after him, see his wipe marks all over the mirrors as her hair curled up around her ears.

He coughed again, closer to the stairs now, and she thought, *Terrific. Your last gift to me will be a cold. My fucking luck, it'll turn into a sinus infection.*

He was hacking up a lung by the sounds of it, so she left the kitchen and crossed the family room, which would remain an ironic description unless they hired the Von Trapps to fill it. And even then there'd be room for one of the smaller African nations and a circus.

He stood at the top of the stairs, naked, coughing blood out of his mouth and onto his chest. He had one hand over the hole in his throat and he kept blinking and coughing, blinking and coughing, like he was pretty sure if he could just swallow whatever was stuck in his throat, this too would pass.

Then he fell. He didn't make it all the way down the stairs – there were a lot of them – but he made it nearly halfway before his right foot got jammed between the balusters. Alan ended his life lying face down and bare-ass, dangling upside down like something about to be dipped.

Nicole only realized she'd been screaming when she stopped.

She heard herself say, "Oh, boy. Jesus. Oh, boy."

Alan's head had landed on the wood between the runner and the balustrade and he'd begun to drip.

"Oh, boy. Wow."

"You got my money?"

To her credit she didn't whip around or let out a yelp. She turned slowly to face him. He stood a couple feet behind her in the family room. He looked every inch the suburban dad out on Saturday errands – light blue shirt untucked over wrinkled khaki cargo shorts, boat shoes on his feet.

"I do," she said. "It's in the kitchen. Do you want to come with me?"

"No, I'm good here."

She started to take a step and stopped. She jerked a thumb toward the kitchen. "May I?"

"What?" he said. "Yeah, sure."

She felt his eyes on her as she crossed the family room to the kitchen. She had no reason to think he had, in fact, turned to watch her go, but she felt it all the same. In the kitchen, her purse was where she'd left it, on one of the high bar stools, and she took the envelope from it, the envelope she'd been instructed to leave in the ivy at the base of the wall by the entrance gate on her way out. But she'd never gone out.

"You cook?" He stood in the doorway, in the portico they'd designed to look like porticos in Tuscan kitchens.

"Me? No. No." She brought him the envelope.

He took it from her with a courteous nod. "Thank you." He looked around the room. "This is a hell of a kitchen for someone who doesn't cook."

"Well, no, it's for the chef."

"Oh, the chef. Well, there you go then. Makes sense again. I always wanted one of those hanging pot things. And those pots, what're they – copper?"

"Some of them, yeah."

He nodded and seemed impressed. He walked back into the family room and stuffed the envelope into the pocket of his cargo shorts. He took a seat by the hearth and smiled in such a way that she knew she was expected to take the seat across from him.

So she did.

Directly behind him was an eight-foot mirror in a marble frame that matched the marble of the hearth. She was reflected in it along with the back of his head and the back of his chair. She suspected she might need work on her lower eyelids. They were growing darker lately, deeper.

"What do you do for a living, Nicole?"

"I'm a homemaker."

"So you make things?"

"No." She chuckled.

"Why's that funny?"

Her smile died in the mirror. "It's not."

"Then why you chuckling?"

"I didn't realize I was."

"You say you're a homemaker; it's a fair question to ask what you make."

"I make this house," she said softly, "a home."

"Ah, I get it," he said. He looked around the room for a moment and his face darkened. "No, I don't. That's one of those things that sounds good – I make the house a home – but is really bullshit. I mean, this doesn't feel like a home, it feels like a fucking monument to, I don't know, hoarding a bunch of useless shit. I saw your bedroom – well one of them, one with the bed the size of Air Force One, that yours?"

She nodded. "That's the master, yeah."

"That's the master's? OK."

"No, I said—"

"Anyway, I'm up there thinking you could hold NFL combines in that room. It's fucking huge. It ain't intimate, that's for sure. And homes to me, always feel intimate. Houses, on the other hand, they can feel like anything."

He pulled a handful of coins out of his pocket for some reason, shook them in his palm.

She glanced at the clock. "Lana's expecting me."

He nodded. "So you don't have a job."

"No."

"And you don't produce anything."

"No."

"You consume."

"Huh?"

"You consume," he repeated. "Air, food, energy—" He looked up at the ceiling and over at the walls: "—space."

She followed his gaze and when she looked back at him, the gun was out on his lap. It was black and smaller than she would have imagined and it had a very long suppressor attached to the muzzle, the kind hit men always used in movies like *Grosse Pointe Blank* or *The Professional*, the kind that went *pffft* when fired.

"I'm meeting Lana," she said again.

"I know." He shook the change in his hand again and she looked closer, realized it wasn't coins at all. Some kind of small metal things that reminded her of snowflake replicas.

"Lana knows who you are."

"She thinks she does, but she actually knew another guy, the real Kineavy. See, they never met. Her father met him, but her father died – what – three years ago, after the stroke."

Her therapist had taught her breathing exercises for tense situations. She tried one now. She took long slow breaths and tried to visualize their colors but the only color that came up was red.

He plucked one of the metal snowflakes from his palm and held it between the thumb and forefinger of his right hand. "So Kineavy, I knew him well, he died too. About two years ago. Natural causes. And faux Kineavy – that's me – sees no point in meeting most clients a second time, which suits them fine. What do you do, Mrs Walford? What do you do?"

She could feel her lower lip start to bubble and she sucked it into her mouth for a moment. "I do nothing."

"You do nothing," he agreed. "So why should I let you live?"

"Because—"

He flicked his wrist and the metal snowflake entered her throat. She could see it in the mirror. About a third of it – three metal points out of eight – stuck out of her flesh. The other five points were on the other side, in her throat. A floss-thin line of blood trickled out of the new seam in her body, but otherwise, she didn't look like someone who was dying. She looked OK.

He stood over her. "You knew what your husband was doing, right?"

"Yes." The word sounded funny, like a whistle, like a baby noise.

"But you didn't stop him."

"I tried. That's why I hired you."

"You didn't stop him."

"No."

"You spent the money."

"Yes."

"You feel bad about it?"

And she had, she'd felt so terribly bad about it. Tears spilled from her eyes and dripped from the edges of her jaw. "Yes."

"You felt bad? You felt sad?"

"Yes."

He nodded. "Who gives a shit?"

And she watched in the mirror as he fired the bullet into her head.

Afterward, he walked around the house for a little bit. He checked out the cars in the garage, the lawn out back so endless you would have thought it was part of the Serengeti. There was a gym and a pool house and a guest house. A guest house for a seven-bedroom main house. He shook his head as he went back inside and passed through the dining room and the living room into the family room where she sat in the chair and he lay on the stairs. All this space, and they'd never had kids. You would have thought they would've had kids.

To kill the silence, if for no other reason.

VOICES THROUGH THE WALL

ALEX GRAY

Voices through the wall. I can hear them, whispering, making insinuations about me. But I'm well used to that now, aren't I? The constant babble of tongues, the sly, invisible eyes looking at the plasterboard that divides them from me, knowing I can sense their disapproval.

It wasn't always like this, though. When he was born, it wasn't thought of as a crime any more; having a wee one out of wedlock had become as common as setting up house together with your man. *Partner*, they call him now, as if he was doing the business all right. There was no parental opposition either, because both of mine were long dead. No grannies to shush the wee fella or to take him off my hands for a brief hour while I caught up with washing his baby clothes. Just him and me. Didn't do too badly, either. Got a wee flat off the council, one floor up, and managed to furnish it with second-hand stuff from the Sally Army shop in Partick. Visiting officer from the Social helped an' all. Nice woman she was, telling me it was my right to have all these things; the layette, the blankets and even the living room decorated at their expense.

So it was nice at first, having this wee man cuddling up, me the centre of his universe. He was never a quiet baby and squirmed and wriggled whenever it was time to change a filthy nappy, but he loved splashing in the blue plastic bath, making damp patches on the worn carpet. Never had any bother from them downstairs, either. No one banging a stick against the ceiling to tell me the racket was too much, making the baby scream even louder. No, the neighbours were lovely; even brought nicely wrapped gifts for Jonnie at Christmas. Made me feel bad 'cos I had nothing to give them back. I remember the yellow rubber duck and that teddy bear with his knitted blue waistcoat: Jonnie played with them for years until they were all but trashed. They disappeared one day after he came home from school and I never found them till just the other day, at the bottom of a box in the hall cupboard. Teddy's head was missing and the duck would never bob in the water any more, its plastic sides stabbed through with a blunt instrument. Holding them in both hands, I wept tears that I had thought could not be shed any more.

Most days I go down to the chapel, but not when Father is in the middle of a service. No, I wait until I'm sure there's nobody left then slip into a pew at the front and have my conversation with the Madonna. Doesn't look as if she could say much, this painted plaster figure, but it does me good to talk to her. She understands, you see. *What was it like for you?* I sometimes ask her. *Did they mock you and whisper behind their hands? "That's his mother. Bad lot, if you ask me. No way to bring up a child. Illegitimate, an' all." Did they point their fingers at you? Wag their self-righteous heads and tell themselves, "It all comes down to the parents, in the end."* Aye, I can guess the sort of pain that pierced your heart after they put him on a cross and killed him.

They didn't kill Jonnie, just put him away. The lawyer told

me he'd get life. Not that it really means life, you know. Just a couple of decades and he could've been back out. But that was before they'd assessed him and found that he wasn't right in the head. Not his fault he'd murdered those wee girls, really. Something in his brain that was never right. But it doesn't stop the voices, on and on, suggesting, wondering whether I was a bad mother to him, making him what he is today.

The newspapers had a field day. This woman came up to see me, promising a load of cash if I would tell them my story. I told her to go to hell. It wasn't any of their business, was it? Even when I had to appear in court as a witness, they wouldn't leave me alone. I saw the wee girls' parents, two mums' and two dads' heads bowed as they entered the High Court. Recognised them from the papers and the telly. Their lives would never be the same again. Never. But neither would mine and the thought that they might just understand that made me want to go up to them and say I was sorry, as if apologising for what Jonnie had done could make it OK. I never did get close enough to catch the eye of any one of them, though their misery cut me to ribbons.

I'd said sorry so many times before. To the weans who'd been bullied by my son and to the parents who'd come knocking at my door, fierce scowls on their unforgiving faces. *Sorry*, I'd say, trying to smile and be friendly to them. *He's just a very active boy*, I'd tell them, thinking to myself: *wild, uncontrollable*, not the wee lad who'd crawled into my bed whenever the thunder crashed and the rain drummed against the windowpanes. When had it all gone wrong? When had Jonnie become this monster living in my home, terrorising me with a look?

Primary Five he'd been escorted home by the head teacher of St Francis. There had been a fight and Jonnie had pulled out a blade. *Was it one that I recognised?*, the man had asked. Looking at my wee vegetable knife, I'd said, yes, it was. Jonnie had hung his head and said nothing at all, nodding his promises to be a better student, never to carry a dangerous weapon like that again. I threw the knife out and bought another one in Woolworth's. Somehow I couldn't bear the thought of cutting up potatoes with the same blade that my son had used to hurt another little boy. But it hadn't stopped there. Money went missing from my purse and into Jonnie's pocket. He must have bought his first switchblade with cash from his very own family allowance. And by the time I challenged him about it, he had grown bigger than me and looked down at his wee Maw with a sneer on his face that was so different from the lovely boy I'd once known.

They said I should have controlled him better. Been a role model for him, whatever that meant. But he left home at sixteen, no qualifications to his name, ready to face a world on his own. I'd cried then, but there was also a sense of pride that my boy could stand on his own two feet. He got a job and came back sometimes for a meal or just to tell me how he was doing. Half of me wanted him back home but the other half felt only relief once he'd gone again.

It was Mother's Day today. For the last week I've seen the shops full of decorated banners and cards, flowers in the doorways. Jonnie made me a card in Primary Two. I took it out this morning and looked at it, his childish scrawl wishing me a *Happy Mother's Day*. I don't have any letters from the place he's in, not even a Christmas card. And I'm not allowed to send anything to Jonnie in case it upsets him. Sometimes I wonder what it's like for him in that place full of mad, bad, sick people and the doctors who have to restrain their violent behaviour. Does Jonnie hear voices through the walls there? And can he hear the whispering coming into his room at night?

The sound of the television stops and the muttering begins, telling me I'm a bad mother, that it's all my fault, that these little girls would be alive if it hadn't been for me and my one lapse of decency.

And they will go on, whispering their insinuations even when my dust blows away and this victim is long forgotten.

WET
WITH
RAIN

LEE CHILD

Births and deaths are in the public record. Census returns and rent rolls and old mortgages are searchable. As are citizenship applications from all the other English-speaking countries. There are all kinds of ancestry sites on the web. These were the factors in our favor.

Against us was a historical truth. The street had been built in the 1960s. Fifty years ago, more or less. Within living memory. Most of the original residents had died off, but they had families, who must have visited, and who might remember. Children and grandchildren, recipients of lore and legend, and therefore possibly a problem.

But overall we counted ourselves lucky. The first owners of the house in question were long dead, and had left no children. The husband had surviving siblings, but they had all gone to either Australia or Canada. The wife had a living sister, still in the neighborhood, but she was over eighty years old, and considered unreliable.

Since the original pair, the house had had five owners, most of them in the later years. We felt we had enough distance. So we went with the third variant of the second plan. Hairl Carter came with me. Hairl Carter the second, technically. His father had the same name. From southeastern Missouri. His father's mother had wanted to name her firstborn Harold, but she had no more than a third-grade education, and couldn't spell except phonetically. So Harold it was, phonetically. The old lady never knew it was weird. We all called her grandson Harry, which might not have pleased her.

Harry did the paperwork, which was easy enough, because we made it all Xeroxes of Xeroxes, which hides a lot of sins. I opened an account at a DC bank, in the name of the society, and I put half a million dollars in, and we got credit cards and a checkbook. Then we rehearsed. We prepped it, like a candidates' debate. The same conversation, over and over again, down all the possible highways and byways. We identified weak spots, but we had no choice but to barrel through. We figured audacity would stop them thinking straight.

We flew first to London, then to Dublin in the south, and then we made the connection to Belfast on tickets that cost less than cups of coffee back home. We took a cab to the Europa Hotel, which is where we figured people like us would stay. We arranged a car with the concierge. Then we laid up and slept. We figured mid morning the next day should be zero hour.

The car was a crisp Mercedes and the driver showed no real reluctance about the address. Which was second from the end of a short line of ticky-tacky row houses, bland and cheaply built, with big areas of peeling white weatherboard, which must have saved money on bricks. The roof tiles were concrete, and had gone mossy. In the distance the hills were like velvet, impossibly green, but all around us the built environment was hard. There was fine cold drizzle in the air, and the street and the sidewalk were both shiny gray.

The car waited at the curb and we opened a broken gate and walked up a short path through the front yard. Carter rang the bell and the door opened immediately. The Mercedes had not gone unnoticed. A woman looked out at us. She was solidly built, with a pale, meaty face. She said, "Who are you?"

I said, "We're from America."

"America?"

"We came all the way to see you."

"Why?"

"Mrs Healy, is it?" I asked, even though I knew it was. I knew all about her. I knew where she was born, how old she was, and how much her husband made. Which wasn't much. They were a month behind on practically everything. Which I hoped was going to help.

"Yes, I'm Mrs Healy," the woman said.

"My name is John Pacino, and my colleague here is Harry Carter."

"Good morning to you both."

"You live in a very interesting house, Mrs Healy."

She looked blank, and then craned her neck out the door and stared up at her front wall. She said, "Do I?"

"Interesting to us, anyway."

"Why?"

"Can we tell you all about it?"

She said, "Would you like a wee cup of tea?"

"That would be lovely."

So we trooped inside, first Carter, then me, feeling a kind of preliminary satisfaction, as if our lead-off hitter had gotten on base. Nothing guaranteed, but so far so good. The air inside smelled of daily life and closed windows. A skilled analyst could have listed the ingredients from their last eight meals. All of which had been either boiled or fried, I guessed.

It wasn't the kind of household where guests get deposited in the parlor to wait. We followed the woman to the kitchen, which had drying laundry suspended on a rack. She filled a kettle and lit the stove. She said, "Tell me what's interesting about my house."

Carter said, "There's a writer we admire very much, name of Edmund Wall."

"Here?"

"In America."

"A writer?"

"A novelist. A very fine one."

"I never heard of him. But then, I don't read much."

"Here," Carter said, and he took Xeroxes from his pocket and smoothed them on the counter. They were faked to look like Wikipedia pages. Which is trickier than people think. Wikipedia prints different than it looks on the computer screen.

Mrs Healy said, "Is he famous?"

"Not exactly," I said. "Writers don't really get famous. But he's very well respected. Among people who like his sort of thing. There's an appreciation society. That's why we're here. I'm the chairman and Mr Carter is the general secretary."

Mrs Healy stiffened a little, as if she thought we were trying to sell her something. She said, "I'm sorry, but I don't want to join. I don't know him."

I said, "That's not the proposition we have for you."

"Then what is?"

"Before you, the Robinsons lived here, am I right?"

"Yes," she said.

"And before them, the Donnellys, and before them, the McLaughlins."

The woman nodded. "They all got cancer. One after the other. People started to say this was an unlucky house."

I looked concerned. "That didn't bother you? When you bought it?"

She said, "My faith has no room for superstition."

Which was a circularity fit to make a person's head explode. It struck me mute. Carter said, "And before the McLaughlins were the McCanns, and way back at the beginning were the McKennas."

"Before my time," the woman said, uninterested, and I felt the runner on first steal second. Scoring position. So far so good.

I said, "Edmund Wall was born in this house."

"Who?"

"Edmund Wall. The novelist. In America."

"No one named Wall ever lived here."

"His mother was a good friend of Mrs McKenna. Right back at the beginning. She came to visit from America. She thought she had another month, but the baby came early."

"When?"

"The 1960s."

"In this house?"

"Upstairs in the bedroom. No time to get to the hospital."

"A baby?"

"The future Edmund Wall."

"I never heard about it. Mrs McKenna has a sister. She never talks about it."

Which felt like the runner getting checked back. I said, "You know Mrs McKenna's sister?"

"We have a wee chat from time to time. Sometimes I see her in the hairdresser's."

"It was fifty years ago. How's her memory?"

"I should think a person would remember that kind of thing."

Carter said, "Maybe it was hushed up. It's possible Edmund's mother wasn't married."

Mrs Healy went pale. Impropriety. Scandal. In her house. Worse than cancer. She said, "Why are you telling me this?"

I said, "The Edmund Wall Appreciation Society wants to buy your house."

"Buy it?"

"For a museum. Well, like a living museum, really. Certainly people could visit, to see the birthplace, but we could keep his papers here, too. It could be a research center."

"Do people do that?"

"Do what? Research?"

"No, visit houses where writers were born."

"All the time. Lots of writers' houses are museums. Or tourist attractions. We could make a very generous offer. Edmund Wall has many passionate supporters in America."

"How generous?"

"Best plan would be pick out where you'd like to live next, and we'll make sure you can. Within reason, of course. Maybe a new house. They're building them all over." Then I shut up, and let temptation work its magic. Mrs Healy went quiet. Then she started to look around her kitchen. Chipped cabinets, sagging hinges, damp air.

The kettle started to whistle.

She said, "I'll have to talk to my husband."

Which felt like the runner sliding into third ahead of the throw. Safe. Ninety feet away. Nothing guaranteed, but so far so good. In fact bloody good, as they say in those damp little islands. We were in high spirits, on the way back in the Mercedes.

The problem was waiting for us in the Europa's lobby. An Ulsterman, maybe fifty years old, in a cheap suit, with old nicks and scars on his hands and thickening around his eyes. A former field operative, no doubt, many years in the saddle, now moved to a desk because of his age. I was familiar with the type. It was like looking in a mirror.

He said, "Can I have a word?"

We went to the bar, which was dismal and empty ahead of the lunchtime rush. The guy introduced himself as a copper, from right there in Belfast, from a unit he didn't specify, but which I guessed was Special Branch, which was the brass-knuckle wing of the UK internal security service. Like the FBI, with the gloves off. He said, "Would you mind telling me who you are and why you're here?"

So Carter gave him the guff about Edmund Wall, and the appreciation society, and the birthplace, but what was good enough earlier in the morning didn't sound so great in the cold light of midday. The guy checked things on his phone in real time as Carter talked, and then he said, "There are four things wrong with that story. There is no Edmund Wall, there is no appreciation society, the bank account you opened is at the branch nearest to Langley, which is CIA headquarters, and most of all, that house you're talking about was once home to Gerald McCann, who was a notorious paramilitary in his day."

Carter said nothing, and neither did I. The guy said, "Northern Ireland is part of the United Kingdom, you know. They won't allow unannounced activities on their own turf. So again, would you mind telling me who you are and why you're here?"

I said, "You interested in a deal?"

"What kind?"

"You want to buy a friend in a high place?"

"How high?"

"Very high."

"Where?"

"Somewhere useful to your government."

"Terms?"

"You let us get the job done first."

"Who gets killed?"

"Nobody. The Healys get a new house. That's all."

"What do you get?"

"Paid. But your new friend in the very high place gets peace of mind. For which he'll be suitably grateful, I'm sure."

"Tell me more."

"First I need to check you have your head on straight. This is not the kind of thing where you make a bunch of calls and get other people involved. This is the kind of thing where you let us do our work, and then when we're gone, you announce your new relationship as a personal coup. Or not. Maybe you'll want to keep the guy in your vest pocket."

"How many laws are you going to break?"

"None at all. We're going to buy a house. Happens every day."

"Because there's something in it, right? What did Gerald McCann leave behind?"

"You got to agree what I said before. You got to at least nod your head. I have to be able to trust you."

"OK, I agree," the guy said. "But I'm sticking with you all the way. We're a threesome now. Until you're done. Every minute. Until I wave you off at the airport."

"No, come with us," I said. "You can meet your new friend. At least shake hands with him. Then come back. Vest pocket or not, you'll feel better that way."

He fell for it, like I knew he would. I mean, why not? Security services love a personal coup. They love their vest pockets. They love to run people. They love to be the guy. He said, "Deal. So what's the story?"

I said, "Once upon a time there was a young officer in the US Army. A bit of a hothead, with certain sympathies. With a certain job, at a certain time. He sold some obsolete weapons."

"To Gerald McCann?"

I nodded. "Who as far as we know never used them. Who we believe buried them under his living room floor. Meanwhile our young officer grew up and got promoted and went into a whole different line of work. Now he wants the trail cleaned up."

"You want to buy the house so you can dig up the floor?"

I nodded again. "Can't break in and do it. Too noisy. The floors are concrete. We're going to need jackhammers. Neighbors need to think we're repairing the drains or something."

"These weapons are still traceable?"

"Weapon, singular, to be honest with you. Which I'm prepared to be, in a spot like this. Still traceable, yes. And extremely embarrassing, if it comes to light."

"Did Mrs Healy believe you about Edmund Wall?"

"She believed us about the money. We're from America."

The guy from Special Branch said, "It takes a long time to buy a house."

It took three weeks, with all kinds of lawyer stuff, and an inspection, which was a pantomime and a farce, because what did we care? But it would have looked suspicious if we had waived it. We were supposed to be diligent stewards of the appreciation society's assets. So we commissioned it, and pretended to read it afterward. It was pretty bad, actually. For a spell I was worried the jackhammer would bring the whole place down.

We stayed in Belfast the whole three weeks. Normally we might have gone home and come back again, but not with the Special Branch copper on the scene, obviously. We had to watch him every minute. Which was easy enough, because he had to watch us every minute. We all spent three whole weeks gazing at each other, and reading crap about dry rot and rising damp. Whatever that was. It rained every day.

But in the end the lawyers got it done, and I got an undramatic phone call saying the house was ours. So we picked up the key and drove over and walked around with pages from the inspection report in our hands and worried expressions on our faces. Which I thought of as setting the stage. The jackhammer had to be explicable. And the neighbors were as nosy as hell. They were peering out and coming over and introducing themselves in droves. They brought old Mrs McKenna's sister, who claimed to remember the baby being born, which set off a whole lot of tutting and clucking among her audience. More people came. As a result we waited two days before we rented the jackhammer. Easier than right away, we thought. I knew how to operate it. I had taken lessons from a crew repairing Langley's secure staff lot.

The living room floor was indeed concrete, under some kind of asphalt screed, which was under a foam-backed carpet so old it had gone flat and crusty. We tore it up and saw a patch of screed that was different than the rest. It was the right size, too. I smiled. Gerald McCann, taking care of business.

I asked, "What actually happened to McCann?"

The Special Branch guy said, "Murdered."

"Who by?"

"Us."

"When?"

"Before he could use this, obviously, whatever it is."

And after that, conversation was impossible, because I got the hammer started. After which the job went fast. The concrete was long on sand and short on cement. Same the world over. Concrete is a dirty business. But even so, the pit was pretty deep. More than just secure temporary storage. It felt kind of permanent. But we got to the bottom eventually, and we got the thing out.

It was wrapped in heavy plastic, but it was immediately

recognizable. A reinforced canvas cylinder, olive green, like a half-size oil drum, with straps and buckles all over it, to keep it closed up tight, and to make it man-portable, like a backpack. A big backpack. A big, heavy backpack.

The guy from Special Branch went very quiet, and then he said, "Is that what I think it is?"

I asked, "Where did you serve?"

"Back then? SAS."

"Then yes, it's what you think it is."

"Jesus Christ on a bike."

"Don't worry. The warhead is a dummy. Because our boy in uniform wasn't."

Carter said, "Warhead? What is it?"

I said nothing.

The guy from Special Branch said, "It's an SADM. A W-54 in an H-912 transport container."

"Which is what?"

"A Strategic Atomic Demolition Munition. A W-54 missile warhead, which was the baby of the family, adapted to use as an explosive charge. Strap that thing to a bridge pier, and it's like dropping a thousand tons of TNT on it."

"It's nuclear?"

I said, "It weighs just over fifty pounds. Less than the bag you take on vacation. It's the nearest thing to a suitcase nuke ever built."

The guy from Special Branch said, "It is a suitcase nuke, never mind the nearest thing."

Carter said, "I never heard about them."

I said, "Developed in the 1950s. Obsolete by 1970.

Paratroops were trained to jump with them, behind the lines, to blow up power stations and dams."

"With nuclear bombs?"

"They had mechanical timers. The paratroops might have gotten away."

"Might have?"

"It was a tough world back then."

"But this warhead is fake?"

"Open it up and take a look."

"I wouldn't know the difference."

"Good point," I said. "Gerald McCann obviously didn't."

The guy from Special Branch said, "I can see why my new friend wants the trail cleaned up. Selling nuclear weapons to foreign paramilitary groups? He couldn't survive that, whoever he is."

We put the thing in the trunk of a rented car, and drove to a quiet corner of Belfast International Airport, to a gate marked GENERAL AVIATION, which meant private jets, and we found ours, which was a Gulfstream IV, painted gray and unmarked except for a tail number. The guy from Special Branch looked a little jealous.

"Borrowed," I said. "Mostly it's used for renditions."

The guy from Special Branch looked a little worried.

I said, "I'm sure they hosed the blood out."

We loaded the munition on board ourselves, because there was no spare crew to help us. There was one pilot and no steward. Standard practice, in the rendition business. Better deniability. We figured the munition was about the size of a fat guy, so we strapped it upright in a seat of its own. Then we all three sat down, as far from it as we could get.

Ninety minutes out I went to the bathroom, and after that I steered the conversation back to rendition. I said, "These planes are modified, you know. They have some of the electronic interlocks taken out. You can open the door while you're flying, for instance. Low and slow, over the water. They threaten to throw the prisoner out. All part of softening him up ahead of time."

Then I said, "Actually, sometimes they do throw the prisoner out. On the way home, usually, after he's spilled the beans. Too much trouble to do anything else, really."

Then I said, "Which is what we're going to do with the munition. We have to. We have no way of destroying it before we land, and we can't let it suddenly reappear in the US, like it just escaped from the museum. And this is the perfect set-up for corroboration. Because there's three of us. Because we're going to get questions. He needs to know for sure. So this way I can swear I saw you two drop it out the door, and you two can swear you saw it hit the water, and you can swear I was watching you do it. We can back each other up three ways."

Which all made sense, so we went low and slow and I opened the door. Salt air howled in, freezing cold, and the plane rocked and juddered. I stepped back, and the guy from Special Branch came first, sidewinding down the aisle, with one of the transport container's straps hefted in his nicked and scarred left hand, and then came the munition itself, heavy, bobbing like a fat man in a hammock, and then came Carter, a strap in his right hand, shuffling sideways.

They got lined up side by side at the open door, their backs to me, each with a forearm up on the bulkhead to steady himself, the munition swinging slackly and bumping the floor between them. I said, "On three," and I started counting the numbers out, and they hoisted the cylinder and started swinging it, and on three they opened their hands and the canvas straps jerked free and the cylinder sailed out in the air and was instantly whipped away by the slipstream. They kept their forearms on the bulkhead, looking out, craning, staring down, waiting for the splash, and I took out the gun I had collected from the bathroom and shot the guy from Special Branch in the lower back, not because of any sadistic tendency, but because of simple ballistics. If the slug went through and through, I wanted it to carry on into thin air, not hit the airframe.

I don't think the bullet killed the guy. But the shock changed his day. He went all weak, and his forearm gave way, and he half fell and half got sucked out into the void. No sound. Just a blurred pinwheel as the currents caught him, and then a dot that got smaller, and then a tiny splash in the blue below, indistinguishable from a million white-crested waves.

I stepped up and helped Carter wrestle the door shut. He said, "I guess he knew too much."

I said, "Way too much."

We sat down, knee to knee.

* * *

Carter figured it out less than an hour later. He was not a dumb guy. He said, "If the warhead was a dummy, he could spin it like entrapment, like taking a major opponent out of the game. Or like economic warfare. Like a Robin Hood thing. He took a lot of bad money out of circulation, in exchange for a useless piece of junk. He could be the secret hero. The super-modest man."

"But?" I said.

"He's not spinning it that way. And all those people died of cancer. The Robinsons, and the Donnellys, and the McLaughlins."

"So?" I said.

"The warhead was real. That was an atom bomb. He sold nuclear weapons."

"Small ones," I said. "And obsolete."

Carter didn't reply. But that wasn't the important part. The important part came five minutes later. I saw it arrive in his eyes. I said, "Ask the question."

He said, "I'd rather not."

I said, "Ask the question."

"Why was there a gun in the bathroom? The Special Branch guy was with us all the time. You didn't call ahead for it. You had no opportunity. But it was there for you anyway. Why?"

I didn't answer.

He said, "It was there for me. The Special Branch guy was happenstance. Me, you were planning to shoot all along."

I said, "Kid, our boss sold live nuclear weapons. I'm cleaning up for him. What else do you expect?"

Carter said, "He trusts me."

"No, he doesn't."

"I would never rat him out. He's my hero."

"Gerald McCann should be your hero. He had the sense not to use the damn thing. I'm sure he was sorely tempted."

Carter didn't answer that. Getting rid of him was difficult, all on my own, but the next hours were peaceful, just me and the pilot, flying high and fast toward a spectacular sunset. I dropped my seat way back, and I stretched out. Relaxation is important. Life is short and uncertain, and it pays to make the best of whatever comes your way.

HAPPY HOLIDAYS

VAL MCDERMID

I

A chrysanthemum burst of colour flooded the sky. "Oooh," said the man, his blue eyes sparking with reflected light.

"Aaah," said the woman, managing to invest the single syllable with irony and good humour. Her shaggy blonde hair picked up colour from the fireworks, giving her a fibre-optic punk look at odds with the conservative cut of her coat and trousers.

"I've always loved fireworks."

"Must be the repressed arsonist in you."

Dr Tony Hill, clinical psychologist and criminal profiler, pulled a rueful face. "You've got me bang to rights, guv." He checked out the smile on her face. "Admit it, though. You love Bonfire Night too." A scatter of green and red tracer raced across the sky, burning after-images inside his eyelids.

DCI Carol Jordan snorted. "Nothing like it. Kids shoving bangers through people's letter boxes, drunks sticking lit fireworks up their backsides, nutters throwing bricks when the fire engines turn up to deal with bonfires that've gone out of control? Best night of the year for us."

Tony shook his head, refusing to give in to her sarcasm. "It's been a long time since you had to deal with rubbish like that. It's only the quality villains you have to bother with these days."

As if summoned by his words, Carol's phone burst into life. "Terrific," she groaned, turning away and jamming a finger into her free ear. "Sergeant Devine. What have you got?"

Tony tuned out the phone call, giving the fireworks his full attention. Moments later, he felt her touch on his arm. "I have to go."

"You need me?"

"I'm not sure. It wouldn't hurt."

If it didn't hurt, it would be the first time. Tony followed Carol back to her car, the sky hissing and fizzing behind him.

The smell of cooked human flesh was unforgettable and unambiguous. Sweet and cloying, it always seemed to coat the inside of Carol's nostrils for days, apparently lingering long after it should have been nothing more than a memory. She wrinkled her nose in disgust and surveyed the grisly scene.

It wasn't a big bonfire, but it had gone up like a torch. Whoever had built it had set it in the corner of a fallow field, close to a gate but out of sight of the road. The evening's light breeze had been enough to send a drift of sparks into the hedgerow and the resulting blaze had brought a fire crew to the scene. Job done, they'd checked the wet smoking heap of debris and discovered the source of the smell overwhelming even the fuel that had been used as an accelerant.

As Tony prowled round the fringes of what was clearly the scene of a worse crime than arson, Carol consulted the lead fire officer. "It wouldn't have taken long to get hold," he said. "From the smell, I think he used a mixture of accelerants – petrol, acetone, whatever. The sort of stuff you'd have lying around your garage."

Tony stared at the remains, frowning. He turned and called to the fire officer. "The body – did it start off in the middle like that?"

"You mean, was the bonfire built round it?"

Tony nodded. "Exactly."

"No. You can see from the way the wood's collapsed around it. It started off on top of the fire."

"Like a Guy." It wasn't a question; the fireman's answer had clearly confirmed what Tony already thought. He looked at Carol. "You do need me."

Tony smashed the ball back over the net, narrowly missing the return when his doorbell rang. He tossed the Wii control on to the sofa and went to the door. "We've got the post-mortem and some preliminary forensics." Carol walked in, not waiting for an invitation. "I thought you'd want to take a look." She passed him a file.

"There's an open bottle of wine in the fridge," Tony said, already scanning the papers and feeling his way into an armchair. As he read, Carol disappeared into the kitchen, returning with two glasses. She placed one on the table by Tony's chair and settled opposite him on the sofa, watching the muscles in his face tighten as he read.

It didn't make for comfortable reading. A male between

twenty-five and forty, the victim had been alive when he'd been put on the bonfire. Smoke inhalation had killed him, but he'd have suffered tremendous pain before the release of death. He'd been bound hand and foot with wire and his mouth had been sealed by some sort of adhesive tape. For a moment, Tony allowed himself to imagine how terrifying an ordeal it must have been and how much pleasure it had given the killer. But only for a moment. "No ID?" he said.

"We think he's Jonathan Meadows. His girlfriend reported him missing the morning after. We're waiting for confirmation from dental records."

"And what do we know about Jonathan Meadows?"

"He's twenty-six, he's a garage mechanic. He lives with his girlfriend in a flat in Moorside—"

"Moorside? That's a long way from where he died."

Carol nodded. "Right across town. He left work at the usual time. He told his girlfriend and his mates at work that he was going to the gym. He usually went three or four times a week, but he never showed up that night."

"So somewhere between – what, six and eight o'clock? – he met someone who overpowered him, bound and gagged him, stuck him on top of a bonfire and set fire to him?"

"That's about the size of it. Anything strike you?"

"That's not easy, carrying out something like that." Tony flicked through the few sheets of paper again. His mind raced through the possibilities, exploring the message of the crime, trying to make a narrative from the bare bones in front of him. "He's a very low-risk victim," he said. "When young men like him die violently, it's not usually like this. A pub brawl, a fight over a woman, a turf war over drugs or prostitution, yes. But not this kind of premeditated thing. If he was just a random victim, if anyone would do, it's more likely to be a homeless person, a drunk staggering home last thing, someone vulnerable. Not someone with a job, a partner, a life."

"You think it's personal?"

"Hard to say until we know a lot more about Jonathan Meadows." He tapped the scene-of-crime report. "There doesn't seem to be much in the way of forensics at the scene."

"There's a pull-in by the gate to the field. It's tarmacked, so no convenient tyre tracks. There's a few footprints, but they're pretty indistinct. The SOCOs think he was wearing some sort of covering over his shoes. Just like the ones we use to preserve the crime scene." Carol pulled a face to emphasize the irony. "No convenient cigarette ends, Coke cans or used condoms."

Tony put down the file and drank some wine. "I don't think he's a beginner. It's too well executed. I think he's done this before. At least once."

Carol shook her head. "I checked the database. Nothing like this anywhere in the UK in the last five years."

That, he thought, was why she needed him. She thought in straight lines, which was a useful attribute in a cop, since, however much they might like to believe otherwise, that was how most criminals thought. But years of training and experience had honed his own corkscrew mind till he could see nothing but hidden agendas stretching backwards like the images in an infinity mirror. "That's because you were looking for a burning," he said.

Carol looked at him as if he'd lost it. "Well, duh," she

said. "That's because the victim was burned."

He jumped to his feet and began pacing. "Forget the fire. That's irrelevant. Look for low-risk victims who were restrained with wire and gagged with adhesive tape. The fire is not what this is about. That's just window dressing, Carol."

Carol tapped the pile of paper on her desk with the end of her pen. Sometimes it was hard not to credit Tony with psychic powers. He'd said there would be at least one other victim, and it looked as if he'd been right. Trawling the databases with a different set of parameters had taken Carol's IT specialist a few days. But she'd finally come up with a second case that fitted the bill.

The body of Tina Chapman, a thirty-seven-year-old teacher from Leeds, had been found in the Leeds–Liverpool canal a few days before Jonathan Meadows' murder. A routine dredging had snagged something unexpected and further examination had produced a grisly finding. She'd been gagged with duct tape, bound hand and foot with wire, tethered to a wooden chair weighted with a cement block and thrown in. She'd been alive when she went into the water. Cause of death: drowning.

A single parent, she'd been reported missing by her thirteen-year-old son. She'd left work at the usual time, according to colleagues. Her son thought she'd said she was going to the supermarket on her way home, but neither her credit card nor her store loyalty card had been used.

Carol had spoken to the senior investigating officer in

charge of the case. He'd admitted they were struggling. "We only found her car a couple of days ago in the car park of a hotel about half a mile from the supermarket her son said she used. It was parked down the end, in a dark corner out of range of their CCTV cameras. No bloody idea what she was doing down there. And no joy from forensics so far."

"Anybody in the frame?"

His weary sigh reminded her of cases she'd struggled with over the years. "It's not looking good, to be honest. There was a boyfriend, but they split up about six months ago. Nobody else involved, it just ran out of road. Quite amicable, apparently. The boyfriend still takes the lad to the rugby. Not a scrap of motive."

"And that's it?" Carol was beginning to share his frustration. "What about the boy's real father?"

"Well, he wasn't what you'd call any kind of father. He walked out on them when the lad was a matter of months old."

Carol wasn't quite ready to let go of the straw she'd grasped. "He might have come round to the idea of having some contact with the boy."

"I doubt it. He died in the Boxing Day tsunami back in '04. So we're back to square one and not a bloody thing to go at."

Carol still couldn't accept she'd reached the end of the road. "What about her colleagues? Any problems there?"

She could practically hear the shrug. "Not that they're letting on about. Nobody's got a bad word to say about Tina, and I don't think they're just speaking well of the dead. She's been working there for four years and doesn't seem to have caused a ripple with other staff or parents. I can't say I share your notion that this has got anything to do with your body, but I tell you, if you come up with anything that makes sense of this, I'll buy you a very large drink."

Making sense of things was what Bradfield Police paid Tony for. But sometimes it was easier than others. This was not one of those occasions. Carol had dropped off the case files on Jonathan Meadows and Tina Chapman at Bradfield Moor, the secure hospital where he spent his days among the criminally insane, a clientele whose personal idiosyncrasies he did not always find easy to distinguish from the population at large.

Two victims, linked by their unlikelihood. There was no evidence that their paths had ever crossed. They lived thirty miles apart. Carol's team had already established that Tina Chapman did not have her car serviced at the garage where Jonathan Meadows worked. He'd never attended a school where she'd taught. They had no apparent common interests. Anyone other than Tony might have been reluctant to forge any link between the two cases. Carol had pointed that out earlier, acknowledging that her counterpart in Leeds was far from convinced there was a connection. Tony's instincts said otherwise.

As he read, he made notes. *Water. Fire. Four elements?* It was a possibility, but admitting it took him no further forward. If the killer was opting for murder methods that mirrored fire, water, earth and air, what did it mean? And why did it apply to those particular victims? Tina Chapman was a French teacher. What had that to do with water? And how was a garage mechanic connected to fire? No, unless he could find more convincing connective tissue, the four elements idea wasn't going anywhere.

He studied the file again, spreading the papers across the living room floor so he could see all the information simultaneously. And this time, something much more interesting caught his attention.

Carol stared at the two pieces of paper, wondering what she was supposed to see. "What am I looking for?" she said.

"The dates," Tony said. "October 31. November 5."

Light dawned. "Hallowe'en. Bonfire Night."

"Exactly." As he always did when he was in the grip of an idea, he paced, pausing by the dining table to scribble down the odd note. "What's special about them, Carol?"

"Well, people celebrate them. They do particular things. They're traditional."

Tony grinned, his hands waving in the air as he spoke. "Traditional. Exactly. That's it. You've hit the nail on the head. They're great British traditions."

"Hallowe'en's American," Carol objected. "Trick or treat. That's not British."

"It is originally. It came from the Celtic Samhain festival. Trick or treat is a variation of the Scottish guising tradition. Trust me, Carol, it only got to be American when the Irish took it over there. We started it."

Carol groaned. "Sometimes I feel the internet is a terrible curse."

"Not to those of us with enquiring minds. So, we've got two

very British festivals. I can't help wondering if that's the root of what's going on here. Tina died like a witch on the ducking stool. Jonathan burned like a bonfire Guy. The murder methods fit the dates." He spun on his heel and headed back towards Carol.

"So I'm asking myself, is our killer somebody who's raging against Britain and our traditions? Someone who feels slighted by this country? Someone who feels racially oppressed, maybe? Because the victims are white, Carol. And the killer's paid no attention to Diwali. OK, we've not had Eid yet, but I'm betting he won't take a victim then. I'm telling you, Carol, I think I'm on to something here."

Carol frowned. "Even if you're right – and frankly, it sounds even more crazy than most of your theories – why these two? Why pick on them?"

Tony trailed to a halt and stared down at what he'd written. "I don't know yet." He turned to meet her eyes. "But there is one thing I'm pretty sure about."

He could see the dread in her eyes. "What's that?"

"If we don't find the killer, the next victim's going to be a dead Santa. Stuffed in a chimney would be my best guess."

Later, Tony's words would echo in Carol's head. When she least expected it, they reverberated inside her. As she sat in the canteen, half her attention on her lasagne and half on the screen of the TV, she was jolted by a newsflash that chilled her more than the November snow: SANTA SNATCHED OFF STREET.

* * *

II

It had been a long time since Tony had been a student but he'd never lost his taste for research. What made his investigations different from those of Carol and her team was his conviction that the truth lay in the tangents. An exhaustive police investigation would turn up all sorts of unexpectedness, but there would always be stuff that slipped between the cracks. People were superstitious about telling secrets. Even when they gave up information, they held something back. Partly because they could and partly because they liked the illusion of power it dealt them. Tony, a man whose gift for empathy was his finest tool and his greatest weakness, had a remarkable talent for convincing people that their hearts would never be at peace till they had shared every last morsel of information.

And so he devoted his attentions to identifying the unswept corners of the lives of Tina Chapman and Jonathan Meadows.

The first thing that attracted his attention about Tina Chapman was that she had only been in her current job for four years. In his world, history cast a long shadow, with present crimes often having their roots deep in the past. He wondered where Tina Chapman had been before she came to teach French in Leeds.

He knew he could probably short-circuit his curiosity with a call to Carol, but her gibe about the internet was still fresh in his mind so he decided to see what he could uncover without her help.

Googling Tina Chapman brought nothing relevant except for a Facebook entry describing her as "everybody's favourite language teacher", an online review of the sixth-form performance of *Le Malade Imaginaire* that she'd directed and a slew of news stories about the murder. None of the articles mentioned where she'd taught previously. But there was an interesting clue in one of them. Tina's son wasn't called Ben Chapman but Ben Wallace. "Lovely," Tony said aloud. If Wallace had been Ben's father's name, there was at least a fighting chance that his mother had used it at some point.

He tried "Tina Wallace" in the search engine, which threw out a couple of academics and a real estate agent in Wyoming. Then he tried "Martina Chapman", "Christina Chapman", "Martina Wallace" and finally, "Christina Wallace". He stared at the screen, hardly able to credit what he saw there.

There was no doubt about it. If ever there was a motive for murder, this was it.

Detective Inspector Mike Cassidy knew Carol Jordan only by reputation. Her major case squad was despised and desired in pretty much equal measure by Bradfield's detectives, depending on whether they knew they would never be good enough or they aspired to join. Cassidy avoided either camp; at forty-two, he knew he was too old to find a niche working alongside the Chief Constable's blue-eyed girl. But he didn't resent her success as so many others did. That didn't stop him showing his surprise when she walked into his incident room with an air of confident ownership.

He stood up and rounded his desk, determined not to be put at a disadvantage. "DCI Jordan," he said with a formal little nod. He waited; let her come to him.

Carol returned the nod. "DI Cassidy. I hear you're dealing with the abduction in Market Street?"

Cassidy's lips twisted in an awkward cross between a smile and a sneer. "The case of the stolen Santa? Isn't that what they're calling it in the canteen?"

"I don't care what they're calling it in the canteen. As far as I'm concerned, there's nothing funny about a man being kidnapped in broad daylight on a Bradfield street."

Cassidy took the rebuke on the chin. "As it happens, I'm with you on that one, ma'am. It's no joke for Tommy Garrity or his family. And apart from anything else, it makes us look like monkeys."

"So where are you up to?"

"Tommy Garrity was dressed in a Santa suit, collecting money for Christmas For Children when two men in balaclavas and blue overalls drove up the pedestrian precinct in a white Transit. They stopped in front of Tommy, bundled him into the Transit and took off. We got the van on CCTV, turns out it was stolen off a building site this morning." Cassidy turned to his desk and excavated a map from the stack of paper by the keyboard. He handed it to Carol. "The red line's the route they took out of the city centre. We lost them round the back of Temple Fields. Once you come off Campion Way, the coverage is patchy."

Carol sighed. "Typical. What about the number plate recognition cameras?"

"Nothing. At least we know they've not left the city on any of the main drags."

"So, Tommy Garrity. Is he known?"

Cassidy shook his head. "Nothing on file. He works behind the bar at the Irish Club in Harriestown, does a lot of charity work in his spare time. He's fifty-five, three kids, two grandkids. Wife's a school dinner lady. I've got a team out on the knocker but so far Garrity's white as the driven."

Carol traced the line on the map. "That's what worries me."

Cassidy couldn't keep his curiosity at bay any longer. "If you don't mind me asking, ma'am, what's your interest? I mean, not to play down the importance of daylight abduction, but it's not major in the sense of being up your street."

Carol dropped the map on Cassidy's desk. "Just something somebody said to me a couple of weeks ago. Can you keep me posted, please?"

Cassidy watched her walk out. She was more than easy on the eye, and normally that would have been all that registered with him. But Carol Jordan's interest had left him perturbed and anxious. What the hell was he missing here?

News generally passed Tony by. He had enough variety in his life to occupy his interest without having to seek out further examples of human shortcomings. But because he'd floated the suggestion of Santa as potential victim, he was more susceptible than normal to the scream of newspaper billboards that announced, SANTA SNATCHED IN CITY CENTRE.

The story in the paper was short on fact and long on frenzy, queasily uncertain whether it should be outraged or amused. Tony, already on his way to Carol's office, quickened his step.

He found her at her desk, reading witness statements from

the Santa kidnap. She looked up and squeezed out a tired smile. "Looks like you were right."

"No, I wasn't. I mean, I think I was, but this isn't him." Tony threw his hands in the air, exasperated at his inability to express himself clearly. "This isn't the next victim in a series," he said.

"What do you mean? Why not? You were the one who told me I should be looking out for Santa. And not in the sense of hanging up my stocking."

"There were two of them. I never said anything about two of them."

"I know you didn't. But it would have made the first two murders a lot easier if they'd been two-handed. And we both know that racially motivated fanatics tend to work in cells or teams. After what you said, I've had my crew looking at all our intel and we're not getting many hits on lone activists." She shrugged. "It may not have been in the profile but two makes sense."

Tony threw himself in the chair. "That's because I was ignoring my own cardinal rule. First you look at the victim. That's what it's all about, and I got distracted because of the eccentricity of the crimes. But I've looked at the victims now and I know why they were killed." He fished some printouts from his carrier bag. "Tina Chapman used to be known by her married name. She was Christina Wallace." He passed the top sheet to Carol. "She taught French at a school in Devon. She took a bunch of kids on a school trip and two of them drowned in a canoeing accident. The inquest cleared her but the bereaved parents spoke to the press, blaming her for what happened. And it does look like they had pretty strong reasons for that. So, she moved away. Reverted to her maiden name and started afresh."

"You think one of the parents did this?"

"No, no, that's not it. But once I knew that about Tina, I knew what I was looking for with Jonathan." He handed over the second sheet. "Seven years ago, a five-year-old girl was killed by a hit-and-run driver. The car was a Porsche that had allegedly been stolen from a garage where it was in for a service. The garage where Jonathan Meadows worked. I went over there and spoke to the local traffic officers. They told me that there was a strong feeling at the time that the Porsche hadn't been stolen at all, that Jonathan had taken it for a ride and had lost control. His DNA was all over the car but his excuse was that he'd been working on it. His girlfriend gave him an alibi and nothing ever came of it."

Carol stared at the two sheets of paper. "You're saying this is some kind of vigilante justice?"

Tony dipped his head. "Kind of. Both victims were implicated in the death of a child but went unpunished because of loopholes in law or lack of evidence. The killer feels they stole children away from their families. I think we should be looking for someone who has lost a child and believes nobody paid the price. Probably in the past year. He's choosing these victims because he believes they're culpable and he's choosing these murder methods because they mark the points in the year where parents celebrate with children."

* * *

Within the hour, Tony and Carol were studying a list of seven children who had died in circumstances where blame might possibly be assigned. "How can we narrow it down?" she demanded, frustration in her voice. "We can't put surveillance on all these parents and their immediate families."

"There's no obvious way," Tony said slowly.

"Santa Garrity could still be a potential victim," Carol said. "We don't know enough about his history and there's nothing in your theory to say it couldn't be two killers working together."

Tony shook his head. "It's emotionally wrong. This is about punishment and pain, not justice. It's too personal to be a team effort." He ran a hand through his hair. "Couldn't we at least go and talk to the parents? Shake the tree?"

"It's a waste of time. Even you can't pick out a killer just by looking at them." They sat in glum silence for a few minutes, then Carol spoke again. "Victims. You're right. It all comes back to victims. How's he choosing his victims? You had to do some digging to come up with what you found. There was nothing in the public domain to identify Jonathan, and Tina had changed her name. That's why the motive didn't jump out at my team."

Tony nodded. "You're right. So who knows this kind of information? It's not the police, there's at least two forces involved here. Not the Crown Prosecution Service either, neither of them ever got that far."

Light dawned behind Carol's eyes. "A journalist would know. They get access to all kinds of stuff. He could have recognized Tina Chapman from the press photographs at the time. If he has local police contacts, he could have heard that

Jonathan Meadows was under suspicion over the hit and run."

Tony scanned the list. "Are any of these journalists?"

DI Cassidy entered the Christmas For Children offices almost at a run, his team at his heels. A trim little woman got to her feet and pointed to her computer screen. "There. Just as it came in."

The e-mail was short but not sweet. *We've got Santa. You've got money. We want £20,000 in cash. You'll hear from us in an hour. No police.*

"I thought I would ignore the bit about 'no police'," the woman said. "It's not as if we're going to be paying the ransom."

Cassidy admired her forthrightness but had to check she was taking all the possibilities into consideration. "You're not frightened they might kill Mr Garrity? Or seriously harm him?"

She gave him a scornful look. "They're not going to hurt Santa. How do you think that would go down in prison? You of all people should know how sentimental criminals are."

Carol's conviction that David Sanders was a serial killer took her no closer to making an arrest. There was a small matter of a complete lack of evidence against Sanders, a feature writer on the Bradfield *Evening Sentinel Times*. Even the apparent miracles of twenty-first-century forensic science couldn't nail this. Water and fire were notorious destroyers of trace evidence. She'd hoped that close analysis might fit together the cut marks on the tape and wire from the previous killings, but the fire had done too much damage. That meant there was no chance of definitively linking them to any materials still in Sanders' possession.

There were no reliable witnesses or meaningful CCTV footage. A couple of homeless men had turned up claiming to have seen Tina Chapman go into the canal. But the person pushing her had been wearing a Hallowe'en mask and the sighting had gone nowhere.

The only option left was to cling to Tony's conviction that the killer would strike again before Christmas. It was always hard to persuade her bosses to mount surveillance operations because they were so costly and because they took so many officers off other cases, but at least this one had a fixed end point.

And so they watched. They watched David Sanders go to work. They watched him drink in the pub with his workmates. They watched him work out at the gym. They watched him do his Christmas shopping. What they didn't watch him do was abduct and murder anyone.

Then it was Christmas Eve, the last day of authorized surveillance. In spite of the privileges of rank, Carol put herself down for a shift. It was already dark when she slid into the passenger seat of the anonymous car alongside DC Paula McIntyre. "Nothing moving, chief. He got home about an hour ago, nobody in or out since."

"The house doesn't look very festive, does it? No sign of a tree or any lights."

Paula, who had known her own share of grief, shrugged. "You lose your only child? I don't expect Christmas is much to celebrate."

The Sanders' four-year-old daughter had drowned during

a swimming lesson back in September. The instructor had been dealing with another kid who was having a come-apart when Sanders' daughter had hit her head on the poolside. By the time anyone noticed, it had been too late. According to a colleague discreetly questioned by Sergeant Devine, it had ripped Sanders apart, though he'd refused to consider any kind of medical intervention.

Before Carol could respond, the garage door opened and Sanders' SUV crawled down the drive. They let him make it to the end of the street before they pulled out of their parking place and slipped in behind him. It wasn't hard to stay on the tail of the tall vehicle and fifteen minutes' driving brought them to a street of run-down terraced houses on the downtrodden edge of Moorside. On the corner was a brightly lit shop, its windows plastered with ads for cheap alcohol. Sanders pulled up and walked into the shop carrying a sports holdall.

"I think this is it," Carol breathed. "Let's go, Paula."

They sprinted down the street and tried the door of the shop. But something was jamming it. Carol took a couple of steps back then charged the door, slamming her shoulder into the wooden surround. Something popped and the door crashed open.

Sanders was standing behind the counter, a cricket bat in his hand, dismay on his face. "Police, drop your weapon," Carol roared as Paula scrambled to the far end of the counter.

"There's someone here, chief. Looks like he's unconscious," Paula said.

The cricket bat fell to the ground with a clatter. Sanders sank to the floor, head in hands. "This is all your fault," he said. "You never make the right people pay the price, do you?"

* * *

Carol collapsed into Tony's armchair and demanded a drink. "He didn't even bother with a denial," she said. "Being arrested seemed almost to come as a relief." She closed her eyes for a moment, memory summoning up Sanders' haggard face.

"It generally does when you're not dealing with a psychopath," Tony said.

Carol sighed. "And a very merry bloody Christmas to you too."

"You stopped him killing again," Tony said, handing her a glass of wine. "That's not an insignificant achievement."

"I suppose. Jahinder Singh's family can celebrate the festive season knowing their father's safe from any further consequences from selling solvents to kids." Before Carol could say more, her phone rang. "What now?" she muttered. She listened attentively, a slow smile spreading from mouth to eyes. "Thanks for letting me know," she said, ending the call. "That was Cassidy. Santa's home free. Two extremely inept kidnappers are banged up and nobody got hurt."

Tony raised his glass, his smile matching hers. In their line of work, making the best of a bad job was second nature. This wasn't exactly a happy ending, but it was closer than they usually managed. He'd settle for that any day.

FOOL YOU TWICE

A LORI ANDERSON STORY

STEPH BROADRIBB

It wasn't the usual kind of job, and he wasn't the usual kind of target.

Back then I was a tadpole bounty hunter. A wet-behind-the-ears, fresh-on-the-scene nobody, just looking for a chance to prove I'd gotten what it took to survive in the game. I was eager to display what I had. And that job, it made me show it all in one way or another.

That first time, I wasn't chasing a bounty. One of the private investigators I'd been doing a little legwork for since arriving in Florida a couple months previously had promised he'd help me make contacts. Because the thing was, although I'd done my training and paid my dues working a few months with my ex-mentor, JT – back in Georgia, before that went all to shit – I needed local experience; form that proved I could do the job the Florida way, else I wasn't never going to get any decent fugitive recovery work.

So I answered the PI's call real eager. "Jason? What have you got for me?"

"Hello yourself," he said, a note of amusement in his voice before his tone turned serious. "I was thinking about what you said, about needing more work. There's a job. Thought on whether to tell you for a while; it's risky, see, and not entirely this side of the line. I wasn't sure that you should—"

I drummed my nails against the cellphone. "Just tell me already."

"Well, alright then." He sounded kind of reluctant. "The thing is, one of my law guy contacts says a buddy of his is looking for a ... private contractor – a female professional, used to working in the field – for a special operation he's running. You interested?"

I was sleeping in a low-rent motel with a pair of loud, sex-crazed folk on one side of the paper-thin walls, and a melancholy guy who played Johnny Cash at max volume all through the night on the other. Worse, I was down to my last ninety bucks. "For sure I am."

"His name's Dirk Ekman. He's working out of room twenty-five at the Sunshine Motel along the beach near the Big Shrimp Shack and Rollers Bar. My contact said if I knew of someone interested they should go round and visit with him."

I frowned, figuring I'd have been going to the precinct. "A motel room? You sure he's legit?"

"He sounds unorthodox for sure, but my contact assures me he's on the level. Wouldn't send you to meet any guy that wasn't."

Jason had been good to me. He was one of the few folks who'd given me work when no one else would. Helped me learn about the way things worked here in Tampa. I figured I could trust him as much as anyone, and doing a job for an officer of the law, well that could be all kinds of helpful.

I should have guessed that it wasn't going to be a cakewalk.

* * *

The Sunshine Motel wasn't exactly fancy, but it was a hell of a step up from the dive I'd been bunking at. The lodgings were housed in three double-storey buildings arranged horseshoe-style around a pool. The stucco exterior was clean and painted pale yellow, and the sign out front advertised large rooms, air-conditioning and an on-site Laundromat. It looked a family-friendly-type place, and as I parked my old Jetta in the lot, I saw that a bunch of young kids were splashing about in the pool.

It seemed an odd choice of location for a cop to conduct his business, but I figured that maybe him choosing this place was less about that, and more down to its location. Because the Sunshine Motel was right on the cusp where mid-rent turned to gold. If I were to stroll out of the parking lot, cross the road, and go down one block, I'd have left the low-rise motels and chain restaurants behind, and entered the world of all-inclusive, five-star luxury hotels.

As I got out of my car, I turned and looked over the road at the huge glass-and-concrete buildings gleaming in the sun. The folks in those places blew more on one vacation than I'd made since I'd arrived in Florida. I shook my head. Something about that seemed real out of whack.

I wore blue jeans, a black tee, and my favourite red pair of cowboy boots. I took my time walking to room twenty-five. Ambling along, looking like I wasn't in any kind of hurry, when in truth I was checking out the place, clocking the maid humming along to her iPod as she cleaned room six on the first floor, and the two guys – one white, one Hispanic – leaning on the railings outside the open door of room twenty-nine, drinking sodas from cans.

Those sodas looked real good. The sun was high overhead, and by the time I'd gotten to number twenty-five my mouth was as dry as gator-hide in August. I rapped my knuckles against the bright blue door and waited.

A shadow passed across the spyhole. Moments later the door opened. The guy was tall and lean, with short salt-and-pepper hair, a deep tan and a neat graying beard. He wasn't in uniform. Instead he was wearing black suit pants with a white shirt, no tie. I figured him for a detective.

"Help you?" he said.

"I'm Lori Anderson."

He smiled, and stepped aside, beckoning me in. "Great, great. Jason's girl, right?"

"Jason's *colleague*. He said you were looking for some help?"

"Well that's true, for sure." He looked me up and down, then pointed toward a couple of chairs positioned either side of a large wooden desk that was overflowing with paperwork and takeout coffee cups. "Sit, please."

I did as he asked. "So what's the job?"

"If I'm honest, and I want to be honest with you, Lori, the job's kind of a honeytrap."

I bristled. Wasn't going to be sleeping with any man for a job, no matter what the payment. And a lawman asking me to do that, well, it didn't sound right to me at all. "Isn't that entrapment? Surely as a cop you can't—"

"Well, I … " He smiled. It looked a little forced. "The thing is, I'm not a cop. I'm a lawyer."

I shook my head. Didn't follow what was going on here. "And this guy's what, a witness for the other side?"

"No, nothing like that. This isn't about a case."

"Then you've lost me."

"Look, this guy, he's real bad news. He's a big shot banker in the city. On weekends he comes out here, checks into a fancy hotel, picks up a woman in the bar, or calls a service if he's had no luck. Once they're up in his suite, he gets rough."

I suppressed a shudder. Knew just how it felt when a man beat down on a woman. I'd been that woman. Swore I'd never be again. I moved to get up. "I'm not the right—"

"Don't decide just yet." The lawyer took a buff folder off his desk and pulled a bunch of pictures from inside. One by one he laid them out on the table in front of me. "Jessie Turner, just nineteen: he broke her jaw and her nose. She reported him, then refused to press charges. Lola Stansfield, twenty-eight: he gave her a black eye and two busted ribs, she never even called the cops. Melly Sharp, twenty-three …" He put the final photo on the table. A woman's torso, covered in eggplant-purple bruises. Exhaled hard. "He needs catching."

I collected the pictures together and handed them back to the lawyer. "Why didn't these women press charges?"

"They were working girls, didn't want to be answering too many questions from the cops about how they'd come to be in his hotel room in the first place. He paid them off. Bought their silence. So he stays free and clear to carry on."

Asshole. "So you want me to let him hit me?"

"I need him to incriminate himself. Get him to admit what he did, to talk about the other women, and what he wants to do to you. Dial me on your cellphone before you enter his room. When he starts getting aggressive I'll call the cops as an anonymous tip-off. He'll get arrested, charged and convicted."

The way Dirk Ekman talked made it sound real easy, but if the man was as violent as he was saying, chances were the cops wouldn't arrive before he'd started using his fists. I figured that's why he wanted a trained professional to do the job; he needed someone who could get into trouble and out of it, too.

I studied the lawyer guy's face. He seemed genuine, like he believed what he was saying, but in truth I knew he needed bruises for a conviction to stick. "How much are you paying?"

He made a steeple with his hands. Resting his chin on his fingertips, he studied me real careful. "Two thousand."

Jeez, that would be enough to keep me going another two months, maybe longer. And I'd get a pocket lawyer to boot, which could be real useful in my line of work. Still, I had to wonder why a lawman would put up that much cash. After all, he wasn't a prosecutor, so he couldn't try the case himself. "What's in this for you?"

He held my gaze, his frown deepening. I thought I saw distress in his eyes. "Melly Sharp's like a daughter to me. What that bastard did to her was …" He exhaled hard. "He can't be allowed to do this again."

I clenched my fists. Knew the lawyer was right. "What's the guy's name?"

The lawyer put a new photograph on the table. In it was a forty-something, broad-shouldered man who was carrying a little more weight than would be good for his blood pressure. "Milton Fraser."

I stared at the picture. Shook my head. Power, money; a man like that thought he was above the law, untouchable.

That people, women, were objects to be used and discarded. I knew the pattern. I'd experienced it up close and real personal at the fists of my ex-husband. A man like that left unchecked would escalate: soon he'd be leaving bodies in his wake rather than bruises. I had to stop soon from coming. "If he goes to hit me, I'll fight back."

The lawyer nodded. "Wouldn't expect any different."

The job went down on Saturday night at the Tampa Bay Grand, a big skyscraper of a hotel right on the beachfront, and the place Milton Fraser – my target – was staying for the weekend. I wore a tight-fitting black dress, strappy heels and a Bluetooth micro-earpiece. As well as a cellphone, I carried a Taser X2 in my purse.

It was gone nine but the temperature was still high, the night air muggy with the humidity of a Florida summer. I climbed out of the cab and stood at the bottom of the steps leading to the hotel entrance. The high-rise glass-sided building stretched up into the darkness of the night sky, looking like it went on forever. Must have been at least forty storeys, a far cry from the Sunshine Motel. I'd never been inside a place like this before.

I took a deep breath to steady myself. Told myself to play it cool. Act like I belonged here. And said just loud enough for my cell to pick up my voice, "I'm going inside now."

"If he gets violent, make sure I can tell. If he doesn't make verbal threats, describe what he's doing so I know to—"

"This isn't my first rodeo. I'll be clear so you know what's happening."

"It's your first time working my rodeo, and I need to know you'll follow the rules." From the tone of his voice, it sounded like the lawman was getting real twitchy about the job. "It's the only way I can keep you safe."

Truth was, he couldn't keep me safe. All he could do was tip off the cops. It was up to me to make this work out. Striding to the entrance, I pushed open the door and stepped into the huge, air-conditioned foyer. Muttered under my breath, "Don't worry. I'll do what's needed."

He said nothing for a long moment. When he spoke, his voice sounded different, kind of breathy and excited. "I'm counting on it that you will."

The hotel bar was all kinds of fancy; soft lighting, velvet couches with glass and chrome tables, and uniformed waiting staff to bring your drinks to you. I clocked my target over in the far corner of the room, sitting alone. Choosing to sit at a table a few away from his, I asked the waiter for an Old Fashioned.

The lawyer hadn't needed to be worried. Milton Fraser made a play for me within minutes. The trap worked perfectly.

Maybe I should have wondered why.

Because I was barely halfway through drinking my cocktail when the waiter brought me a second. "From the gentleman by the window," he said, gesturing to Fraser. "With his compliments."

I smiled. "How kind."

Taking the drink, I turned to Fraser, caught his eye, and raised the glass in thank-you.

He was out of his seat and asking if I fancied company in less than twenty seconds. I batted my lashes and told him I'd like to go someplace more private. We took the elevator to his room.

His room turned out to be the penthouse; furnished in a minimalist style, with a balcony that ran the full length of the suite and looked out over the ocean, it was quite a place. I walked out onto the balcony, and gazed down at the lights of Tampa twinkling below us, and listened to the faint noise of the waves breaking on the beach. "It's beautiful."

Fraser wasn't interested in the outside view. "Take off your clothes."

Well that wasn't going to happen. I gave a little laugh. "Shouldn't we get to know each other a little better first?"

From his expression it was real clear that hadn't been a part of his plan. He lunged for me. Put his hands around my throat and pressed. "Get naked."

I slapped his hands off me, and moved back inside. "Don't do that."

In my ear I heard the lawman telling me to describe what was going on.

"I'm paying you. I own you." Fraser grabbed for me.

I moved away fast. Feigned surprise; my eyes wide. "Paying me? Oh my …" I injected some upset into my tone. "You think I'm an escort?"

For the first time since we'd come up to the room, he looked back-footed. Then he laughed, a real belly laugh. "I *am* paying you."

I frowned. Didn't understand.

"You might not be a hooker, but that two grand Dirk promised you is mine."

Now I was the one on the back-foot. I heard laughing in my ear. The douche lawman had set me up. Pulling out the earpiece, I backed away from Fraser. "What the hell is this?"

"I needed more of a challenge," he said, stepping toward me. "Dirk said he'd find me one."

He'd fooled me. I'd not checked his lawman credentials. I'd fallen for a sob story and a kindly face; two things that my ex-mentor had lectured me on real often. *Never trust no one*, he'd oftentimes told me. *Your compassion, Lori. It's a weakness in this job. It'll get you killed.*

They'd hooked me into whatever sick game they were playing. But I damn well wasn't going to let them keep me on the line. I reached into my purse.

Before I could pull out the Taser, he flew at me. Fraser was a solid guy. His momentum shoved me backward and I fell hard. Landed on my back, Fraser on top of me. He tried to pin my arms but I rolled away, faster than him, and scrambled to my feet. Wouldn't let him win.

All penthouse suites have panic buttons. I just needed to find this one's.

Fraser bellowed and came after me.

I dodged around the couch, scanning the room, looking for the button. Checked the space behind the couches, the wall by the huge flat-screen television. Then I spotted it on the opposite side of the room. A black button, blending in perfectly with the black-and-white flocked wallpaper print.

"Come here you little—" There was a sheen of sweat over his face, and he wore a smug, self-satisfied grin. He thought he'd gotten me cornered.

I slammed the heel of my hand into his nose. Heard the bone crack as he recoiled. The shock on his face made me realize Dirk must have figured I wasn't tough enough to fight back, and on that I was glad I'd fooled them, as it'd given me an advantage.

As Fraser cried out in pain, his hands clutching at his nose, I used that advantage. I sprinted out from the corner, along the glass, to the opposite wall. Pressed my palm against the button, then kept moving, back to the spot where I'd dropped my purse.

Fraser let out a roar and lumbered toward me. He looked one hell of a mess; blood smeared over his face and pouring down his chin. "You're going to pay for—"

I heard knocking at the door, loud and insistent. I yelled for help. Grabbed for my purse as I felt Fraser's hands on my shoulders, spinning me round to face him.

Fraser's eyes were bloodshot and unfocused, but he looked plenty mad. I scrambled for my purse, and he screamed cusses at me, lashing out with weak-assed punches. One, a glancing blow to the side of my face, stung and would be hard enough to bruise, no doubt.

Then he put his hands around my throat again and squeezed.

As the security guards broke down the door, I gave them just long enough to see what he was doing. Then I tasered him in the balls.

I watched as he convulsed and jerked, flapping around like a fish on an electrified line, and thought about the two thousand dollars I wouldn't be getting.

Shaking my head, I kept my voice dead serious. "Nobody owns me, honey."

* * *

I'd reckoned that'd be the last time I'd see Milton Fraser, but I was wrong. The second time was after he skipped his bail.

The call came from Quinn, a new contact I'd made at C.F. Bonds – a mid-sized independent bond shop that I'd been trying to get work from for a few weeks, but up to that point had gotten no joy.

Jason, the PI, tried to dissuade me from taking the job. He was still feeling real cut up over telling me about Dirk Ekman. Said he'd never had cause before to doubt the contact who'd told him about the double-crossing douche lawman, but that he'd torn a strip off them after what happened, and that he'd never take work from them again. He said he'd gone round to have it out with the douche the day after it'd gone down, but it didn't work out. Word was, Fraser had named Ekman as an accomplice in an attempt to share the blame for what had happened. Ekman must've caught wind that there was a warrant out on him, because when Jason got to his motel room, the douche was already in the wind.

But still, a girl's got to eat, and jobs from C.F. Bonds would be real useful for me, so I took the skip trace. See, a guy like Milton Fraser runs to someplace he feels safe, and old patterns die hard. An escort-beating asshole fugitive is still an escort-beating asshole. I figured he'd revert to type sooner or later, and I had the idea it'd most likely be sooner.

After a couple of nights looking, I spotted him in the bar of the Bay View Plaza, a real fancy five-star hotel on the beachfront. And that time the lawman was in the bar with him.

I wore a dark wig, shades and a blood-red dress. I didn't sit in the bar that time, instead I gave the barman a good tip, bought a bottle of champagne, and wrote a note for him to deliver with it – *Looking for some fun?* I folded the keycard for the room I'd just rented into the note, and had the waiter take it and the champagne over to Fraser's table.

I timed it real careful. So that as Fraser and Ekman read the note I was walking away toward the elevator. They couldn't see my face. Wouldn't be able to recognize me. Right then, my dark bobbed hair and tight dress would be the only things they'd be giving a look-see. And I knew the pair of them were self-satisfied enough to believe that their luck was in.

The knock on my door came six minutes later. I could hear them guffawing in the corridor, thinking that they were about to get their rocks off. Unaware that, this time, the trap was set to fool *them*. Keeping my shades on, I opened the door, smiled, and beckoned them inside. I didn't speak, and they didn't recognize me.

Trouble started when I shut the door, stood blocking their escape, and pulled out my cuffs. "Milton Fraser," I said, my voice real clear. "I'm a bail runner acting on behalf of C.F. Bonds."

He looked confused. Glanced at Ekman. I started telling them the legalities of what was happening.

That's when their fight or flight response kicked in.

Fraser decided fight. Ekman went for flight.

As Fraser launched himself at me, Ekman made a run for the door.

Scooting sideways, I dodged Fraser's bulk. Unable to stop,

his momentum slammed him against the door. He recovered fast, but I was quicker. A jab to the throat, and knee to the balls, and he was winded. Grabbing my cuffs, I reached for his wrist. That was the moment Ekman dodged around us, reaching for the door handle.

But this time I hadn't taken any chances. When I'd spotted Milton Fraser and Dirk Ekman in the bar, I'd rented the room and then called Jason for backup. As Ekman opened the door, he found Jason and his friend waiting outside. Grabbing him, they pushed him back inside. Jason, all eager to make amends for connecting me with the douche lawman in the first place, held him down and the semi-retired PI he'd roped in to help, a guy called Red, slapped on the cuffs.

Then Jason helped me with Fraser, who was struggling to get free, only one wrist in cuffs. He flailed around, sent a lamp crashing to the floor, and got a lucky punch into Jason's belly, but the victory was short-lived. I grabbed my Taser and dry-fired it into his neck. Fraser howled and crumpled to the floor. Made it real easy to fix the second cuff into place.

Cuffed and subdued, I drove them down to the precinct and got them booked.

I looked from one to the other as the cops hauled them away and smiled. I'd just successfully completed my first job as a bounty hunter in Florida. Fraser's bond percentage was worth over four thousand dollars, and putting Dirk Ekman in jail was priceless.

They might have taken me for a fool one time. But me, I'd fooled them twice.

LEBENSRAUM

CHRISTOPHER FOWLER

It was a lovely sunny morning in late summer. The sky was so bright it made your eyes hurt. They rang the doorbell, two short rings, just like anyone would. Ten past nine, just after the milkman had been. I was dressed, you understand, just about to go down to the shop for some bread. I wasn't expecting anyone, and at that time in the morning you don't expect—

You don't expect.

A boy and a girl. She was a little thin, he a little pale, but a clean and healthy-looking couple, just a bit impoverished. Down at heel, I thought, fallen on hard times. Or perhaps they had never known good times. She looked about sixteen, he was two or three years older. Not from around here. Eric and Betty, they'd come about the room. What room? I asked them. They pointed to the front room. They'd seen it through the street window. I still called it the front room but I hardly ever went in there, except to clean. I liked to keep it well polished. Well, I suppose I might have thought about renting it, might even have said something about it down at the post office. Even so, it was odd that they mentioned it. Fortuitous, I might have thought at the time.

The girl was in a pink cardigan two sizes too small, like a little girl wearing something her mother might have knitted, with her thin blonde hair done up in bangs. We used to call them bangs, anyway. They looked so anxious and hopeful. How could I refuse them?

Hard times, he said, something about hard times. Well. This whole neighbourhood has fallen on hard times. I like to think I'm a good person. I try to help where I can. They had a little money for rent, not a lot, but he had expectations and could get some. Just a room. What about the toilet and kitchen? I asked, you'd need to use those. You won't know we're here, said the girl, we're very quiet. It won't be for long.

I suppose I must have wondered what had brought them here, if they'd left home and had come to this city with a purpose. But the girl's eyes were so blue and wide, and the boy's face was so pale and lean. He had a crimson rash on his neck that needed treatment. You feel sorry for the younger ones, how can they get a start in life now? Nothing around here is affordable for people like them. Money goes nowhere. Luckily Sam had left me savings, otherwise I would have been in the same boat. You have to put yourself in another's place.

I had room to spare. The house had three floors and was hard for me to keep clean these days. A semi-detached residence, built in 1902. Even when Sam was alive we never used all the rooms, they cost too much to heat. With him gone and hardly anyone visiting, I lived mostly at the back on the ground floor, and used the first-floor bedroom. What need had I for a front room with a piano I had to keep polished every week, and so many of my grandmother's ornaments in the glass cabinet, and the best china and the rugs, and the air so still you could see motes of dust hovering on sunny afternoons, not even circulating through the light?

I thought I might be glad of the company, and let them move in.

I gave them a key, the only one I had spare, Sam's old key. At first I hardly knew they were there, they were so quiet. One day Betty left me a cake, came through and shyly put it on my kitchen table. Shop bought, just sponge and blue icing, but a sweet gesture. Betty and I ate some together with tea, and she told me she was pregnant, and had been thrown out of her stepfather's flat. She had no money. Eric had no job. How were they to live? Some people had so much and others had so little.

I moved my things to the first floor so that they could have the bathroom to themselves. We could share the kitchen. I thought it was only fair. She said they would pay me back once they got on their feet.

Eric often went out late. I watched him go from the upstairs window. He left Betty alone, but I didn't go downstairs. I didn't like to pry. Who wants an old lady interfering and making a nuisance of herself? Young people live differently now. They live in ways that would have frightened us.

It's a quiet street, run-down and rather dirty, so much litter lying about, but you should have seen it when Sam was still alive; smart and neat with tidy little courtyards and plants in pots, not like today with broken glass and people yelling and screaming late at night. Now they leave their belongings right on the pavement. They move in and move out without saying hello or goodbye. A woman was beaten in broad daylight for no reason. How can you be beaten for no reason? The police do nothing. I write and write, but all I ever get back is a form letter – thank you for bringing this matter to our attention, and so on.

It snowed early that year and Eric stopped going out so much. That was when the doorbell started ringing more often. At first it was just during the day. Strangers would call and ask for him. I would hear Betty answer the door, see her usher them in. They would stay for an hour or so and then leave. Sometimes people called quite late at night. They were the same age as him, and wore the same clothes, grey jackets, black trousers, brown boots. When did clothes become so colourless? When I was a girl there were so many colours, embroidery and lace.

One night the house was cold because someone had left the front door open. I wanted to check that everything was all right, and knocked on the door to the front room but there was no answer. I could hear sounds inside. Him arguing, her crying.

I still did my own cleaning then. One day I was sweeping the hall carpet and found a needle, a nasty-looking thing, and I showed it to the girl, and she explained that Eric was a diabetic, and had forgotten to take his insulin before he went out – he hadn't been able to get a regular job but he was helping at the community centre, and then there was his group. I asked what group? She said a political group. Sometimes they held their meetings here, it was about getting rid of the greedy ones and changing society for the better so that there were fair shares for all, and it was very interesting and perhaps I'd like to sit in one evening, although sometimes the language got very strong. I said no, I had been on enough protests and marches in my time, thank you, and although things get better eventually it usually takes a long time for change to happen, and sometimes for the unlikeliest reasons, things out of your control, things you just don't see coming. But I could tell she didn't understand what I was talking about, so we went back to discussing what she would do when the baby arrived.

The lady from social services came to call to see how I was, and I told her everything was fine. My neighbour Mary called, a Methodist lady who lived across the road, who always came over after Sam died. She said she was moving, and would I be all right without her popping in to see me, and I said I'd be fine. I didn't mention my lodgers, I don't know why. I wanted to sort things out for myself. I hadn't seen Betty for a few days, and neither she nor Eric had offered me any money lately. They were probably embarrassed because they had none to give. I knew I would have to say something eventually, just to know where I stood.

A few mornings later I knocked at the door, and found myself confronted by a heavily built man dressed in one of my husband's old shirts. He told me he was staying with Eric and Betty for a while, and who was I? Well, I hardly knew what to say. When I was growing up, no one would have ever behaved in such a way. I was trembling, but I demanded to see the room.

This man – I never found out who he was – opened the door. It was a shock to find the place in such a state, rubbish on the floor, food and beer bottles and filth, everything so dirty, the smell was terrible, and Eric lying in an armchair half asleep, dressed in a short-sleeved shirt, with terrible bruises on his arms.

What happened? I asked.

Betty told me that some of the people in Eric's group disagreed with him and that there had been a fight, then she apologised for the state of the room. She'd meant to clean it but she hadn't been well. Her stomach was large now, but when I asked her about the baby she didn't seem interested in talking about it.

I went back to my bedroom on the first floor to think things through. I was sure Eric's heart was in the right place and, like so many people of his age, he was just trying to make a better world for his family, but I couldn't have that kind of disorder in the house. With a heavy heart I decided it was probably best to ask them to leave, but how was the best way to broach the subject?

I decided to talk the matter over with Mary, my neighbour, and went over the road to see her, but she wasn't there; I'd forgotten she was moving, and when I looked in through the ground-floor windows I saw that the floorboards were bare. It was odd because some of her belongings were still in the hall, a pair of shoes, a hat and a small bag, as if she'd simply left them behind without a care in the world.

The next day Eric came in carrying one of those portable music players, and started playing it all the time, popular music, awful sentimental stuff. I asked him to turn it down but the volume always went back up.

One morning I saw him put on his grey jacket and go out, watched through the banisters as he shut the front door, then I went downstairs. Betty was sitting against the wall with a rubber cord tied around her arm. She and a man I had never seen before were boiling something in spoons over Sam's old primus stove. Well, of course I knew it was drugs, I wasn't born yesterday, so I had to put my foot down. No drugs in this house, I told her, I'm afraid I will have to ask you and your friends to leave. And with your baby coming too, how could you think of such a thing?

You don't understand, she said, the pressures we're under, the problems we're having, we'll be quieter and I'll clean up the rooms, I promise. We'll go soon, when circumstances change. But I found it hard to believe her now.

The other man, he told me to go away – only he was much ruder than that, he actually swore at me, told me to eff off and mind my own effing business. Told me not to come downstairs again, that it was off-limits from now on. Betty tried to calm him down but he shook his fist in my face. I was shaking when I went back upstairs. I would not be spoken to in that way, not in my own house.

I waited until the next morning and went to the police. I waited for ages to see someone, and this very abrupt man told me I was to make a report, and although they were busy he would deal with the matter, so I filled out a form, giving them my name and address, and handed it to him, but I could tell he was not interested in doing anything, so I came home.

When Sam was alive the house was filled with plants: aspidistras, ferns and palms in round white china bowls. Everything gleamed; silverware, crockery, my best tea service, the framed photographs on the walls. In the month that followed everything disappeared: the cutlery, the pictures, the books, the silverware. They sold it all piece by piece, became quite brazen about it.

Betty wouldn't talk to me any more. She seemed distant and only half alive. Eric avoided me. One day, I came back from the shops to find two new men, one with a scar right across his face, and another girl, a great lump of a thing with piggy eyes lost in too much flesh. She had thick make-up and an awful screeching laugh, so common and brazen, I could not bring myself to look at her. I knew Sam would have been ashamed to have someone like her in the house. The men said they were friends of Eric's and were working for the cause, and had come to stay, but they would need more room. They would need my first floor.

I wouldn't have let them, but all I could think was that perhaps there were redeeming circumstances, perhaps there was still a reason to be kind, that they saw their cause as more important than a silly, selfish old lady with too many empty rooms in her house. But at night, I couldn't sleep for worry. I heard noises through the floor, strange thumps and muffled crying. I put my head under the pillow.

I was still determined to return to the police, as no one had called to talk to me, but meanwhile I moved up to the top floor. It was a bitter winter, and the radiators weren't working all the time. Sam had always done something to them to get rid of the air bubbles, but I didn't know how to do it and in any case I had no strength in my hands to turn the taps. When the ice came I put on more clothes, and wrapped myself in blankets.

The stairs to the top floor were steeper, and although there was a toilet, the kitchen was no more than a cubbyhole. I heard them on my stairs at night. They stole everything that was left out. I heard them laughing and fighting and crashing into things. I saw disreputable-looking young men hanging around outside the house, and wondered what the neighbours must think.

Then one morning I caught sight of myself in the mirror on the landing. I looked so old and ill. I realised that I was scared, really scared. I had survived a war and seen my husband die, so of course I wasn't scared for myself, but these people hurt themselves and each other; they were so in the grip of their beliefs I suppose, always making plans and ranting about the future when everything would be different, and this thing that had got hold of them had cracked them into pieces, making them behave like animals. Always they talked about change, as if people could simply be moved around like chess pieces and made to do what others wanted.

Sometimes when I couldn't get back to sleep I went to the big staircase and sat at the top, looking down at the closed doors, listening to the noises behind them. The record player, the laughter, the crack of bottles, the angry shouting. Once the man with the scar pushed past me on the stairs and held his fist up to me, his fist! Just because I asked him to make less noise, because I couldn't sleep.

Then the water went off. Nobody came to fix it, and I was too frightened to go downstairs because I did not wish to run into the man with the scar again. They wouldn't let me wash, or sleep. I became ashamed of myself.

I had to start sneaking downstairs to use the main bathroom while they slept – I didn't want to have to confront them – and had trouble getting back to my room because it was cold and my joints didn't move like they used to. The worst time was when I came out on to the landing and saw them in the hall. One of them was cutting a young man's face with a razor blade. Blood was falling on to the old Persian runner like drops of red ink from a fountain pen. I cried that night – buried my face in my pillow and pretended it was not happening. I would dream Sam was still alive, and the house was still warm and filled with beautiful plants, and I would wake up with a terrible sinking sensation when I realised that all my fears were real.

It frightened me to leave the house, but one day I kept watch on the closed doors and took a chance. I put on my quietest shoes and crept out, and went back to the police station and told them what was happening. They seemed surprised that no one had come to visit, and insisted on coming back with me, two of them. They said there had been complaints from the neighbours. I didn't know about that. I hadn't talked to my neighbours in a long time: a young couple on one side, hardly ever at home; some new rough people on the other. The police told me they had "initiated eviction procedures", and put the water back on. But when they left, the people in my house were still there. They won't do anything to you if you stay out of their way, said one of the policemen, just let us know if you have any more trouble, they'll be gone soon. These things pass.

A few days later one of them called to inform me that a county court eviction order had been applied for. The police returned with a warrant and shouted at the doors until they opened. Then they evicted everyone from my house. One man jumped over my garden fence and broke it.

I was alone for the first time in four months, but I felt no relief. I had terrible nightmares. The lady from the council called and told me that she could get someone in to help clean up the mess, but it would take a while for the application to be processed. She didn't think they would be able to get my belongings back. I only cared about the things that had sentimental value.

A few nights later, they moved back in. I heard them banging around, not even bothering to be quiet. They had nothing to be scared of. I couldn't believe anyone could be so brazen. You hear about such things but never think it can happen to you. I am seventy-five years old, and all of my friends had gone. I had no one to turn to.

The police came back later that week, and this time they were armed. Troublemakers, said one of the officers, they would get rid of them. He made it sound like I had mice or an infestation of cockroaches. But these men and their women, they still came back. This time the one with the scar lifted me up and carried me to the top floor, and told me to stay there if I knew what was good for me. Every night I heard them banging through the house, looking for things to sell until there was nothing left. They cleared out my wardrobe and took my jewellery, my wedding necklace, the earrings Sam had given me on our silver wedding anniversary. They emptied out my purse, even took all my old dresses.

I couldn't go out, and I didn't dare to answer the door because I never knew who might be there. One afternoon I heard the knocker – the doorbell had been taken out, and all that was left was a rectangle of old paint – and I tiptoed out into the hall to my usual spot between the banisters.

I recognised the shape behind the glass at once. I didn't know what to do. Should I risk going downstairs? Finally I decided I had to be brave, and crept down as quietly as I could.

The doors were all shut, and the house seemed quiet because everyone had a habit of sleeping at odd hours, so I carefully opened the front door.

Dear God in Heaven, said Mary, look at you! You told me you'd be all right. I came back to see my sister. When did you last eat? You look terrible. Why are you still here all alone?

I said did you know you left some of your things behind? She said you must know what's been going on, it's a disgrace. Her voice was so loud that I was frightened she would wake them up, so I told her I had the flu, and would call her when I was feeling better, and I quickly shut the door.

I made my way upstairs and went to bed, and stayed there. There was little point in doing anything else, not when the rest of my house was out of bounds. The next day I received a letter from the bank warning me about an overdraft, and asking me to place extra funds into the account at once. I had never had such a letter in my life! My pension was paid in by Sam's old company, and I always had enough to see me through the month because I suppose I spent so little on myself – you save, don't you, when you're eating for one. It was a shock, and when I searched for the box that held my chequebook I couldn't find it anywhere. Anger drove me downstairs. I went to see Betty.

She opened the door in her usual sleepy state, only looking worse this time. Her face was yellow with jaundice, and her eyes had sunk so deep that I could hardly tell if she was looking at me in the candlelight. She said she had lost the baby, and for a moment my heart went out to her.

Then she told me that Eric had drawn out my savings and paid some men off with my money, that he had to because they needed funds for the cause, only now it was all gone, and what did I have that I could sell? I felt my face burn hot and said, how can you live like this, what is wrong with you people? You're not fighting for a cause, when you steal from people you become nothing more than common criminals, and you get away with it because the police turn a blind eye. When I was your age nobody lived in this terrible way, lying and stealing and hurting each other, and soon she was crying and saying I know, I know, we're sorry, and hugging me like a baby wanting to be nursed.

Then Eric came back with his friends now all in their matching uniforms, the insignias gleaming, I would have thought them very smart if they weren't so frightening, and I could tell they had been drinking, so I scuttled back upstairs, but I heard what they said to Betty. Do you think she's got more money hidden away? We really need it. You could get it out of her, she likes you. And Betty said no, leave her alone, she's so old she won't live if you hurt her. She's not like the rest; there are bad Jews like the bankers and there are good Jews, almost as good as Aryans. And Eric said a house is like a nation, it needs to spread out, it needs space to grow. We could tie her up and leave her without food until she tells us if she has more money, that's not like actually torturing her, is it. They'll take her away eventually. They'll take all of them away, good and bad, and then it'll be too late. Then I heard them coming up the stairs.

I held my breath. The footsteps stopped. Something distracted them and they started arguing. After a few minutes they went back downstairs and closed the front room door once more. That was when I decided I couldn't stay on the top floor any longer. I would have to move.

I quickly decided that the only place left was the cupboard in the top room. I hadn't used it for years because it was tucked in a corner and hard to get at. It went under the attic, but if I dragged my blankets in there I could make myself a bed. I could come out at night and take food from their kitchen, perhaps use my old oven because it was quiet and they hadn't come to sell it because it wasn't worth anything. I worked quickly and quietly, taking only the things I needed, and made myself a new little home. I would not be hurt if nobody could find me.

I did a clever thing. I put away everything in the top floor rooms, then crept downstairs and left the front door wide open so they would think I had gone out, so they would think I had gone away for good. Of course I couldn't, because I had no money and no clean clothes, and anyway where would I go now that the city was filled with strangers? In my day you knew all your neighbours but now there were only men and uniforms. When the house was quiet I stole some food from their kitchen. I found a tin of condensed milk, some bread and an apricot, not very fresh but better than nothing. I was careful not to take too much, otherwise they would notice. Then I went back up to my cupboard. And there I stayed.

I thought for a while I would escape, but I couldn't get much further than the toilet and the cubbyhole kitchen, and certainly couldn't manage the main staircase to the front door any more: it was far too long and the stairs were too deep.

They overran the house, barking and chasing each other like dogs, and nobody thought of looking in the cupboard because you wouldn't, it was so insignificant, and they didn't notice details. At night they smashed things up and screamed at each other, screamed terrible things, and once there were gunshots, but nobody ever came round to complain. I think the only ones left were too frightened to go out any more, like me.

The food did not last long. I forced myself to stretch my legs and got as far as the kitchen, where I found some tins of potted meat, and bread. I noticed that the house next door, the one belonging to the young couple, was now empty. They had got out, or been taken out.

I still live here in my old house. I don't know how long I've been here. The worst thing is when the people downstairs leave and I hope against hope that this is all over, and then I realise that if they don't come back I'll have no food. I need them to feed me. But they always return, smoking their little pipes and leaving plates of half-eaten sausage on the floor, which I can take when they're asleep.

Of course I am scared. I've been scared before, but when you are scared all the time, the sensation fades away into a dull ache that you hardly remember any more, like losing Sam or any other sadness that is always with you. They talked about needing room to move and grow, but they were far more confined than I, quarantined by the house and their narrow thoughts. Me, I was free to think anything I wanted. I was the one with all the space now.

Sometimes I remember the house the way it was. With polished lino and ticking clocks and china dogs on the mantelpiece, and the Bach playing on the wireless, the smell of fresh-baked jam puddings and lavender polish, washed net curtains, everything dusted and tidy and bright, children in the street, mothers in gardens; but those days have gone, and I would rather be old and filled with memories and living in this little dark room than be downstairs in the bare, hard light, young and raw and screaming inside, facing the daily terror of being alive in a world that can no longer tell decency from corruption or right from wrong, a world that no longer notices if you are even there at all.

———✳———

DANCING TOWARDS THE BLADE

MARK BILLINGHAM

He was always Vincent at home.

At school there were a few boys who called him "Vince", and "Vinny" was yelled more often than not across the playground, but his mother and father never shortened his name and neither did his brothers and sisters whose own names, in turn, were also spoken in full.

"Vincent" around the house then, and at family functions. The second syllable given equal weight with the first by the heavy accent of the elder members. Not swallowed. Rhyming with "went".

Vincent was not really bothered what names people chose to use, but there were some things it was never pleasant to be called.

"Coon!"

"Black coon!"

"Fucking black bastard …"

He had rounded the corner and stepped into the passageway to find them waiting for him, like turds in long grass. A trio of them in Timberland and Tommy Hilfiger. Not shouting, but simply speaking casually. Saying what they saw. Big car. Hairy dog. Fucking black bastard.

Vincent stopped, caught his breath, took it all in.

Two were tallish – one abnormally thin, the other shaven-headed, and both cradled cans of expensive lager. The third was shorter and wore a baseball cap, the peak bent and pulled down low. He took a swig of Smirnoff Ice, then began to bounce on the balls of his feet, swinging the frosted glass bottle between thumb and forefinger.

"What you staring at, you sooty fucker?"

Vincent reckoned they were fifteen or so. Year eleven boys. The skinny one was maybe not even that, but all of them were a little younger than he was.

From somewhere a few streets away came the noise of singing; tuneless and incoherent, the phrases swinging like bludgeons. Quick as a flash, the arms of the taller boys were in the air, lager cans clutched in pale fists, faces taut with blind passion as they joined in the song.

"No one likes us, no one likes us, no one likes us, we don't care …"

The smaller boy looked at Vincent and shouted above the noise. "Well?"

It was nearly six o'clock and starting to get dark. The match had finished over an hour ago but Vincent had guessed there might still be a few lads knocking about. He'd seen a couple outside the newsagent's as he'd walked down the ramp from the Tube station. Blowing onto bags of chips. Tits and guts moving beneath their thin replica shirts. The away fans were long gone and most of the home supporters were already indoors, but there were others, most who'd already forgotten the score, who still wandered the streets, singing and drinking. Waiting in groups, a radio tuned to 5 Live. Standing in lines on low walls, the half-time shitburgers turning to acid in their stomachs, looking around for it.

The cut-through was no more than fifteen feet wide, and ran between two three-storey blocks. It curled away from the main road towards the block where Vincent lived at the far end of the estate. The three boys that barred his way were gathered around a pair of stone bollards, built to dissuade certain drivers from coming onto the estate; from setting fire to cars on people's doorsteps.

Vincent answered the question, trying to keep his voice low and even, hoping it wouldn't catch. "I'm going home."

"Fucking listen to him. A posh nigger."

The skinny boy laughed and the three came together, shoulders connecting, forearms nudging one another. When they were still again, they had taken up new positions. The three now stood, more or less evenly spaced across the walkway, one in each gap. Between wall and bollard, bollard and bollard, bollard and wall.

"Where's home?" the boy in the cap asked.

Vincent pointed past the boy's head. The boy didn't turn. He raised his head and Vincent got his first real look at the face, handsome and hard, shadowed by the peak of the baseball cap. Vincent saw something like a smile as the boy brought the bottle to his lips again.

"This is the shortcut," Vincent said. "My quickest way."

The boy in the cap swallowed. "Your quickest way home is via the airport." The smile that Vincent had thought he'd seen now made itself very evident. "You want the Piccadilly line to Heathrow, mate."

Vincent chuckled softly, pretending to enjoy the joke. He saw the boy's face harden, watched him raise a hand and jab a finger back towards the main road.

"Go round."

Vincent knew what he meant. He could walk back and take the path that led around the perimeter of the estate, approach his block from the other side. It would only take a few minutes longer. He could just turn and go and he would probably be home before they'd finished laughing.

"You heard." The skinny boy leaned back against a bollard. He could *easily* turn and go round.

"Now piss off …"

The edges of Vincent's vision began to blur and darken and the words that spewed from the mouth of the boy with the shaven head became hard to make out. A distant rhythm was asserting itself and as Vincent looked down at the cracked slabs beneath his feet, a shadow seemed to fall across them. A voice grew louder, and it was as if the walls on either side had softened and begun to sway above him like the tops of trees.

The voice was one Vincent knew well. The accent, unlike his own, was heavy, but the intonation and tone were those that had been passed on to him and to his brothers and sisters. It was a rich voice, warm and dark, sliding effortlessly around every phrase, each dramatic sentence of a story it never tired of telling.

His father's voice …

Looking out from his bedroom window, the boy could see the coffee plants lying like a deep green tablecloth across the hillside, billowing down towards the canopy of treetops and the dirty river beneath. If he raised his eyes *up*, he saw the mountain on the far side of the valley, its peaks jutting into the mist, the slopes changing colour many times a day according to the cloud and the position of the sun. Black or green or blood red. Other colours the boy had no name for.

A dozen views for the price of one, and he'd thought about all of them in the time he'd been away. He'd tried to picture each one during the bone-shaking, twelve-hour bus ride that had brought him home from school five days before.

"Hey! Stand still, boy. This is damn fiddly."

Uncle Joseph, on his knees in front of him, his thick fingers struggling with the leather fastenings, as they had every morning since they'd begun. It was hard to tie the knots so that the strings of beads clung to the calves without slipping, but not so tightly that they would cut into the flesh.

When he'd finished with the beads on the lower legs, Uncle Joseph would move on to the thick bands of dried goatskin, each heavy with rows of bells and strapped around the thighs. These were expensive items, hand-made like everything else. Lastly, Joseph would wrap the dark highly polished belt around the boy's waist. On three out of the last four mornings, much to the boy's amusement, he'd sliced a finger on one of the razor-sharp shells sewn into the leather.

Behind him, Uncle Francis worked on attaching the beads that crossed his back and chest in an X, like brightly coloured bandoliers. Francis was always cheerful, and the boy imagined that he too looked forward to that moment when Joseph would cry out, curse and stick a bleeding finger into his mouth. It was always Francis and Joseph that dressed him. The rest of his uncles waited outside. He'd been amazed at quite how *many* uncles he had, when they'd gathered on the night after he'd got back; when the family committee had met to organise it all.

There had been lots to decide.

"Do we have drummers?"

"Of course. This is important. *He* is important."

"Grade A. Definitely Grade A."

"These drummers are not cheap. Their damn costumes alone are a fortune."

"I think they should come *with* their costumes. It isn't fair. We shouldn't have to pay for the costumes separately."

"We should have *lots* of drummers …"

And on and on, deep into the night, arguing and getting drunker while the boy listened from his bedroom. Though he didn't understand everything, the passion in the voices of these men had caused excitement to swell in his chest. Yes, and an equal measure of dread to press down on it, like one of the huge flat stones that lay along the riverbed at the bottom of the valley. He'd lain awake most of that night thinking of his friends, his *age-mates* in the other villages, wondering if they were feeling the same thing.

"All set, boy," Uncle Joseph said.

Uncle Francis handed him the headdress, rubbed the back of his neck. "Feeling fit?"

Outside, he was greeted with cheers and whoops. This was the last day of gathering and there was more noise, more gaiety than there had been on any day previously. This was the eve of it all; the final, glorious push.

He took his place in the middle of the group, acknowledged

the greetings of his brothers, of uncles, and cousins whose names he could never remember. Though no one was dressed as extravagantly as he was, everyone had made the necessary effort. No man or boy was without beads or bells while the older ones were all draped in animal skins – monkey, zebra and lion. All had painted faces and strips of brightly coloured cloth attached to the edges of their leather vests.

A huge roar went up as the first drum was struck. A massive bass drum, its rhythm like a giant's heartbeat. The smaller drums joined then, and the whistles, and the yelps of the women and children, watching from the doorways of houses, waving the gatherers goodbye.

The boy cleared his throat and spat into the dirt. He let out a long, high note, listened to it roll away across the valley. The rhythm became more complex, more frantic, and he picked up his knees in time to it, the beads rattling on his legs and the shells clattering against the belt around his waist.

He began to dance.

The procession started to move. A carnival, a travelling circus, a hundred or more bare feet slapping into the dirt in time to the drummers. A cloud of dust rose up behind them as they picked up speed, moving away along the hard, brown track that snaked out of the village.

The mottled grey of the slabs was broken only by the splotches of dog-shit brown and dandelion yellow.

Vincent looked up from the floor of the walkway.

The eyes of the two taller boys darted between his face

and that of their friend. It seemed to Vincent that they were waiting to be told what to do; that they were looking for some sort of signal.

The boy in the cap raised his eyes up to Vincent's. He took a long, slow swig from his bottle, his gaze not shifting from Vincent's face. Then, he snatched the bottle from his lips, wiped a hand across his mouth and glared, as if suddenly affronted.

"*What?*"

Vincent smiled, shook his head. "I didn't say anything."

"Yes, you fucking did."

The boy with the shaved head took a step forward. "What did you say, you cheeky black fucker?"

The smaller boy nodded, pleased, and took another swig. Vincent shrugged, feeling the tremble in his right leg, pressing a straight arm hard against it.

"Listen, I don't want any trouble. I'm just trying to get home."

Home.

Vincent blinked and saw his brother's face, the skin taken off his cheek and one eye swollen shut. He saw his mother's face as she stood at the window all the next afternoon, staring out across the dual carriageway towards the lorry park and the floodlights beyond. He saw her face when she turned finally, and spoke.

"We're moving," she'd said.

One more blink and he saw the resignation that had returned to her face after a day doing the maths; scanning newspapers, and estate agents' details from Greenwich and Blackheath. As the idea of moving *anywhere* was quickly forgotten.

"I've already told you," the boy with the bottle said. "If

you're so desperate, just go round."

Vincent saw the face of his father then. As it had been that day when his brother had come home bleeding, and then, as he imagined it to have been twenty-five years before. In a country Vincent had only ever seen pictures of.

The boy sat at the back of the house, beneath the striped awning that his father had put above his bedroom window. Rose rubbed ointment on to his blisters. They stared across the valley at the sun dropping down behind the mountain, the slopes cobalt blue beneath a darkening sky.

He knew that they should not have been sitting together, that his uncles would not have approved. Contact with young women was frowned upon in the week leading up to the ritual. He would regret it, his uncles would have said, in the days afterwards, in the healing time after the ceremony. "Talk to young women," Joseph had told him, "let them smile at you now, and shake their hips, and you will *pay*."

He didn't care. He had known Rose since before he could walk and besides, Joseph, Francis and the others would be insensible by now. They had sat down around the pot as soon as they had finished eating supper. Talking about the day, filling in the elders on how "the boy" was doing, and getting slowly drunker. Sucking up powerful mouthfuls of home-brew from the pot through long, bamboo straws.

The boy had watched them for a while, no longer jealous, as he would have been before. Once it was all over, he would have earned the right to sit down and join them.

"Fine, but not yet you haven't," Rose had said, when he'd mentioned it to her.

It had been a hard day and the boy was utterly exhausted. He reckoned they had danced twenty miles or more, visited a dozen villages, and he had sung his heart and throat out every step of the way. He was proud of his song, had been since he'd written it months before. Even Rose had been forced to concede that it was pretty good. He'd practised it every day, knowing there was prestige and status attached to the best song, the best performance. He'd given that performance a hundred times in the last week and now his voice was as ragged as the soles of his feet.

It had been a successful day too. Uncle Philip had not announced the final tally, but it had certainly been a decent haul. Relatives close and distant in each homestead had come forward dutifully with gifts: earthenware dishes piled high with cash; chickens or a goat from cousins; cattle from those of real importance. Philip had made a careful note of who'd given what, in the book that was carried with them as they criss-crossed the district, each village ready to welcome them, each able to hear them coming from a mile or more away.

Everyone had been more than generous. By sundown the following day, the boy would be a rich man.

"Are you scared?" Rose asked.

He winced as she dropped his foot to the floor. "No," he said.

The boy wasn't sure why he lied. Being frightened was fine, it was *showing* the fear that was unacceptable, that would cost you. He remembered the things that had scared him the most that day, scared him far more than what was to come the following afternoon. He had been sitting with the elders in the village where his father had been born. Squatting in the shade, stuffed full of roasted goat and green bananas, with barely the energy to nod as each piece of advice was given, each simple lesson handed out.

"You will not fear death."

"You will defend your village against thieves."

Then he'd been handed the baby.

"There are times when your wife will be sick, and you must look after yourself and your children."

"You will learn to cook."

"You will learn to keep a fire burning all day."

They roared as the baby began to piss on his lap, told him it was good luck. They were still laughing as the boy turned and danced his way out of the village. All he could think about, as he began his song again, was how being unafraid of death and of thieves sounded easy compared with taking care of children.

He thought about telling Rose this, but instead told her about what had happened in the first village they'd visited that day. Something funny and shocking. A distant cousin of his father's had been discovered hiding in the fields on the outskirts of the village. Trying to dodge the handover of a gift was a serious matter and not only had the offering been taken from him by force, but he had brought shame upon himself and the rest of his family.

"Can you believe it?" the boy said. "That man was Grade A! Cowering in the tall grass like a woman, to avoid handing over a bowl. A *bowl* for heaven's sake."

Rose pushed her shoulder against his. "So, you think *you're* going to be Grade A? Grade B maybe? What d'you think, boy?"

He shrugged. He knew what he was hoping for. All he could be certain about was that this was the last time anybody would call him "boy".

The one with the bottle stood a foot or so forward from his two friends. He reached over his shoulder for the lit cigarette that he knew would be there, took three quick drags and handed it back. "What team do you support anyway?"

"Fucking Man U, I bet."

For a moment, Vincent thought about lying. Giving them their own team's name. He knew that he'd be caught out in a second. "I don't follow a team."

"Right. Not an *English* team."

"Not any team," Vincent said.

"Some African team, yeah? Kicking a fucking coconut around."

"Bongo Bongo United FC!"

"Headers must be a nightmare, yeah?"

The skinny one and the one with the shaved head began to laugh. They pursed their lips and stuck out their bum-fluffy chins. They pretended to scratch their armpits.

"You know what FC stands for don't you? Fucking coon."

Vincent looked away from them. He heard the monkey noises begin softly, then start to get louder.

"Look at him," the one in the cap said. "He's shitting himself. You *should* be, mate, because it's our country again, now." He said something else after that, but Vincent didn't hear it.

* * *

Dawn, at the river, on the final morning.

Dotted for a mile or more along the flat, brown riverbank were the other groups. Some were smaller than his own, while others must have numbered a hundred, but at the centre of each stood one of the boy's age-mates. Each ready to connect with the past, to embrace the future. Each asking for the strength to endure what lay ahead of him.

The boy was called forward by an elder. As he took his first steps, he glanced sideways, saw his age-mates along the riverbank moving in a line together towards the water.

This was the preparation.

In the seconds he spent held beneath the water, he wondered whether a cry would be heard if he were to let one out. He imagined it rising up to the surface, the bubbles bursting in a series of tiny screams, each costing him grades.

He emerged from the river purified and ready to be painted with death.

The sun was just up but already fierce, and the white mud was baked hard within a minute or two of being smeared across his face, chest and belly. The mist was being burned away and, looking along the bank, the boy saw a row of pale statues. A long line of ghosts in the buttery sunlight.

He watched an old man approach each figure, as one now approached him. The elder took a mouthful of beer from a pumpkin gourd and spat, spraying it across the boy's chest. The beer ran in rivulets down the shell of dried mud as prayers were said and his uncles stepped towards him.

The group that had been nearest to him jogged past, already finished, and he looked at his age-mate, caked in white mud as he was. The boy had known him, as he'd known most of them, for all of their sixteen years, but his friend was suddenly unrecognisable. It was not the mask of mud. It was the eyes that stared out from behind it. It was the eyes that were suddenly different.

The boy was nudged forward, was handed his knife, and the group began loping away in the same direction as his friend. Drumming again now, and singing, heading for the marketplace. All of them, all the ghost-boys, moving towards the moment when they would die and come back to life.

"Shut up!" Vincent shouted.

After a moment or two, the skinny one and the one with the shaved head stopped making their monkey noises, but only after a half-glance in their direction from the one in the cap.

"Turn your pockets out," he said.

Vincent's hands were pressed hard against his legs to keep them still. He slowly brought each of them up to his pockets, slipped them inside.

"Maybe we'll let you *pay* to go home. Let me see what you've got."

Vincent's left hand came out empty. His right emerged clutching the change from his train ticket. He opened his hand and the one in the cap leaned forward to take a look.

"Fuck that, mate. Where's the notes?"

Vincent shook his head. "This is all I've got."

"You're a liar. Where's your wallet?"

Vincent said nothing. He closed his hand around the coins and thrust his fist back into his trouser pocket.

The one in the cap took a step towards him. He was no more than a couple of feet away. "Don't piss me about. I don't like it, yeah?"

He could easily turn and go round …

"Where's his phone?" the skinny one said.

"Get his fucking phone, man. They always have wicked phones."

The one in the cap held out his hand. "Let's have it."

It suddenly seemed to Vincent that the phone might be the way out of it, his way past them. Handing it over, giving them something and then trying to get past was probably a good idea.

The mobile was snatched from his grasp the second he'd produced it. The one in the cap turned and swaggered back towards his friends. They cheered as he held it up for them to look at.

The three gathered around to examine the booty and Vincent saw a gap open up between the far right bollard and the wall. He thought about making a run for it. If he could stay ahead of them for just a minute, half a minute maybe, he would be virtually home. He reckoned he could outrun the two bigger ones anyway. Perhaps his mother or father, one of his brothers might see him coming.

He took a tentative step forward.

The one in the cap wheeled round suddenly, clutching the phone. "Piece of cheap shit." His arm snapped back, then forward and Vincent watched the phone explode against the wall, shattering into pieces of multicoloured plastic.

The crack of the phone against the bricks changed something.

By the time Vincent looked again the gap had been filled. The three stood square on to him, their bodies stiff with energy despite their efforts to appear relaxed.

The space between them all was suddenly charged.

Vincent had no idea how he looked to them, what his face said about how he felt at that moment. He looked at *their* faces and saw hatred and excitement and expectation. He also saw fear.

"Last chance," the one in the cap said.

The boy was stunned by the size of the crowd, though it was nothing unusual. He could remember, when he'd been one of the onlookers himself as a child, thinking that there couldn't possibly be this many people in the whole world. Today, as at the same moment every year, those that could not get a clear view were standing on tables and other makeshift platforms. They were perched on roofs and clustered together in the treetops.

He and his age-mates were paraded together, one final time, carried aloft like kings. His eyes locked for a few seconds with a friend's as they passed each other.

Their Adam's apples were like wild things in their throats.

While the boy moved on shoulders above the teeming mass of bodies, the dancing and the drumming grew more frenzied. Exhausted, he summoned the strength to sing one final time, while below him the basket was passed around and each relative given a last chance to hand over more money or pledge another gift.

Now, it was only the fizzing in the boy's blood that was keeping him upright. There were moments – a sickening wave of exhaustion, a clouding of his vision as he reached for a high note – when he was sure he was about to pass out, to topple down and be lost or trampled to death. He was tempted to close his eyes and let it happen.

At the moment when the noise and the heat and the *passion* of the crowd was at its height, the boy suddenly found himself alone with Joseph and Francis at the edge of the marketplace. There was space around him as he was led along a track towards a row of undecorated huts.

"Are you a woman?" Joseph asked.

"No," the boy said.

The boy wondered if thinking about his mother and father made him one. He knew that they would be waiting, huddled together among the coffee plants, listening for the signal that it was over. Did wishing that he was with them, even for the few moments it would take to shake his father's hand and smell his mother's neck, make him less than Grade A?

"Are you a woman?" Francis repeated.

"No!" the boy shouted.

His uncles stepped in front of him and pushed open a door to one of the peat latrines.

"This will be your last chance," Joseph said.

The boy moved inside quickly, dropped his shorts and squatted above the hole formed by the square of logs. He looked up at the grass roof, then across at his uncles who had followed him inside. He knew that they had sworn to stay with him until the final moment, but honestly, what did they think he was going to do? Did they think he would try to kill himself by diving head first into the latrine?

Did they think he would try to run?

Joseph and Francis smiled as the shit ran out of him like water.

"Better now than later," Francis said.

The boy knew that his uncle was right.

He stood and wiped himself off. He felt no shame, no embarrassment at being watched. He was no more or less than a slave to it now.

A slave to the ritual.

The beer can hit him first, bouncing off his shoulder. It was almost empty, and Vincent was far more concerned by the beer that had sprayed onto his cheek and down his shirt. The can was still clattering at his feet when the cigarette fizzed into his chest. He took a step back, smacking away the sparks, listening to the skinny one and the one with the shaved head jabbering.

"I don't believe it, he's still fucking here."

"Is he? It's getting dark, I can't see him if he isn't smiling."

"He said he wasn't looking for trouble."

"Well he's going to get a fucking slap."

"He's just taking the piss now."

"We gave him every chance."

"They're *all* taking the piss."

"He's the one that's up for it, if you ask me. It's *him* who's kicking off, don't you reckon? He could have walked away and he just fucking stood there like he's in a trance. He's trying to face us down, the twat, like he still belongs here. Yeah? Don't you reckon?"

"Come on then."

"Let's fucking well. Have. It."

Vincent became aware that he was shifting his weight slowly from one foot to the other, that his fists were clenched, that there was a tremor running through his gut.

A hundred yards away, on the far side of the estate, he saw a figure beneath a lamp post. He watched it move inside the cone of dirty orange light. Vincent wondered if whoever it was would come if he shouted.

His eyes darted back to the boy in the cap.

To the boy's hand, which tilted slowly as he emptied out what drink there was left in his bottle.

The noise in the marketplace died as each one stepped forward, then erupted again a minute or two later when the ritual had been completed.

It was the boy's turn.

The crowd had moved back to form a tunnel down which he walked, trancelike, his uncles slightly behind. He tried to focus on the two red splodges at the far end of the tunnel and when his vision cleared he saw the faces of the cutters for the first time. Their red robes marked them out as professionals – men who travelled from village to village, doing their jobs and moving on. They were highly skilled, and had to be. There were stories, though the boy had never seen such a thing happen, of cutters being set upon by a crowd and killed if a hand was less than steady; if a boy were to die because of one of them.

The boy stopped at the stone, turned to the first cutter and handed over his knife. He had sharpened it every day on the soft bark of a rubber tree. He had confidence in the blade.

In three swift strokes, the knife had sliced away the fabric of the boy's shorts. All he could feel was the wind whispering at the top of his legs. All he could hear was the roaring of the blood, loud as the river, inside his head.

He was offered a stick to clutch, to brace against the back of his neck and cling on to. This was the first test, and with a small shake of the head it was refused. No Grade A man would accept this offer.

He was hard as stone.

His hands were taken, pressed into a position of prayer and placed against his right cheek. His eyes widened, and watered, fixed on the highest point of a tree at the far end of the marketplace.

Repeating it to himself above the roaring of the river. *Hard as stone.*

The boy knew that this was the moment when he would be judged. This was everything – when the crowd, when his family would be watching for a sign of fear. For blinking, for shaking, for shitting ...

He felt the fingers taking the foreskin, stretching it.

Focused on the tree ... chalk-white ghost-boy ... stiff and still as any statue.

He felt the weight of the blade, cold and quick. Heavy,

then heavier and he *heard* the knife pass through the skin. A boom and then a rush …

This was when a Grade A man might prove himself, jumping and rubbing at his bloody manhood. The crowd would count the jumps, clap and cheer as those very special ones asked for alcohol to be poured into the wound.

The boy was happy to settle for Grade B. His eyes flicked to his uncle Joseph, who signalled for the second cutter to come forward. The knife was handed across and with three further cuts the membrane, the "second skin", was removed.

A whistle was blown and the boy started slightly at the explosion of noise from the crowd. It was all over in less than a minute.

Everything took on a speed – underwater slow or blink-quick – a dreamlike quality of its own as the pain began.

A cloth was wrapped around the boy's shoulders.

He was gently pushed back onto a stool.

He lowered his eyes and watched his blood drip onto the stone at his feet.

There was a burning then, and a growing numbness as ground herbs were applied, and the boy sat waiting for the bleeding to stop. He felt elated. He stared down the tunnel towards the far side of the marketplace, towards what lay ahead.

He saw himself lying on a bed of dried banana leaves, enjoying the pain. Only a man, he knew, would feel that pain. Only a man would wake, sweating in the night, crying out in agony after a certain sort of dream had sent blood to where it was not wanted.

He saw himself healed, walking around the marketplace

with other men. They were laughing and talking about the different grades that their friends had reached. They were looking at women and enjoying the looks that they got back.

The boy looked down the tunnel and saw, clearer than anything else, the baby that he'd been handed the day before. He watched it again, happily pissing all over him.

He saw its fat, perfect face as it stared up at him, kicking its legs.

The skinny one and the one with the shaved head were drifting towards him.

Vincent knew that if he turned and ran they would give chase, and if they caught him they would not stop until they'd done him a lot of damage. He felt instinctively that he had a chance of coming off better than that if he stood his ground. Besides, he didn't want to run.

"I bet he's fucking carrying something," the skinny one said.

The one with the shaved head reached into his jacket pocket, produced a small, plastic craft knife. "Blacks always carry blades."

Vincent saw the one with the cap push himself away from the bollard he was leaning against. He watched him take a breath, and drop his arm, and break the bottle against the bollard with a flick of his wrist.

Vincent took a step away, turned and backed up until he felt the wall of the block behind him.

Hard as stone …

"Stupid fucker."

"He can't run. His arse has gone."

"I bet he's filling his pants."

Vincent showed them nothing. As little as his father had shown when the blade sang against his skin. He tensed his body but kept his face blank.

"Three points in the bag, lads," the one with the broken bottle said. "Easy home win."

Vincent had learned a lot about what you gave away and what you kept hidden. They could have his phone and whatever money they could find. He would give them a little blood and a piece of his flesh if it came to it, and he would try his hardest to take some of theirs.

Vincent looked down the tunnel and saw them coming. He would not show them that he was afraid though. He would not give them that satisfaction.

He was Grade A.

———✳———

KITTENS

DEAN KOONTZ

The cool green water slipped along the streambed, bubbling around smooth brown stones, reflecting the melancholy willows that lined the bank. Marnie sat on the grass, tossing stones into a deep pool, watching ripples spread in ever-widening circles and lap at the muddy banks. She was thinking about the kittens. This year's kittens, not last year's. A year ago, her parents had told her that the kittens had gone to Heaven. Pinkie's litter had disappeared the third day after their squealing birth.

Marnie's father had said, "God took them away to Heaven to live with Him."

She didn't exactly doubt her father. After all, he was a religious man. He taught Sunday school every week and was an officer or something in the church, whose duty it was to count collection money and mark it down in a little red book. He was always picked to give the sermon on Laymen's Sunday. And every evening, he read passages to them from the Bible. She had been late for the reading last night and had been spanked. "Spare the rod and spoil the child," her father always said. No, she didn't actually doubt her father, for if anyone would know about God and kittens, it was he.

But she continued to wonder. Why, when there were hundreds upon thousands of kittens in the world, did God have to take all four of hers? Was God selfish?

This was the first that she had thought of those kittens for some time. In the past twelve months, much had happened to make her forget. There was her first year in school, the furore of getting ready for the first day – the buying of paper, pencils, and books. And the first few weeks had been interesting, meeting Mr Alphabet and Mr Numbers. When school began to bore her, Christmas rushed in on polished runners and glistening ice: the shopping, the green and yellow and red and blue lights, the Santa Claus on the corner who staggered when he walked, the candlelit church on Christmas Eve when she had had to go to the bathroom and her father had made her wait until the service was over. When things began to lose momentum again in March, her mother had given birth to twins. Marnie had been surprised at how small they were and at how slowly they seemed to grow in the following weeks.

Here it was June again. The twins were three months old, finally beginning to grow a great deal heavier; school was out, and Christmas was an eternity away, and everything was getting dull again. Therefore, when she heard her father telling her mother that Pinkie was going to have another litter, she grasped at the news and wrenched every drop of excitement from it. She busied herself in the kitchen, preparing rags and cotton for the birth and a fancy box for the kittens' home when they arrived.

As events ran their natural course, Pinkie slunk away and had the kittens during the night in a dark corner of the barn. There was no need for sterilized rags or cotton, but the box came in handy. There were six in this litter, all gray with black spots that looked like ink hastily blotted.

She liked the kittens, and she was worried about them. What if God was watching again like last year?

"What are you doing, Marnie?"

She didn't have to look; she knew who was behind her. She turned anyway, out of deference, and saw her father glaring down at her, dark irregular splotches of perspiration discoloring the underarms of his faded blue work coveralls, dirt smeared on his chin and caked to the beard on his left cheek.

"Throwing stones," she answered quietly.

"At the fish?"

"Oh, no, sir. Just throwing stones."

"Do we remember who was the victim of stone throwing?" He smiled a patronizing smile.

"Saint Stephen," she answered.

"Very good." The smile faded. "Supper's ready."

She sat ramrod stiff in the old maroon easy chair, looking attentive as her father read to them from the ancient family Bible that was bound in black leather, all scuffed and with several torn pages. Her mother sat next to her father on the dark blue corduroy couch, hands folded in her lap, an isn't-it-wonderful-what-God-has-given-us smile painted on her plain but pretty face.

"Suffer the little children to come to Me, and forbid them not; for such is the Kingdom of God." Her father closed the book with a gentle slap that seemed to leap into the stale air and hang there, holding up a thick curtain of silence. No one spoke for several minutes. Then: "What chapter of what book did we just read, Marnie?"

"Saint Mark, chapter ten," she said dutifully.

"Fine," he said. Turning to his wife, whose smile had changed to a we've-done-what-a-Christian-family-should-do expression, he said, "Mary, how about coffee for us and a glass of milk for Marnie?"

"Right," said her mother, getting up and pacing into the kitchen.

Her father sat there, examining the inside covers of the old holy book, running his fingers along the cracks in the yellow paper, scrutinizing the ghostly stains embedded forever in the title page where some great-uncle had accidentally spilled wine a million-billion years ago.

"Father," she said tentatively.

He looked up from the book, not smiling, not frowning.

"What about the kittens?"

"What about them?" he countered.

"Will God take them again this year?"

The half-smile that had crept onto his face evaporated into the thick air of the living room. "Perhaps," was all that he said.

"He can't," she almost sobbed.

"Are you saying what God can and cannot do, young lady?"

"No, sir."

"God can do anything."

"Yes, sir." She fidgeted in her chair, pushing herself deeper into its rough, worn folds. "But why would He want my kittens again? Why always mine?"

"I've had quite enough of this, Marnie. Now be quiet."

"But why mine?" she persisted.

He stood suddenly, crossed to the chair, and slapped her delicate face. A thin trickle of blood slipped from the corner of her mouth. She wiped it away with the palm of her hand.

"You must not doubt God's motives!" her father insisted. "You are far too young to doubt." The saliva glistened on his lips. He grabbed her by the arm and brought her to her feet. "Now you get up those stairs and into bed."

She didn't argue. On the way to the staircase, she wiped away the re-forming stream of blood. She walked slowly up the steps, allowing her hand to run along the smooth, polished wood railing.

"Here's the milk," she heard her mother saying below.

"We won't be needing it," her father answered curtly.

In her room, she lay in the semidarkness that came when the full moon shone through her window, its orange-yellow light glinting from a row of religious plaques that lined one wall. In her parents' room, her mother was cooing to the twins, changing their diapers. "God's little angels," she heard her mother say. Her father was tickling them, and she could hear the "angels" chuckling – a deep gurgle that rippled from down in their fat throats.

Neither her father nor her mother came to say goodnight. She was being punished.

Marnie was sitting in the barn, petting one of the gray kittens, postponing an errand her mother had sent her on ten minutes earlier. The rich smell of dry, golden hay filled the air. Straw covered the floor and crackled underfoot. In the far end of the building, the cows were lowing to each other – only two of them, whose legs had been sliced by barbed wire and who were being made to convalesce. The kitten mewed and pawed the air below her chin.

"Where's Marnie?" her father's voice boomed from somewhere in the yard between the house and the barn.

She was about to answer when she heard her mother call from the house: "I sent her to Brown's for a recipe of Helen's. She'll be gone another twenty minutes."

"That's plenty of time," her father answered. The crunch of his heavy shoes on the cinder path echoed in military rhythm.

Marnie knew that something was wrong; something was happening that she was not supposed to see. Quickly, she put the kitten back in the red and gold box and sprawled behind a pile of straw to watch.

Her father entered, drew a bucket of water from the wall tap, and placed it in front of the kittens. Pinkie hissed and arched her back. The man picked her up and shut her in an empty oat bin from which her anguished squeals boomed in a ridiculously loud echo that belonged on the African veldt and not on an American farm. Marnie almost laughed, but remembered her father and suppressed the levity.

He turned again to the box of kittens. Carefully, he lifted one by the scruff of the neck, petted it twice, and thrust its head under the water in the bucket! There was a violent thrashing from within the bucket, and sparkling droplets of water sprayed into the air. Her father grimaced and shoved the entire body under the smothering pool. In time, the thrashing ceased. Marnie found that her fingers were digging into the concrete floor, hurting her.

Why? Why-why-why?

Her father lifted the limp body from the bucket. Something pink and bloody hung from the animal's mouth. She couldn't tell whether it was the tongue or whether the precious thing had spewed its entrails into the water in a last attempt to escape the heavy, horrible death of suffocation.

Soon six kittens were dead. Soon six silent fur balls were dropped in a burlap sack. The top was twisted shut. He let Pinkie out of the bin. The shivering cat followed him out of the barn, mewing softly, hissing when he turned to look at her.

Marnie lay very still for a long time, thinking of nothing but the execution and trying desperately to understand. Had God sent her father? Was it God who told him to kill the kittens – to take them away from her? If it was, she didn't see how she could ever again stand before that gold and white altar, accepting communion. She stood and walked toward the house, blood dripping from her fingers, blood and cement.

"Did you get the recipe?" asked her mother as Marnie slammed the kitchen door.

"Mrs Brown couldn't find it. She'll send it over tomorrow." She lied so well that she surprised herself. "Did God take my kittens?" she blurted suddenly.

Her mother looked confused. "Yes," was all that she could say.

"I'll get even with God! He can't do that! He can't!" She ran out of the kitchen toward the staircase.

Her mother watched but didn't try to stop her.

Marnie Caufield walked slowly up the stairs, letting her hand run along the smooth, polished wood railing.

At noon, when Walter Caufield came in from the field, he heard a loud crash and the tinkling of china and the shattering of glass. He rushed into the living room to see his wife lying at the foot of the stairs. A novelty table was overturned, statuettes broken and cracked.

"Mary, Mary. Are you hurt?" He bent quickly to her side.

She looked up at him out of eyes that were far away in distant mists. "Walt! My Good God, Walt – our precious angels. The bathtub – our precious angels!"

TAKE MY HAND

A. K. BENEDICT

"And this is my favourite exhibit," Dr Ruth Irving said, stopping in front of a closed cabinet. The tour guide turned to the group of fourteen-year-olds, her eyes sparking. "Has anyone heard of a Hand of Glory?"

Some shook their heads. Most didn't bother – it was hot, and they'd already trudged round six rooms of dead things. There were better things to do, like drinking. What's a school trip without an educational pop to the nearest pub?

"You'll like this one," Ruth said, taking the key out of her pocket.

"Don't bet on it," Matilda muttered to her best friend, Tara. Tara snorted.

Ruth's eyebrows raised. "You won't be laughing when you see what's inside."

Which just made Tara laugh harder. Giggles can't be gagged by a woman in half-mast trousers.

Her right cheek twitching, Ruth unlocked the cabinet and opened the door. Inside, on a glass plinth, was a hand. Its remaining skin clung, sunken, to the bones. Tea-coloured and skeletal, each finger was tipped with a yellow nail.

"*Urgh*," Tara said. "That's gross."

Ruth's hands shot to her hip pockets as if she were in a dusty desert gunfight not a musty museum. "*That* is a valuable artefact," she said.

"I'll give yer a pound," Matilda said, rootling through her pockets and pulling out a gum-covered coin.

"Funny thing to have as your favourite, Miss," Tara said. "Have you not got a dildo at home?"

Some of the class laughed. Ruth's face flushed to the red of her jacket. She breathed in, closed her eyes, breathed out. "Doctor," she said.

"What?" Tara replied.

"My title is Doctor, not Miss. Let's get on, shall we? According to seventeenth- and eighteenth-century sources, a Hand of Glory came from a hanged convict, severed while they were still on the gibbet."

"Cool," said Brandon.

Ruth smiled at him. "Very cool. The hand, usually the left, would then be dried and pickled for a month. A candle, made from the fat of the dead criminal, was balanced on the severed hand then used in one of two ways. The most famous use is by a burglar. The legend states that householders remain asleep for as long as the candle burns. When they wake, their precious items have been stolen and the house smells of molten human tallow."

"Disgusting," Matilda said.

"Fascinating," Ruth replied. "The perfect combination of folklore and crime."

"Your dad could've done with one," Tara shouted over to Brandon. "Then maybe he wouldn't've gone down for five years."

Brandon looked down at the chequered floor.

"You're not the one who should be ashamed," Ruth said

to him quietly. "We can't be blamed for the actions of those close to us."

Brandon gave her a grateful grin.

"Now," Ruth continued, "any questions about the exhibit?"

"Where's the candle?" Brandon asked, his voice hardly audible.

Ruth managed to catch it, though. "That is an excellent question. Very well observed. Another way to use the Hand of Glory is to dip the fingertips in wax and light them. It's thought that this is one example, although it's never been used."

The group pressed closer to the cabinet, staring intently at the withered fingers.

"What did he do to get himself hanged?" Matilda asked.

"That, sadly, isn't in our records," Ruth said. Her fingers trailed the shelf on which the Hand of Glory sat. "We received the hand by anonymous donation. We don't know its provenance."

"Are you French, Miss?" Tara asked.

"Doctor," Ruth said again. "And no, I'm from Rotherham."

"Only my uncle went to Provence. Said he saw a prostitute lying on a sofa in a window. Was it you?"

Ruth's nostrils flared. "I said *provenance*, a word meaning 'evidence of where something comes from'. Your provenance, for example, is clearly a family of Pringles-eating, sofa-shaped ingrates trapped in tracksuit trousers."

Tara's lips opened but no words came out.

"Not so mouthy now, are you?" said Ruth. "You really don't want to mess with me."

Matilda squared up to Ruth. "You can't say that."

"You'd think so, wouldn't you?" Ruth replied. "Turns out you can."

"Come on," Tara said, grabbing Matilda's elbow. "Let's leave her to her manky hand." She stalked off, followed by Matilda.

Ruth watched them go, then smiled at the rest of the group as she locked the cabinet. "Shall we continue?"

The museum toilets were furnished with dark wood and hissing cisterns. Tara stood in front of the mirror, swiping a contour stick from her right earlobe down to the corner of her mouth. Smudging the dark stripe into her skin, she watched as her cheekbone popped. "We can't let that bitch get away with speaking to me like that," she said.

"Are you going to tell Mrs Crabbe?" Matilda asked.

"Mrs Crabbe wouldn't care," Tara replied, sculpting the other side of her face. "The lazy cow couldn't even be bothered to come in with us."

"What are you gonna do, then?"

"What are *we* going to do," Tara corrected.

"Fine, what are *we* going to do?"

"We get revenge, that's what." Tara turned to Matilda. "And what do you do to someone to get revenge?" She didn't wait for an answer. "You take something they love." Tara waggled the red-tipped fingers of her left hand.

"Excuse me, Miss," Matilda said, tapping Ruth on the shoulder when the tour had finished.

Ruth spun round. "Doctor, not Miss. I thought you two had left."

Tara sidled up next to her, real close. "We couldn't go before we made up with you. Say sorry and that."

"That's not necessary," Ruth said. She tried to back away but was blocked by a display case containing a frozen pandemonium of taxidermy parrots. Tara put her arm round Ruth's shoulders.

Matilda stepped in, breathing spearmint and tooth decay in Ruth's face as she slowly said: "We're really, really sorry."

"That's OK," Ruth replied, trying to smile.

"We wouldn't want to make you uncomfortable," Tara said into Ruth's ear.

Ruth's breath became ragged. She went to reach for her inhaler, but the girls had pinned her hands to her sides. "I'm fine," she said. The muscles in her jaw clenched.

"That's alright, then. See ya, Miss," Tara said, stepping away so quickly that Ruth slumped against the display case. A parrot rocked on its branch.

When the girls were out of sight, their laughter echoing in the corridors, Ruth walked into the staffroom. Put on a pot of coffee. Sank into the armchair. Her hands were still shaking. Sometimes she didn't know why she still worked here.

The door opened. For one dust-moted moment, she thought that the girls had followed her, then Lyron, the museum curator, shuffled into the room.

"Good tour, Ruth?" he asked.

"Please don't give me the GCSE students, Lyron," she said. "I find it hard to hold back. Today, I'm ashamed to say, I didn't."

"They probably deserved it," he said, coming over to sit next to her. He had fuzzy down on his otherwise bald head and blinked a lot, like an exhibit surprised to come to life.

"They definitely deserved it," she replied.

"Michael would be proud of you, then," Lyron said. "If he were here rather than …"

"Rather than swanning off on a research trip without telling me." Ruth looked down at her lap, linking her fingers together. She tried to blink back her tears, but it just made them spill over the sides.

"Sorry," Lyron said, softly. "I shouldn't have mentioned him."

"Glad you did," Ruth told him. "I only volunteer here to feel close to him but no one else will mention him."

"He was the best curator this museum ever had," Lyron said, touching her shoulder.

"If not the best husband."

"Have you heard from him?" he asked.

"Only a postcard." Ruth fished the card out of her inside jacket pocket and handed it to him. "No phone calls, no letters."

Lyron squeezed her shoulder. He knew Michael of old. He looked at the picture on the front: Angel Falls, captured mid fall. "Venezuela, now, eh? Very nice." He turned the card over. "Michael at his usual verbose best."

Ruth's husband never wrote on postcards. Far too prosaic. He melted dried-blood-red sealing wax on the back, sprinkled on soil or sand from the country he was visiting and pressed his thumbprint on top. That way he owned the place. So many places. He went away every year for research, even after they got married. The staffroom notice board was filled with decades' worth of these cards, now their home was as well. He'd stayed away for longer than expected before, but never for so many weeks.

Lyron handed the card back and Ruth placed it in her pocket. It was a tight fit. She liked the way the edge of the card dug into the skin above her heart.

"He'll be home soon, bringing back something wonderful from his travels," Lyron said.

"Hmm," Ruth replied.

In York, at night, the streets take on the yellow of a little owl's eyes. Ruth's walk home passed the meat hooks of The Shambles then followed a series of snickelways that echoed with other people's footsteps. Her house was at the end of an unfinished road, and if that wasn't a metaphor for her marriage then she didn't know what was.

She felt a rush of relief as she entered the house. The walls seemed to swell and exhale too, like wallpapered ribcages. She loved these walls. They contained so much that was important to her: furniture inherited from her grandparents, books on seventeenth-century history, photos and mementoes of Michael and, best of all, Rigby.

Rigby figure-eighted her ankles, rubbing his head against her boots. His purr was fur-soft. Ruth emptied a tin of cat food into Rigby's bowl and watched as he lapped at the meat. Now nearly nineteen, Rigby didn't like to go outside unless Ruth was with him, so she made herself a gin and tonic and opened the kitchen door.

Rigby trotted out, turning his head to make sure she was following.

"I'm right behind you, Rigby," Ruth said, aware that she talked mainly for her own benefit.

Outside, in the courtyard, the sun was sitting on the fence, September strength, and about to go down fighting. She watered the flowerpots and sipped gin that tasted of rosemary, sage and redcurrants. There was not much to do, other than wait for Michael to come home.

At the far end of the unfinished road, Tara and Matilda leant against a wall. "What time do you think she goes to bed?" Matilda asked.

"Really early," Tara replied. "Ten? Half ten? She's got no one to shag – her husband is off on holiday for ages or something and I can't see her having an affair. Not in those shoes. She doesn't have any friends, either."

"How do you know all that?"

"Looked at her Facebook page. Always do your research. No one comments on her stuff. Not even her husband."

"Ouch, burned by your own bloke," said Matilda.

"Yeah. Still, this'll cheer her up," Tara said, reaching into her bag and pulling out the Hand of Glory.

"Put it away," Matilda said, giggling as Tara used the hand to tickle her under the armpit. "Someone'll see."

Tara placed the hand carefully back in her bag. "As long as *she* doesn't see until we've finished. And if the Hand of Glory does what it's supposed to do, she won't."

* * *

Hours later, the sun had died for the day and Ruth was in bed. It was cold enough for the autumn duvet now. It felt safer, somehow, underneath these covers. There were often times that she didn't feel safe here. It was probably paranoia, but, since Michael went away, she felt watched. Vulnerable.

Ruth turned onto her side and Rigby snuggled into her – the little furry spoon. Her head swam with Bathtub Gin. Sometimes, drinking stopped the dreams from coming. Sometimes, it let them in.

"You sure this is going to work?" Matilda whispered as they climbed over the back fence. The conditions were perfect. Nobody was about. Even the moon was hiding its face in the clouds.

"I've broken into my own house loads of times and they've never caught me," Tara said. "Out all hours and they think I'm fast asleep."

"I suppose," Matilda said.

"*And* I climbed onto your garage when you were grounded to get you out," Tara said, landing on the decking like a TK Maxx-clad cat. Avoiding pots, treading carefully on the gravel, she moved to the back door and took the Hand of Glory out of her shoulder bag.

"I still can't believe we took it," Matilda said as she brought out her lighter.

"She shouldn't leave the keys to 'valuable artefacts' in her pocket, should she? Asking to be robbed, she was."

"Yeah," whispered Matilda. "We're just teaching her not to be so rude. We're the customers. Oh, and to look after her possessions."

"'Xactly. Maybe next time her husband won't fuck off for so long," Tara replied. "Go on then, it's time."

Matilda flipped her lighter. Tara held out the Hand of Glory and dipped the little fingertip in the yellow of the flame until it caught light.

Matilda gasped as each of the fingers was lit. The flames spread no further than the smallest knuckle of each finger yet lit up the midnight courtyard. The Hand of Glory smelled of herbs and beeswax and pickled onions.

"Right, then," Tara said. "Let's break this door in."

Neither Ruth nor Rigby stirred as glass hit the floor of the kitchen downstairs and the back door was forced open. Nor did they move when Matilda stood upon the creaky floorboard on the landing. They didn't even twitch an eyelid when Ruth's clothes were tipped out of the chest of drawers in the room next door, quietly to start with, and then, as it became clear that the Hand of Glory was in action, with no thought to noise at all.

The girls stood in Ruth's bedroom doorway. Ruth was face down in the pillows, breathing deeply. Her cat was stretched out in black alongside her. An empty glass on her bedside table. "We could do anything, as long as the Hand is still burning," Tara said, her head tilted on one side.

"We could shave her eyebrows," Matilda said, giggling.

"We could do that. Or we could kill her," Tara said. Her eyes showed the light of five fingertips blazing.

Matilda turned to Tara. "You're joking, right?" Her voice trembled like a flame.

"We could, though." Hand of Glory in one hand, Tara took a knife out of her shoulder bag with the other.

"I thought we were just going to scare her a bit, get her back for saying those things," Matilda said. She looked very young by candlelight.

"We don't need to use the knife," Tara said.

"Good," Matilda said. "Then let's take stuff and—"

"You could just sit on her back, push her head into the pillows," Tara said. "She's got enough of them."

"That thing's infected you," Matilda said, staring at the Hand of Glory. "You wouldn't talk like that otherwise. It must be a murderer's hand. It's speaking through you."

"Maybe it is," Tara said. "And it feels amazing. You should try it." She thrust the Hand of Glory at Matilda.

"I don't want it," Matilda said, backing out of the room. "I don't like it."

"What's the problem?" Tara said. "I thought you'd want to feel powerful for once." She followed Matilda down the corridor, the burning hand held out.

"Stop it, Tara," Matilda said, turning her head away from the heat. "It's not funny." She reached behind her, found a door frame and fumbled for the handle. The door opened into another room, and Matilda stumbled inside. She tried to close the door, but Tara was too quick, darting through, candles flaring.

The Hand of Glory lit up that room, too. Matilda screamed. Tara turned. In the corner, hanging from the ceiling, was what once was a man. He was tea-coloured and withered. Smelled of rosemary and sage and pickled redcurrants. It only had one hand, and its thumb was covered in blood-coloured wax.

Tara dropped the Hand of Glory. The fingers flared against the carpet, then died.

Matilda ran for the door, rattled it. "It's locked!" she said.

Tara tried. The door was firmly shut.

"Thanks for giving Michael back his hand," Ruth called through the door.

"Let us out, you mad old bitch!" Tara screamed.

"I warned you about messing with me," Ruth said. "And you didn't listen. Just like I warned Michael when he was about to leave me. I said he'd made a vow and it'd be a crime to break it. I took his hand in marriage and, when he left, I took his hand in death. The museum wanted a Hand of Glory, now they have one."

"What about us?" Matilda said. "What are you going to do with us?"

"That is an excellent question," Ruth said.

A few months later, Dr Ruth Irving was giving her tour to a WI group. Practical women, good with their hands. They stood staring at the Hand of Glory.

"What's the other way?" one of them asked.

"What do you mean?" asked Ruth.

"You said that there were two ways to use a Hand of Glory,

but only mentioned one." The WI woman looked pleased, as if she had caught Ruth out.

Ruth smiled. "The other way is to prevent burglary. A householder can burn a Hand of Glory, and they shall not be disturbed in their own home. No one will be able to enter without the owner's knowledge."

"We could all do with that," another woman said.

They all laughed.

"Shall we continue with the tour?" Ruth said, locking Michael's hand back in its cabinet.

At home, Ruth got into bed and pulled the winter duvet up to her neck. Snuggled up next to her, Rigby's deaf ears twitched from things heard in dreams. Outside, the wind rushed and sirened like police cars, but it couldn't get in. Nor could anything, or anyone, else.

Relaxing into her pillows, she stared at the flickering shapes on her ceiling. On either side of the bed, fingers curling, red-tipped and on fire, the severed hands kept her safe.

DRESSED
TO KILL

JAMES OSWALD

"It's absolutely perfect!"

She stands in the tiny changing room at the back of the shop, staring in the mirror as she twirls. The dress is old, older than her mum. Older even than her gran. Something she imagines a flapper girl in the 1920s might wear. And yet it feels like it was made for her. Nothing has ever flattered her figure so much, nothing has been quite so comfortable. She can hardly contain her joy.

"You sure, hen? Don't you think it's a bit cheap, you know? Second-hand dress and all that?"

She stares past her reflection at the figure standing behind her. Trust Susan to get the wrong end of the stick, best friend or no.

"It's no' second hand, it's vintage. There's a difference, see?"

"That mean it's cheap, aye?"

"Cheaper than that outfit you've got your eye on, Suze." She reluctantly shrugs herself out of the dress, pulls on her normal clothes. Somehow they don't feel right any more. They're too tight around the arms, chafe in uncomfortable places she hadn't noticed before. It's no matter. She can change when she gets home.

Carefully, she gathers up the dress, trying hard to ignore the dangling price tag. She lied. It's more than Susan's paying for her outfit, more than she can really afford. But hey, that's what credit cards were invented for, right?

"What have we got here, Bob? Sounded pretty awful when Control called me."

Detective Chief Inspector Tony McLean stood at the open doorway of an unassuming suburban terrace house, and watched as a small army of forensic technicians came and went.

"Looks like a murder-suicide, sir. Possibly a domestic gone wrong." Detective Sergeant "Grumpy Bob" Laird had been waiting for him outside. "Mr and Mrs Johnson, at least we think it's them. Neighbours called it in. Said there'd been a lot of shouting, things being thrown at the wall. We sent a squad car round to have a word, and they found the front door open. Inside, well …" He nodded his head once in the direction of the open door, said nothing else.

Usually the one to bring a little gallows humour to help everyone through the trauma of investigating deaths, Grumpy Bob's unease suggested something terrible inside. It would have to be something utterly gruesome to be worse than the truck crash that had brought the city to a standstill earlier in the summer. McLean couldn't suppress the involuntary shudder that ran through him at the memory. Twenty dead, and some had taken days to identify. He pushed aside the thought. That was done, now he had this to deal with.

"I guess I'd better have a look, then."

* * *

The house had probably been built sometime in the 1960s, and was surprisingly spacious inside. Not like the modern apartments going up all over Edinburgh, scarcely large enough to stun a kitten. McLean followed the clear path set out by the forensic team, through a wide hall and into a kitchen at the back of the house. The main focus of attention was beyond that, in a much more modern conservatory. At first he thought the floor was made from dark-stained wood, but then he saw the chair, and the body sprawled in it, the details resolving themselves piece by horrifying piece.

She was young, that was the first thing he noticed. Her blonde hair splayed out from her head as if blown by an invisible fan. Sightless eyes stared up at the sky through the glass of the conservatory roof, but no amount of sun could tan the terrible paleness of her skin. It contrasted horribly with the ruddy-brown mess that spilled out over her once white blouse, slicked her frayed jeans and covered the cheap laminate flooring all around her. It never ceased to amaze him how much blood was in a person. How far it could go.

"Pathologist been?" McLean asked of a passing technician. She was holding a camera and treading very carefully in her attempts to record the scene.

"Upstairs, sir. With the husband."

"Thanks." He backtracked gratefully out, then followed the sound of voices up the stairs and into a large bedroom. It looked like a hurricane had swept through, turning furniture upside down, knocking pictures askew, breaking the mirrored doors on a built-in wardrobe and scattering clothes everywhere. It had also picked up a man and thrown him bodily at the wall, if the mess above him was anything to go by. He lay on the bed, broken and twisted, dark bloody holes where his eyes had been, a ragged gaping mess all that was left of his throat. Crimson stained the sheets and duvet, all but obscuring a yellow floral pattern that only made the scene worse.

"Thought you might appear soon, Tony." Angus Cadwallader, city pathologist, stood up from beside the body, knees popping in protest.

"What's the story? Looks like he was attacked by a wild animal."

"Aye. He's been beaten about a fair bit." Cadwallader had always been the master of understatement.

McLean took a step closer even though his every instinct was to run. "I take it he bled out from that." He pointed at the man's ruined neck.

"Looks like it, given the amount of blood and where it's gone. Reckon it's the same knife as cut the wifey downstairs." Cadwallader let out a long sigh quite at odds with his normally cheery demeanour. "We'll confirm it at autopsy, but I'm fairly sure she killed him, then turned the knife on herself."

McLean looked around the room again, trying to wind back time and see the events as they had unfolded. "She's just a wee slip of a thing, Angus. How could she do all this?"

The pathologist shrugged. "That's your job, Tony, not mine. And I can't say I envy you."

"They were such a lovely couple. Always a kind word when you saw them. Never any bother, really. Until last night."

McLean glanced briefly past the two people sitting on

the sofa, through the window to the street beyond. Thomas and Bethany Ackroyd held each other's hands as if they were newly in love, although from what he had gathered so far the two of them had been married almost forty years and spent the best part of that living in this house, just a thin wall away from where Peter and Mary Johnson had met their grisly ends. Outside, a couple of TV news vans had arrived already, ghouls circling around the tragedy. He'd have to see about making sure they didn't start harassing his key witnesses.

"You called the emergency number at ten forty-eight last night." Grumpy Bob consulted his notebook as he spoke. "Said there was screaming, sounds of things being thrown about. Had there ever been any other incidents like that?"

Thomas Ackroyd shook his head. "Not in all the years they've been there. Must be, what? Almost three now."

"And did you know them well?"

"Aye. Well, I thought so. But this …"

"Anything changed recently? Either of them had a new job, perhaps? Or were they expecting a baby?" McLean tried not to think about the young woman he had seen in the conservatory, imagining her alive and happy. It wasn't easy.

"Mary couldn't have children." It was the first time Bethany Ackroyd had spoken since McLean and Grumpy Bob had knocked on the front door. "She wasn't upset about it or anything. And Pete never mentioned it at all."

"There was that wedding they went to, though. Remember? What was it, three months ago? Pete was a bit quiet for a while after that." Thomas Ackroyd frowned as if the memory were too strange to accept.

Quiet was the exact opposite of what McLean wanted to hear, but it was a start. "You don't happen to know whose wedding it was? Family? Friend?"

"A friend of Mary's," Bethany Ackroyd said. "Close friend, I think. She was very excited about it. Had a lovely dress picked out, too. She was so pleased with it, came round wearing it and showed me. Said she'd found it in a vintage clothes shop."

"Was that unusual?" McLean asked. "For her to come round like that, I mean?"

"Oh no. Mary was always popping in for a cup of tea. Or I'd go round there. She worked from home mostly, and I'm retired." Bethany Ackroyd paused a moment as if considering her words. "It was a bit strange, though, now I think about it. She was very happy with the dress, I could tell. But it was meant to be for the wedding. Only, she wore it round the house for days before that. And afterwards too. Almost like she didn't want to take it off."

McLean wasn't sure how relevant that was, although the body, he was going to find it hard to forget, wore a blood-stained blouse and jeans, not the kind of dress you might put on for a friend's wedding.

"She wasn't wearing it yesterday," he said.

"No. That was the thing. I remember Pete telling me now." Thomas Ackroyd leaned forward in his chair, arms on his knees and wrinkled old hands held together almost in prayer. "He took it away to be cleaned. At least, that's what he told Mary. He said to me he was taking it back to the vintage clothes shop before she wore it out completely."

"And when was this?" McLean asked. Not that it was enough to warrant a murder-suicide.

Thomas Ackroyd paused a while before answering, his old face creasing with thought. "Wasn't all that long ago, now I think about it," he said. "Do you know, it might have been the last time I spoke to him?"

"You got any further with that murder-suicide?"

Another day, and McLean had been walking to the canteen in search of tea, possibly cake, but the open door to one of the unused offices had caught his attention. Grumpy Bob sat at a desk inside, staring at a computer that was almost as old as he was. He rubbed at his eyes before looking up at the detective chief inspector.

"Still waiting on the pathology and forensics reports, sir. Thought I'd do a bit of background on the Johnsons. Record of violence, medical problems, that sort of thing."

"Any luck?"

"Not really, no. Seem to be a perfectly normal and happy couple. He worked in finance, she was a freelance virtual assistant, whatever that is. They don't have any money problems, no family history of instability. Nothing to suggest what happened would happen."

"What about family? We found any relatives yet?"

"Aye. Mr Johnson doesn't seem to have anyone, but Mrs Johnson's sister lives in Manchester. She's on her way up to deal with it all. Looks like she's the one who'll be inheriting the lot, too."

"You don't think …?"

Grumpy Bob shook his head. "No. It's not motive, and there wasn't any evidence of a third person at the house that night. Something else is bothering me, though."

"Aye?" McLean stepped further into the room and closed the door behind him.

"Aye. Something about it rang a bell, so I went on the database, looked for murder-suicides with a similar MO. Didn't take long to find one. Almost identical. Young couple, happy, well enough off, good neighbours. Then there's a report of an argument and when our lot turn up, he's had his eyes put out and throat cut, she's bled out on the kitchen floor."

"When was this?" McLean felt the all-too-familiar cold in his gut.

"Eighty-six. I vaguely remember. I'd not long moved to plain clothes, but it was another team looked into it."

"Coincidence?" McLean didn't see how it could be anything else.

"You'd think, but there was another one, twenty-four years earlier."

"Another murder-suicide?"

"Same MO, everything. Wife goes off the rails, cuts husband's throat and puts out his eyes, then kills herself. I've only got the bare details so far. Just a record on the database. Everything else is in the archives. If we're lucky." Grumpy Bob turned his attention back to his elderly screen.

"Do me a favour, will you, Bob? Dig them out and go over them. See if there's anything that got missed first time round."

"You think the cases might all be connected?"

"I don't know. One might just be a grim coincidence, but two? My gut says something's not right here." McLean patted his stomach. "Either that or I need to eat something."

"Still wearing that old thing, hen?"

She lets out a snort of annoyance, but it's short-lived. Susan is always like this when they meet up for a coffee. Jealous, probably.

"I like it. Cost me enough, too. Might as well make the most of it while the sun's shining."

"Aye, fair enough."

She watches her old friend as she clumsily pulls out a chair and slumps into it. Susan was never the slimmest, but she's let herself go recently.

"How's Mike?" she asks, and knows the answer by the scowl that squeezes itself across Susan's features.

"How d'you think he is, cuckolded at his own wedding reception?"

"Oh God. If I'd known …"

"That your boyfriend was going to shag the bride 'fore the groom had a chance? It's no' your fault. Katie. None of us knew."

"Aye, well. Doesn't say much for my taste in men, does it."

"We all make mistakes, hen." Susan raises an arm to call over the waiter. Orders something with a stupid name. "You wanting anything?"

"Nah, I'm good." She reaches for her coffee, and that's when it happens. Stupid flimsy handle snaps clean off in her fingers. She can see it in slow motion, the half-full cup tumbling towards her lap, treacly-black espresso already spreading in the air, the better to ruin her favourite dress.

She can only sit there, damp and distraught as Susan fusses over her with paper napkins, water from the glass she wishes she'd picked up instead. It's too late, the perfect fabric ruined. Even now the dress feels wrong, uncomfortable, the clothing of a dead woman. There are voices behind Suze's inane reassurances, hoarse whispers telling her it's all over. The sun still casts shadows, but the world feels darker, colder.

"C'mon, hen. It's no' far to my place. Let's get you changed, aye? Get that old thing off to the dry cleaners."

The words scarcely register, and she is powerless to resist as Susan pulls her to her feet, guides her from the little café. All she knows is that the dress is ruined. Her life is ruined.

What has she done?

"Christ, this is depressing."

McLean sat in his over-large office on the third floor, sifting through the endless paperwork that was the most tedious part of his job as a senior officer. Across the room, Grumpy Bob stared at the screen of a tablet computer that had been found at the house of Peter and Mary Johnson. It had taken a few days for forensics to check it over and break the password protection. Now they were going through the contents to try and establish something, anything, that might explain why Mary Johnson had so brutally murdered her husband, then opened up her own throat.

"Depressing how?" He closed the folder he'd been working on and went to peer over Grumpy Bob's shoulder.

"Knowing they're dead, I guess." The detective sergeant swiped away a photograph, bringing up another to replace it. "These pictures show them so happy."

"Pictures can lie though, Bob. You know that as well as I do."

"Aye, you're right. Still can't find anything – oh, hang on." Grumpy Bob craned his neck, then pinched at the image on the screen to make it bigger. Looking over his shoulder, McLean saw a photograph clearly taken at a wedding, Mary Johnson in an old-fashioned dress, laughing. She looked so full of life, it was hard to reconcile the image with that of the woman in the conservatory, but the date stamp on the photograph showed it had been taken just a few weeks before she had killed her husband and then herself.

"What is it?" he asked, as Grumpy Bob put the tablet down and reached for a thick archive folder. The detective sergeant said nothing, flicking through a bundle of reports hand-typed on paper turned sepia with age. Eventually he came up with a selection of photographs, black-and-white but clear enough.

"This is Angela Pemberton, taken a few weeks before she murdered her husband and then killed herself, back in 1962. According to the file, this was an undeveloped roll of film in her husband's camera."

McLean stared at the image, another young woman, smiling at a joke. Then he picked up the tablet and held it alongside the photograph. The people were different, but the obvious joy and happiness of both occasions was the same.

As was the dress worn by both women.

* * *

"It'll take a couple of days, but we should be able to shift this. They made things properly back in the day, didn't they?"

She stands at the counter in the dry cleaners, her head a whirl of noise and conflicting emotion. Susan's old sweat pants and hoody make her feel like a character from one of those terrible daytime television shows, but the thought of being parted from her dress is worse.

"A couple of days? Can you no' do it in an hour like the sign says?"

The young man holds her dress gently, and that soothes her a little. It would be worse if it was another woman holding it, she couldn't have that.

"That's for shirts and the like. Normal washes. This ..." He lifts the stained garment up as if it were a living person. "This needs special care."

Something about the way he says "special" is reassuring, but still her instinct is to grab the dress from him, run away. She can wear it at home and nobody will see the coffee stain all down the front. But no, that's being silly. It's just a dress. She can do without it. At least for a little while.

"As quickly as you can, then." She gives the man a nervous smile. "And be careful with it."

"Don't worry. It'll be like new."

"There's nothing in the inventory, sir. You want me to go through this lot?"

McLean looked at the stack of boxes, filled with neatly bagged items from the Johnsons' home. Everything had been collected, examined, catalogued. He knew that the team working on the house were meticulous, so if the inventory didn't list the dress, it wasn't there.

"I don't think there's much point. Is that everything, though?"

Detective Constable Janie Harrison consulted the printout listing all the items taken, as if that would answer the question for her.

"Everything forensics thought worth looking at, aye. They stripped the bedroom and conservatory bare, since that's where the bodies were. Don't think there were clothes anywhere else."

"You know if people rent wedding outfits like that one?" McLean held up the tablet with its photograph, even though Harrison had seen it before.

"I don't know, sir. Looks kind of old? There's plenty other outfits here, and it wasn't like she couldn't afford to buy a new one if she wanted."

"Second-hand, though? Seems a bit … cheap?"

"Well, if you put it that way, aye. But some of that vintage stuff's worth a bomb. Much better made than most of the crap you can buy today, too. And fashion keeps on coming round. Something like that dress might've been popular two or three times since it was first made, right enough."

McLean stared at the photograph, then at the detective constable. A horrible thought forming in his mind.

"You seen Grumpy Bob recently?"

"Think he's in the CID room, sir. You want me to find him?"

"Aye, if you would, thanks. Then we'll see if he can find someone for me."

* * *

When did it all start to go wrong? She finds it so hard to think, the well of despair pulling her down, the darkness so overwhelming despite the sun that shines in mockery through her window. She hasn't set a foot outside in days, too overwhelmed at the thought of all those people staring at her, expecting things of her, judging her.

She's never been happy. Not really. It's always been about other people. Even when she thought she was having a good time, it wasn't really her. Like the wedding. She put herself in so much debt to celebrate Jen and Michael getting married. So many expectations, so much hope. And what came of it? Single again, after wasted years living with a man who showed how little he cared for her and her friends by screwing the bride at the reception. The partner she brought to the party quite literally fucked it up for everyone. Jesus, how can she live with herself after that?

She should call Suze. Get her to come round like she used to. Maybe bring a bottle of wine and some corny rom-com to watch. Except that Suze is Mike's friend, and it's all too terrible to think about. Suze will be better off without her. They'll all be better off without her. Nobody needs reminding of that horrible, agonising, embarrassing incident. It's too much to bear.

Too much to live with.

* * *

"I've not thought about it in a very long time. Not properly. Something like that never really goes away though, does it?"

McLean sat in an uncomfortable chair in a nursing home on the outskirts of the city. Across a small coffee table from him sat an elderly woman wearing dark glasses that were almost completely black, her gnarled hands gripping a white cane as if her life depended on it. Audrey Maidstone had been surprisingly hard to track down, not helped by the two marriages and changes of name she had gone through since her sister had killed herself in 1962.

"I'm sorry to dredge up old memories, especially unpleasant ones."

"Well, I'm sure you wouldn't unless you thought it was necessary, although I thought the case was closed long ago."

"It was. It is. But I was hoping you might be able to remember what became of all their possessions, your sister and her husband? Did they go to other family members? I'm thinking of your sister's clothes, in particular."

"You're thinking of that bloody dress, I take it." She pulled off her dark glasses with a wavering hand. The eyes that stared at McLean were almost completely white, and yet they held his gaze with a fierce intensity, reading him as if he were an open book. After what felt like an hour, but was more likely the most uncomfortable fifteen seconds of McLean's life, she slowly put them back on again.

"Angie was obsessed with that dress. Found it in a junk shop or something. I thought it was hideous, but she loved it. Bought it to wear to a wedding. Bertie Smythe, I think it was. Only, she never took the damned thing off. Every time I saw her she was wearing it, and laughing her head off. Drove poor Derek round the bend. That's why it was so strange when she … did what she did. If I'd guessed anyone would have gone off the deep end, it'd have been Derek."

"She wasn't wearing the dress when she was found." McLean had seen the photographs from the case archive, along with the report that told him it had been Audrey who had discovered the bodies. "Do you know what became of it?"

"There's the thing, Inspector. I remember it quite clearly. None of the family wanted mementoes, as I'm sure you'll understand. Once you lot had closed the case and we could get on with our lives, I sorted through all Angie's clothes and sent them off to a charity shop. But that dress wasn't with them."

"You're sure of that?"

"Oh, quite sure. If it had been, I'd have burned the bloody thing."

"What do you suppose happened to it, then?"

"I've no idea. Maybe Derek lost his temper and threw it away."

Lazy blue light strobed through the closed blinds, flickering like a faulty fluorescent tube as McLean sat in a tidy kitchen in a tiny Bruntsfield tenement flat. Across the table from him, a large blonde woman cried into her hands, black mascara running down her ample cheeks. Through the open door, they could see a procession of forensic technicians making their way to the living room, where the body of a young woman lay.

"I'm very sorry for your loss, Miss …?"

"Edwards. Susan Edwards." The large woman sniffed, then

wiped her eyes with the sleeve of her hoody. "My friends all call me Suze."

"I take it you know Miss Hatley well?" McLean tilted his head ever so slightly in the direction of the living room. He'd been in there and seen the body, had no great desire to see it again. There was no doubting it was suicide, though. Another young life needlessly lost.

"We've been best friends since primary school. Grew up together."

"You have a key to her flat?"

"Aye. Only for emergencies, like? See, if she loses hers? She's got keys to mine, too. Never thought I'd need to use them."

"And why did you use them?"

"'Cos she weren't answering her phone, didn't turn up to work. Nobody knew where she was. That's no' like her."

"So you wouldn't have said she was depressed, then."

"No. Well, maybe a bit. She split up wi' her boyfriend no' that long ago, but she was better off wi'out him."

"Oh yes?"

"We was all at a friend's wedding, only it turns out Kate's boyfriend and the bride had a thing going on nobody knew about. Least, not until the groom found them at it."

"Sounds like a good reason to be depressed."

"Kate? No way, man. See, if I'd come in and found him on the floor like that, her standing over him wi' a knife, I'd no' be surprised. But cut her own ..." Susan gulped, and for a moment McLean thought she was going to be sick. He couldn't really blame her.

"So you don't think that would be the reason, then?"

"Hell no. Kate? She wouldnae. She couldnae. She was more upset about spilling coffee on her dress than splitting up wi' that prick. Aw, man. Kate."

It's cleaned up nicely, scarcely a mark on the thing despite its age. There were some other stains, around the hems and hidden in the pleats, that he'd noticed when he prepared the dress for the cleaning process. Not really surprising, given its age, he guesses. They've gone too. Modern dry cleaning is so much more effective than it was even five years ago.

"You still obsessing over that thing?"

Maureen comes through from the back, a pile of suits draped over her arm, a warm smile on her face.

"Just checking the date on the card. Been here almost six months now. Think it's fair to say no one's coming to pick it up." He teases the plastic sheet back over the dress and takes it to the rack at the end of the counter, hanging it with the other uncollected garments. "Seems a shame. It's a lovely dress. Must be worth a fair bit, too."

"Aye. Well. Happens sometimes. Bag it up for the charity shop. Sheila's coming in tomorrow."

He takes one last look at it, hanging there among the other unloved and unwanted items. There's a story behind it, he's sure. Not one he'll ever know, though.

"Aye, the charity shop will do well from it. Nice to think it can bring someone else some joy."

BOOTY
AND THE
BEAST

JOE R. LANSDALE

"Where do you keep the sugar?" Mulroy said, as he pulled open cabinet doors and scrounged about.

"Go to hell," Standers said.

"That's no way to talk," Mulroy said. "I'm a guest in your house. A guest isn't supposed to be treated that way. All I asked was where's the sugar?"

"And I said go to hell. And you're not a guest."

Mulroy, who was standing in the kitchen part of the mobile home, stopped and stared at Standers in the living room. He had tied Standers' hands together and stretched them out so he could loop the remainder of the lamp cord around a doorknob. He had removed Standers' boots and tied his feet with a sheet, wrapped them several times. The door Standers was bound to was the front door of the trailer and it was open. Standers was tied so that he was sitting with his back against the door, his arms stretched and strained above him. Mulroy thought he ought to have done it a little neater, a little less painful, then he got to thinking about what he was going to do and decided it didn't matter, and if it did, tough.

"You got any syrup or honey?"

This time Standers didn't answer at all.

Mulroy neatly closed the cabinet doors and checked the refrigerator. He found a large plastic see-through bear nearly full of syrup. He squeezed the bear and shot some of the syrup on his finger and tasted it. Maple.

"This'll do. You know, I had time, I'd fix me up some pancakes and use this. I taste this, it makes me think pancakes. They got like an IHOP in town?"

Standers didn't answer.

Mulroy strolled over to Standers and set the plastic bear on the floor and took off his cowboy hat and nice Western jacket. He tossed the hat on the couch and carefully hung his jacket on the back of a chair. The pistol in the holster under his arm dangled like a malignancy.

Mulroy took a moment to look out the open door at the sun-parched grass and the fire ant hills in the yard. Here was a bad place for a mobile home. For a house. For anything. No neighbors. No trees, just lots of land with stumps. Mulroy figured the trees had been cut down for pulp money. Mulroy knew that's what he'd have done.

Because there were no trees, the mobile home was hot, even with the air-conditioner going. And having the front door open didn't help much, way it was sucking out what cool air there was.

Mulroy watched as a mockingbird lit in the grass. It appeared on the verge of heat stroke. It made one sad sound, then went silent. Way, way out, Mulroy could hear cars on the highway, beyond the thin line of pine trees.

Mulroy reached down and unbuckled Standers' pants. He tugged down the pants and underwear, exposing Standers. He got hold of the bear and squeezed some of the syrup onto Standers' privates.

Standers said, "Whatcha doin', fixin' breakfast?"

"Oh ho," Mulroy said. "I am cut to the quick. Listen here. No use talkin' tough. This isn't personal. It's business. I'm going to do what I got to do, so you might as well not take it personal. I don't have anything against you."

"Yeah, well, great. I feel a hell of a lot better."

Mulroy eased down to Standers' feet, where his toes were exposed. He put the syrup on Standers' toes. He squirted some on Standers' head.

Mulroy went outside then. The mockingbird flew away. Mulroy walked around and looked at the fire ant hills. Fire ants were a bitch. They were tenacious bastards, and when they stung you, it was some kind of sting. There were some people so allergic to the little critters, one bite would make them go toes up. And if there were enough of them, and they were biting on you, it could be Goodbye City no matter if you were allergic or not. It was nasty poison.

Mulroy reached in his back pocket, pulled out a half-used sack of Red Man, opened it, pinched some out and put it in his mouth. He chewed a while, then spit on one of the ant hills. Agitated ants boiled out of the hill and spread in his direction. He walked off a ways and used the toe of his boot to stir up another hill, then another. He squirted syrup from the bear on one of the hills and ran a thin, dribbling stream of syrup back to the mobile home, up the steps, across the floor and directed the stream across Standers' thigh and onto his love apples. He said, "A fire ant hurts worse than a regular ant, but it isn't any different when it comes to sweets. He likes them. They like them. There're thousands of ants out there. Maybe millions.

Who the hell knows. I mean, how you gonna count mad ants, way they're running around?"

For the first time since Mulroy first surprised Standers – pretending to be a Bible salesman, then giving him an overhand right, followed by a left uppercut to the chin – he saw true concern on Standers' face.

Mulroy said, "They hurt they bite you on the arm, leg, foot, something like that. But they get on your general, crawl between your toes, where it's soft, or nip your face around the lips, eyes and nose, it's some kind of painful. Or so I figure. You can tell me in a minute."

Suddenly, Mulroy cocked his head. He heard a car coming along the long road that wound up to the trailer. He went and looked out the door, came back, sat down on the couch and chewed his tobacco.

A few moments later the car parked behind Mulroy's car. A door slammed, a young slim woman in a short tight dress with hair the colour of fire ants came through the door and looked first at Mulroy, then Standers. She pivoted on her high heels and waved her little handbag at Standers, said, "Hey, honey. What's that on your schlong?"

"Syrup," Mulroy said, got up, pushed past the woman and spat a stream of tobacco into the yard.

"Bitch," Standers said.

"The biggest," she said. Then to Mulroy: "Syrup on his tallywhacker?"

Mulroy stood in the doorway and nodded toward the yard. "The ants."

The woman looked outside, said, "I get it. Very imaginative."

She eyed the plastic bear where Mulroy had placed it on the arm of the couch. "Oh, that little bear is the cutest."

"You like it," Mulroy said. "Take it with you." Then to Standers he said, "You think maybe now you want to talk to us?"

Standers considered, decided either way he was screwed. He didn't tell, he was going to suffer, then die. Maybe he told what they wanted, he'd just die. He could make that part of the deal, and hope they kept their side of the bargain. Not that there was any reason they should. Still, Mulroy, he might do it. As for Babe, he couldn't trust her any kind of way.

Nonetheless, looking at her now, she was certainly beautiful. And his worm's-eye view right up her dress was exceptional, considering Babe didn't wear panties and was a natural redhead.

"I was you," Mulroy said, "I'd start talking. Where's the loot?"

Standers took a deep breath. If he'd only kept his mouth shut, hadn't tried to impress Babe, he wouldn't be in this mess.

During World War II his dad had been assigned to guard Nazi treasure in Germany. His dad had confiscated a portion of the treasure, millions of dollars' worth, and shipped it home to East Texas. A number of religious icons had been included in the theft, like a decorated box that was supposed to contain a hair from the Virgin Mary's head.

Standers' father had seen all this as spoils of war, not theft. When he returned home, much of the treasure was split up between relatives or sold. After the war the Germans had raised a stink and the US government ended up making

Standers' dad return what was left. The Germans offered to pay his father a price for it to keep things mellow. A flat million, a fraction of what it was worth.

Divided among family members, that million was long gone. But there was something else. Standers' dad hadn't given up all the treasure. There were still a few unreturned items; gold bars and the so-called hair of the Virgin Mary.

Early last year the Germans raised yet another stink about items still missing. It had been in the papers and Standers' family had been named, and since he was the last of his family line, it was assumed he might know where this treasure was. Reporters came out. He told them he didn't know anything about any treasure. He laughed about how if he had treasure he wouldn't be living in a trailer in a cow pasture. The reporters believed him, or so it seemed from the way it read in the papers.

A month later he met Babe, in a store parking lot. She was changing a tire and just couldn't handle it, and would he help her? He had, and while he did the work he got to look up the line of her leg and find out she wore nothing underneath the short dresses she preferred. And she knew how to talk him up and lead him on. She was a silver-tongued, long-legged slut with heaven between her legs. He should have known better.

One night, after making love, Babe mentioned the stuff in the papers, and Standers, still high on flesh friction, feeling like a big man, admitted he had a large share of the money socked away in a foreign bank, and the rest, some gold bars, and the box containing the hair from the Virgin Mary, hidden away here in East Texas.

The relationship continued, but Standers began to worry when Babe kept coming back to the booty. She wanted to know where it was. She didn't ask straight out; she danced around matters; he didn't talk. He'd been stupid enough, no use compounding the matter. She was after the money, and not him, and he felt like a jackass. He doubled up on the sex for a while, then sent her away.

This morning, posing as a Bible salesman, Mulroy had shown up, clocked him, tied him up, introduced himself and tried to get him to tell the whereabouts of the loot. When Babe came through the door, it all clicked in place.

"I got a question," Standers said.

"So do we," Mulroy said. "Where's the spoils? We don't even want the money you got in a foreign bank … Well, we want it, but that might be too much trouble. We'll settle for the other. What did you tell Babe it was? Gold bars and a cunt hair off the Virgin Mary?"

"I just want to know," Standers continued, "were you and Babe working together from the start?"

Mulroy laughed. "She was on her own, but when she couldn't get what she wanted from you, she needed someone to provide some muscle."

"So you're just another one she's conned," Standers said.

"No," Mulroy said, "you were conned. I'm a business partner. I'm not up for being conned. You wouldn't do that to me, would you, Babe?"

Babe smiled.

"Yeah, well, I guess you would," Mulroy said. "But I ain't gonna let you. You see, I know she's on the con. Knew it from the start. You didn't. Conning the marks is what I do for a living."

"It was all bullshit," Standers said. "I just told her that to sound big. She gets you in bed, she makes your dick think it's the president. I was tryin' to keep that pussy comin', is all. I had money, you think I'd be living like this?"

"If you were smart, you would," Mulroy said.

"I'm not smart," Standers said. "I sell cars. And that's it."

"Man," Mulroy said, "you tell that so good I almost believe it. Almost. Shit, I bet you could sell me an old Ford with a flat tire and missing transmission. Almost … hey, let's do it like this. You give the location of the stuff, and we let you go, and we even send you a little of the money. You know, ten thousand dollars. Isn't much, but it beats what you might get. I think that's a pretty good deal, all things considered."

"Yeah, I'll wait at the mailbox for the ten thousand," Standers said.

"That's a pretty hard one to believe, isn't it?" Mulroy said. "But you can't blame me for tryin'. Hell, I got to go to the can. Watch him, Babe."

When Mulroy left the room, Standers said, "Nice, deal, huh? You and him get the loot, split it fifty–fifty."

Babe didn't say anything. She went over and sat on the couch.

"I can do you a better deal than he can," Standers said. "Get rid of him, and I'll show you the loot and split it fifty–fifty."

"What's better about that?" Babe said.

"I know where it is," Standers said. "It'd go real easy."

"I got time to go less easy, I want to take it," she said.

"Yeah," Standers said. "But why take it? Sooner you get it, sooner we spend it."

Mulroy came back into the room. Babe picked the plastic bear off the couch arm and went over to the refrigerator and opened it. She put the bear inside and got out a soft drink and pulled the tab on the can. "Man, I'm hungry," she said, then swigged the drink.

"What?" Mulroy said.

"Hungry," Babe said. "You know. I'd like to eat. You hungry?"

"Yeah," Mulroy said. "I was thinking about pancakes, but I kinda got other things on my mind here. We finish this, we'll eat. Besides, there's food here."

"Yeah, you want to eat this slop?" Babe said. "Go get us a pizza."

"A pizza?" Mulroy said. "You want I should get a pizza? We're fixin' to torture a guy with fire ants, maybe cut him up a little, set him on fire, whatever comes to mind that's fun, and you want me to drive out and get a fuckin' pizza? Honey, you need to stop lettin' men dick you in the ear. It's startin' to mess up your brain. Drink your soda pop."

"Canadian bacon, and none of those little fishies," Babe said. "Lots of cheese, and get the thick chewy crust."

"You got to be out of your beautiful red head."

"It'll take a while anyway," Babe said. "I don't think a couple of ant bites'll make him cave. And I'd rather not get tacky with cuttin' and burnin', we can avoid it. Whatever we do, it'll take some time, and I don't want to do it on an empty stomach. I'm tellin' you, I'm seriously and grown-up hungry here."

"You don't know fire ants, Baby," Mulroy said. "It ain't gonna take long at all."

"It's like, what, fifteen minutes into town?" Babe said,

sipping her drink. "I could use a pizza. That's what I want. What's the big deal?"

Mulroy scratched the back of his neck, looked out the doorway. The ants were at the steps, following the trail of syrup.

"They'll be on him before I get back," he said.

"So," Babe said, "I've heard a grown man scream before. He tells me somethin', you get back, we'll go, eat the pizza on the way."

Mulroy used a finger to clear the tobacco out of his cheek. He flipped it into the yard. He said, "All right. I guess I could eat." Mulroy put on his coat and hat and smiled at Babe and went out.

When Mulroy's car was way out on the drive, near the highway, Babe opened her purse and took out a small .38 and pointed it at Standers. "I figure this will make you a more balanced kind of partner. You remember that. You mess with me, I'll shoot your dick off."

"All right," Standers said.

Babe put the revolver in her other hand, got a flick blade knife out of her purse, used it to cut the sheets around Standers' ankles. She cut the lamp cord off his wrist.

Standers stood, and without pulling his pants up, hopped to the sink. He got the hand towel off the rack and wet it and used it to clean the syrup off his privates, his feet and head. He pulled up his pants, got his socks, sat on the couch and put his boots back on.

"We got to hurry," Babe said. "Mulroy, he's got a temper. I seen him shoot a dog once for peeing on one of his hub caps."

"Let me get my car keys," Standers said.

"We'll take my car," she said. "You'll drive."

They went outside and she gave him the keys and they drove off.

As they drove onto the highway, Mulroy, who was parked behind a swathe of trees, poked a new wad of tobacco into his mouth and massaged it with his teeth.

Babe had sold out immediately, like he thought she would. Doing it this way, having them lead him to the treasure, was a hell of a lot better than sitting around in a hot trailer watching fire ants crawl on a man's balls. And this way he didn't have to watch his back all the time. That Babe, what a kidder. She was so greedy, she thought he'd fall for that lame pizza gag. She'd been winning too long; she wasn't thinking enough moves ahead anymore.

Mulroy rode well back of them, putting his car behind other cars when he could. He figured his other advantage was they weren't expecting him. He thought about the treasure and what he could do with it while he drove.

Until Babe came along, he had been a private detective, doing nickel and dime divorces out of Tyler; taking pictures of people doing the naked horizontal mambo. It wasn't a lot of fun. And the little cons he pulled on the side, clever as they were, were bullshit money, hand to mouth.

He made the score he wanted from all this, he'd go down to Mexico, buy him a place with a pool, rent some women. One for each day of the week, and each one with a different sexual skill, and maybe a couple who could cook. He was damn sure tired of his own cooking. He wanted to eat a lot and get fat and lay around and poke the *señoritas*. This all fell through, he thought he might try and be an evangelist or some kind of politician or a lawman with a regular check.

Standers drove for a couple of hours, through three or four towns, and Mulroy followed. Eventually, Standers pulled off the highway, onto a blacktop. Mulroy gave him time to get ahead, then took the road too. With no cars to put between them and himself, Mulroy cruised along careful like. Finally he saw Standers way up ahead on a straight stretch. Standers veered off the road and into the woods.

Mulroy pulled to the side of the road and waited a minute, then followed. The road in the woods was a narrow dirt one, and Mulroy had only gone a little ways when he stopped his car and got out and started walking. He had a hunch the road was a short one, and he didn't want to surprise them too early.

Standers drove down the road until it dead-ended at some woods and a load of trash someone had dumped. He got out and Babe got out. Babe was still holding her gun.

"You're tellin' me it's hidden under the trash?" she said. "You better not be jackin' with me, honey."

"It's not under the trash. Come on."

They went into the woods and walked along awhile, came to an old white house with a bad roof. It was surrounded by vines and trees and the porch was falling down.

"You keep a treasure here?" she said.

Standers went up on the porch, got a key out of his pocket and unlocked the door. Inside, pigeons fluttered and went out holes in the windows and the roof. A snake darted into a hole in the floor. There were spiders and spider webs everywhere. The floor was dotted with rat turds.

Standers went carefully across the floor and into a bedroom. Babe followed, holding her revolver at the ready. The room was better kept than the rest of the house. She could see where boards had been replaced in the floor. The ceiling was good here. There were no windows, just plyboard over the spots where they ought to be. There was a dust-covered desk, a bed with ratty covers, and an armchair covered in a faded flower print.

Standers got down on his hands and knees, reached under the bed and tugged diligently at a large suitcase.

"It's under the bed?" Babe said.

Standers opened the suitcase. There was a crowbar in it. He got the crowbar out. Babe said, "Watch yourself. I don't want you should try and hit me. It could mess up my makeup."

Standers carried the crowbar to the closet, opened it. The closet was sound. There was a groove in the floor. Standers fitted the end of the crowbar into the groove and lifted. The flooring came up. Standers pulled the trap door out of the closet and put it on the floor.

Babe came over for a look, careful to keep an eye on Standers and a tight grip on the gun. Where the floor had been was a large metal-lined box. Standers opened the box so she could see what was inside.

What she saw inside made her breath snap out. Gold bars

and a shiny wooden box about the size of a box of cigars.

"That's what's got the hair in it?" she asked.

"That's what they say. Inside is another box with some glass in it. You can look through the glass and see the hair. Box was made by the Catholic Church to hold the hair. For all I know it's an armpit hair off one of the Popes. Who's to say? But it's worth money."

"How much money?"

"It depends on who you're dealing with. A million. Two to three million. Twenty-five million."

"Let's deal with that last guy."

"The fence won't give money like that. We could sell the gold bars, use that to finance a trip to Germany. There're people there would pay plenty for the box."

"A goddamn hair," Babe said. "Can you picture that?"

"Yeah, I can picture that." Babe and Standers turned as Mulroy spoke, stepped into the room cocking his revolver with one hand, pushing his hat back with the other.

Mulroy said, "Put the gun down, Babe, or I part your hair about two inches above your nose."

Babe smiled at him, lowered her gun. "See," she said. "I got him to take me here, no trouble. Now we can take the treasure."

Mulroy smiled. "You are some kind of kidder. I never thought you'd let me have fifty percent anyway. I was gonna do you in from the start. Same as you were with me. Drop the gun, Babe."

Babe dropped the revolver. "You got me all wrong," she said.

"No I don't," Mulroy said.

"I guess you didn't go for pizza," Standers said.

"No, but I tell you what," Mulroy said. "I'm pretty hungry

right now, so let's get this over with. I'll make it short and sweet. A bullet through the head for you, Standers. A couple more just to make sure you aren't gonna be some kind of living cabbage. As for you, Babe. There's a bed here, and I figure I might as well get all the treasure I can get. Look at it this way. It's the last nice thing you can do for anybody, so you might as well make it nice. If nothing else, be selfish and enjoy it."

"Well," Standers said, looking down at Babe's revolver on the floor. "You might as well take the gun."

Standers stepped out from behind Babe and kicked her gun toward Mulroy, and no sooner had he done that, than he threw the crowbar.

Mulroy looked down at the revolver sliding his way, then looked up. As he did, the crowbar hit him directly on the bridge of the nose and dropped him. He fell unconscious with his back against the wall.

Soon as Mulroy fell, Babe reached for her revolver. Standers kicked her legs out from under her, but she scuttled like a crab and got hold of it and shot in Standers' direction. The shot missed, but it stopped Standers.

Babe got up, pulled her dress down and smiled. "Looks like I'm ahead."

She turned suddenly and shot the unconscious Mulroy behind the ear. Mulroy's hat, which had maintained its position on his head, came off as he nodded forward. A wad of tobacco rolled over his lip and landed in his lap. Blood ran down his cheek and onto his nice Western coat.

Babe smiled again, spoke to Standers. "Now I just got you. And I need you to carry those bars out of here."

Standers said, "Why should I help?"

"'Cause I'll let you go."

Standers snorted.

"All right then, because I'll shoot you in the knees and leave you here if you don't. That way, you go slow. Help me, I'll make it quick."

"Damn, that's a tough choice."

"Let's you and me finish up in a way you don't have to suffer, babycakes."

Standers nodded, said, "You promise to make it quick?"

"Honey, it'll happen so fast you won't know it happened."

"I can't take the strain," Standers said. He pointed to the room adjacent to the bedroom. "There's a wheelbarrow in there. It's the way I haul stuff out. I get that, we can make a few trips, get it over with. I don't like to think about dying for a long time. Let's just get it done."

"Fine with me," Babe said.

Standers started toward the other room. Babe said, "Hold on."

She bent down and got Mulroy's gun. Now she had one in either hand. She waved Standers back against the wall and peeked in the room he had indicated. There was a wheelbarrow in there.

"All right, let's do it," she said.

Standers stepped quickly inside, and as Babe started to enter the room, he said sharply, "Don't step there!"

Babe held her foot in midair, and Standers slapped her closest gun arm down and grabbed it, slid behind her and pinned her other arm. He slid his hands down and took the guns from her. He used his knee to shove her forward. She stumbled and the floor cracked and she went through and spun and there was another crack, but it wasn't the floor. She screamed and moaned something awful. After a moment, she stopped bellowing and turned to Standers; she opened her mouth to speak, but nothing came out.

Standers said, "What's the matter? Kind of run out of lies? There ain't nothing you can say would interest me. It's just a shame to have to kill a good-lookin' piece like you."

"Please," she said, but Standers shot her in the face with Mulroy's gun and she fell backwards, her broken leg still in the gap in the floor. Her other leg flew up and came down and her heel hit the floor with a slap. Her dress hiked up and exposed her privates.

"Not a bad way to remember you," Standers said. "It's the only part of you that wasn't a cheat."

Standers took the box containing the hair out of the closet, put the closet back in shape, got the wheelbarrow and used it to haul Babe, her purse, and the guns out of there and through the woods to a pond his relatives had built fifty years ago.

He dumped Babe beside the pond, went back for Mulroy and dumped him beside her. He got Mulroy's car keys out of his pocket and Babe's keys out of her purse.

Standers walked back to Babe's car and drove it to the edge of the pond, rolled down the windows a little, put her and Mulroy in the back seat with her purse and the guns, then he put the car in neutral. He pushed it off in the water. It was a deep, dirty pond. The car went down quick.

Standers waited at the shack until almost dark, then took the box containing the hair, walked back, found Mulroy's car and drove it out of there. He stopped the car beside a dirt road about a mile from his house and wiped it clean with a handkerchief he found in the front seat. He got the box out of the car and walked back to his trailer.

It was dark when he got there. The door was still open. He went inside, locked up and set the box with the hair on the counter beside the sink. He opened the box and took out the smaller box and studied the hair through the smeary glass.

He thought to himself: *What if this is the Virgin Mary's hair? It could even be an ass hair, but if it's the Virgin Mary's … well, it's the Virgin Mary's. And what if it's a dog hair? It'll still sell for the same. It was time to get rid of it.* He would book a flight to Germany tomorrow, search out the right people, sell it, sock what he got from it away in his foreign bank account, come back and fence the gold bars and sell all his land, except for the chunk with the house and pond on it. He'd fill the pond in himself with a rented backhoe and dozer, plant some trees on top of it, let it set while he lived abroad.

Simple, but a good plan, he thought.

Standers drank a glass of water and took the box and lay down on the couch snuggling it. He was exhausted. Fear of death did that to a fella. He closed his eyes and went to sleep immediately.

A short time later he awoke in pain. His whole body ached. He leaped up, dropping the box. He began to slap at his legs and chest, tear at his clothes.

Jesus. The fire ants! His entire body was covered with the bastards.

Standers felt queasy. *My God*, he thought. *I'm having a reaction. I'm allergic to the little shits.*

He got his pants and underwear peeled down to his ankles, but he couldn't get them over his boots. He began to hop about the room. He hit the light switch and saw the ants all over the place. They had followed the stream of syrup, and then they had found him on the couch and gone after him.

Standers screamed and slapped, hopped over and grabbed the box from the floor and jerked open the front door. He held the box in one hand and tugged at his pants with the other, but as he was going down the steps, he tripped, fell forward and landed on his head and lay there with his head and knees holding him up. He tried to stand, but couldn't. He realised he had broken his neck, and from the waist down he was paralyzed.

Oh God, he thought. *The ants.* Then he thought: *Well, at least I can't feel them*; but he found he could feel them on his face. His face still had sensation.

It's temporary, the paralysis will pass, he told himself, but it didn't. The ants began to climb into his hair and swarm over his lips. He batted at them with his eyelashes and blew at them with his mouth, but it didn't do any good. They swarmed him. He tried to scream, but with his neck bent the way it was, his throat constricted somewhat, he couldn't make a good noise. And when he opened his mouth the furious little ants swarmed in and bit his tongue, which swelled instantly.

Oh Jesus, he thought. *Jesus and the Virgin Mary.*

But Jesus wasn't listening. Neither was the Virgin Mary.

The night grew darker and the ants grew more intense, but Standers was dead long before morning.

* * *

About ten a.m. a car drove up in Standers' drive and a fat man in a cheap blue suit with a suitcase full of Bibles got out; a real Bible salesman with a craving for drink.

The Bible salesman, whose name was Bill Longstreet, had his mind on business. He needed to sell a couple of moderate-priced Bibles so he could get a drink. He'd spent his last money in Beaumont, Texas on a double, and now he needed another.

Longstreet strolled around his car, whistling, trying to put up a happy Christian front. Then he saw Standers in the front yard supported by his head and knees, his ass exposed, his entire body swarming with ants. The corpse was swollen up and spotted with bites. Standers' neck was twisted so that Longstreet could see the right side of his face, and his right eye was nothing more than an ant cavern, and the lips were eaten away and the nostrils were a tunnel for the ants. They were coming in one side, and going out the other.

Longstreet dropped his sample case, staggered back to his car, climbed on the hood and just sat there and looked for a long time.

Finally, he got over it. He looked about and saw no one other than the dead man. The door to the trailer was open. Longstreet got off the car. Watching for ants, he went as close as he had courage and yelled toward the open door a few times.

No one came out.

Longstreet licked his lips, eased over to Standers and moving quickly, stomping his feet, he reached in Standers' back pocket and pulled out his wallet.

Longstreet rushed back to his car and got up on the hood. He looked in the wallet. There were two ten-dollar bills and a couple of ones. He took the money, folded it neatly and put it in his coat pocket. He tossed the wallet back at Standers, got down off the car and got his case and put it on the back seat. He got behind the wheel, was about to drive off, when he saw the little box near Standers' swollen hand.

Longstreet sat for a moment, then got out, ran over, grabbed the box, and ran back to the car, beating the ants off as he went. He got behind the wheel, opened the box and found another box with a little crude glass window fashioned into it. There was something small and dark and squiggly behind the glass. He wondered what it was.

He knew a junk store bought stuff like this. He might get a couple bucks from the lady who ran it. He tossed it in the back seat, cranked up the car and drove into town and had a drink.

He had two drinks. Then three. It was nearly dark by the time he came out of the bar and wobbled out to his car. He started it up and drove out onto the highway right in front of a speeding semi.

The truck hit Longstreet's car and turned it into a horseshoe and sent it spinning across the road, into a telephone pole. The car ricocheted off the pole, back onto the road and the semi, which was slamming hard on its brakes, clipped it again. This time Longstreet and his car went through a barbed wire fence and spun about in a pasture and stopped near a startled bull.

The bull looked in the open car window and sniffed and went away. The semi driver parked and got out and ran over and looked in the window himself.

Longstreet's brains were all over the car and his face had lost a lot of definition. His mouth was dripping bloody teeth.

He had fallen with his head against an open Bible. Later, when he was hauled off, the Bible had to go with him. Blood had plastered it to the side of his head, and when the ambulance arrived, the blood had clotted and the Bible was even better attached; way it was on there, you would have thought it was some kind of bizarre growth Longstreet had been born with. Doctors at the hospital wouldn't mess with it. What was the point. Fucker was dead and they didn't know him.

At the funeral home they hosed his head down with warm water and yanked the Bible off his face and threw it away.

Later on, well after the funeral, Longstreet's widow inherited what was left of Longstreet's car, which she gave to the junkyard. She burned the Bibles and all of Longstreet's clothes. The box with the little box in it she opened and examined. She couldn't figure what was behind the glass. She used a screwdriver to get the glass off, tweezers to pinch out the hair.

She held the hair in the light, twisted it this way and that. She couldn't make out what it was. A bug leg, maybe. She tossed the hair in the commode and flushed it. She put the little box in the big box and threw it in the trash.

Later yet, she collected quite a bit of insurance money from Longstreet's death. She bought herself a new car and some see-through panties and used the rest to finance her lover's plans to open a used car lot in downtown Beaumont, but it didn't work out. He used the money to finance himself and she never saw him again.

THE NEW LAD

PAUL FINCH

Adam had always supposed the most important thing about being a policeman was behaving like one. OK, that might sound profound – hell, it might sound like the only thing you really needed to know – but now that he was *in*, so to speak, now that he was wearing the actual uniform, he wasn't at all sure what it meant.

If he was honest, he was confident that he looked the part. He was a youngish guy, tall, with chiselled, handsome looks – or so he'd been told – and short spiky hair that was totally in regulation. He was lean, but not thin, a physique ideally suited to the paramilitary look the job affected these days: combat trousers, the duty belt adorned with its various bits of kit, the radio harness, the stab vest, the black, padded anorak with POLICE stencilled across the back. He didn't have a mirror to check himself in, and theoretically he shouldn't need one – everything fitted as it should. But when you were as new to the role as Adam was, you couldn't help wondering: *Am I right for it? Is this really me?*

Not that he'd ever expected his very first shift to maroon him for a whole night in a mobile command post out in the woods. He strode up and down the narrow interior, the soles of his boots clipping the worn linoleum floor, hands clamped behind his back. *I'm alert!* was the image he sought to project.

It might be after two in the morning, but I've got a job to do here and I'm ready for anything!

It was a pointless exercise, of course. Adam was alone, so there was no one to impress. His one job was to hold the fort, a task so simple at this time of night in midweek that even a brand new constable could manage it. He occasionally had to step outside to check on the crime scene, but there was nothing going on at this ungodly hour. If anyone needed him, they'd call him on the radio, but that was unlikely to happen, the small device clipped to Adam's collar giving off nothing but a steady hiss of dead air. He might as well just sprawl in the chair next to the desk or make himself another cup of coffee; he'd had several of those already, but the sticky jar of Nescafé contained enough granules to see him through till morning, and there was milk left in the fridge.

Sit down, then. Put your boots up. Have another brew.

No harm there at all. Except that to Adam it would feel slovenly and unpolice-like. Not only that; if he relaxed, he might doze. And what would happen if some senior rank arrived?

He walked up and down again, finally deciding to have another snoop around outside. The interior of the command post was heated, which made it warm even with the square skylight in the ceiling jammed open a couple of inches. But outside it was a different story. Adam zipped his anorak up, fitted his helmet in place and pulled his gloves on before stepping out into the crisp autumn night.

It was halfway through November, but the encircling wood was not damp. It was a deep, dry kind of chill, almost frosty – the sort that indicated winter was well on its way.

Adam's vaporous breath plumed as he explored around the outside of the command post, feet crunching bracken when he got to the rear. He couldn't go much further as thorns and thickets came up to the back in such density that there was barely room to slide past them. Everything looked to be in order, though.

The command post was boldly marked with the distinctive Greater Manchester Police logo, but was little more to look at, in truth, than an overlarge and somewhat battered caravan with wire mesh over its single letter-box window. It was about thirty yards long and ten yards wide, but there was *less* room inside than you'd expect. This had taken Adam by surprise on first entering a few hours ago, though the mystery was explained when he'd seen how much of its interior was taken up by cupboards and storage lockers, the bulk of them crammed with traffic cones, visi-flashers, POLICE STOP signs and the like. In comparison, the living quarters – if that was what you called them – were spartan. Apart from the desk and the chair, the coffee-making equipment and the fridge, and the complex-looking radio set on the wall – which Adam didn't dare touch, having already found the personal radio a difficult enough thing to work out – there was nothing of interest.

Either way, it was a basic object both inside and out. There wasn't much to attract thieves or vandals, so he hadn't expected anyone to be hanging around, looking to cause mischief.

Satisfied with that, he walked out to the leaf-strewn road.

It was deafeningly quiet. Which was what he'd expected all the way out here.

Springburn Wood was located almost exactly halfway

between the former coal-mining townships of Tyldesley and Leigh, on the dividing line between two separate subdivisions – and that made it a fifteen-minute walk from the nearest bunch of houses. At one time, all this had been colliery spoil land; but nature had long ago reclaimed it – there were trees, bushes, even fishing ponds. Footpaths and wildlife trails sneaked through it. Some local folk regarded it as a beauty spot, though it wouldn't have won a prize tonight.

Adam crossed the small road, stopping at the verge and squinting as he tried to peer into the tangled, skeletal undergrowth. *There ought to be mist here*, he thought; *thick drifts of it hanging shroud-like between the twigs*. But an absence of such didn't reduce the "creep" factor. The branches overhead were leafless, but interlaced into a roof, intensifying the darkness at ground level, only hints of moonlight glimmering on gnarly bark or strips of forest floor. Adam knew that his vision would adjust, but not by much. The autumnal woods would be dim rather than dark, but it still wouldn't pay to go tramping off the road; you'd never see the root that tripped you, or the low-slung branch that hooked you in the eye.

Not that strolling forward from here was an option anyway. The strand of blue-and-white incident tape drawn horizontally across his path prevented it. If you really wanted to go further from this point, and that privilege was restricted solely to police personnel, you had to walk thirty yards north to the "common entryway", and even this had been laid with forensic duckboards which you must rigidly stick to.

Adam hovered with indecision. He wasn't entirely sure which parts of the scene he, as a simple sentry, was permitted access to, but hell – he was the one in charge and he *had* to check the place out every so often.

So, he wandered left, one hand gripping the hilt of his baton, head pivoting. Springburn Wood wasn't an ideal place for a crime scene; this late at night, it would be easy for some interloper to get close. But again, Adam didn't anticipate that. Mainly because by now there was nothing here of interest. Gillian Howes had been murdered over five weeks ago. As far as he knew, the forensics teams had just about finished on the site. There might be one or two additional things they needed to check, but mostly it was done – which was why there was only one person, an ordinary uniform like him, standing guard.

They took these things pretty seriously, though.

As Adam started along the entryway, boots clomping on PVC, he switched on his Maglite to ensure that he didn't accidentally step off it. Thus far, he was only inside what they referred to as the "outer-cordon", but already, his powerful torch shed light over numbered flags planted in the woodland floor on either side.

A short distance in, the duckboards ended at a small forensics tent, the entrance to which was zip-locked closed. As far as he knew, this was the changing room, where detectives and SCIs gloved up and put on their coveralls and overshoes before entering the "inner cordon", and after that the actual murder scene. That area lay further away still, and was distinguishable by the squarish, boxy outline of the much larger forensics tent covering the place where the body had been found.

Several dozen yards beyond that, vaguely discernible through the twisted, naked branches, stood the infinitely taller and more ruined outline of Springburn Special Hospital. From this distance, there wasn't much of it visible; it was an immense, monolithic structure, a stark, angular blot of darkness lowering among the trees, which more than hinted that the vast bulk of the old building, though gutted now and empty, remained intact.

Adam regarded it coolly.

Special hospital.

That was quite a name, given the place's history.

He supposed it would have been funny if it hadn't been sad, the way the unlikely legends surrounding this drear edifice had suddenly dovetailed with reality.

Formerly a facility for the criminally insane, Springburn Special Hospital had once provided confinement for men and women so mentally disabled that they'd never even faced trial for their crimes. But it had closed down nine years ago after a scandal that shook the entire country. No one in the outside world had known what the conditions were like inside that place until an undercover reporter penetrated it, and discovered a regime that was harsh beyond imagining, run by bullying, sadistic staff (several of whom would go on to be prosecuted not just for physically assaulting their charges, but for sexually assaulting them too). With mass overcrowding, neglect and brutality at every level, and living accommodation bereft of hygiene, the so-called hospital was later described by the local MP as a "den of filth and hopelessness".

When the story broke, the resulting uproar saw the institution closed and the patients removed to other facilities, such as the new, state-of-the-art Woodhatch Centre, located not twenty miles from here and regarded as one of the best and most modern in the UK. But alas, the sad tale wasn't over. Not long after that, rumours had started spreading that one of Springburn's most dangerous patients had escaped from Woodhatch and returned to live in the rotted shell of the rathole he'd once called home, and that this person was not just demented, but horribly disfigured – that he had a hook for a hand, and would slaughter anyone who came close.

It was the substance of nightmares, but it was slasher-movie stuff too.

Adam shook his head at the lack of seriousness with which so many people responded to the tragic and seemingly insoluble problem of mental illness.

A disfigured madman … *with a hook for a hand, for God's sake!*

He knew that he was inclined to be an idealist when it came to his fellow men, perhaps more than was sensible for a policeman, but really, that stuff was all so demeaning.

Of course, the chance was that the whole grisly story would gradually have faded into that morass of urban mythology popular mainly with school kids if Gillian Howes had not gone and got herself killed a few weeks ago. That unexpected event had started the whole thing up again. Suddenly, it was all over the papers, the news, the internet.

Mythical Woodland Monster May Be Real! one hysterical headline read.

Search On For Hook-handed Killer! screamed another.

Nubile Teens Beware! had been a real doozy, accompanied as it was by the strapline underneath: *Lovers' Lane Maniac Butchers Babe in Hollywood Horror Scenario!*

That last headline had been a particularly irresponsible one, because as far as Adam knew, Springburn Wood was not and never had been a lovers' lane. The eerie presence of the abandoned asylum had seen to that. The ominous shape of that sinister place supposedly prevented anyone coming here at night, let alone gangs of horny teens. From what Adam had heard, the Howes girl, who was in her late twenties, had come here with her boyfriend to carry out an amateur investigation. They'd called themselves "urban explorers", which apparently was the big new thing online; those involved investigating abandoned structures and complexes, and documenting whatever they found on photograph and video. From a law enforcement perspective, it was unacceptable given that it involved trespassing and maybe causing damage, while the danger of accident and injury had to be high. Plus, there was the ghoulishness factor. These guys claimed to be creating an invaluable record of forgotten sites, but so often their focus was on the lurid: places guaranteed to disturb or distress because once they'd been famous for pain and suffering. Like prisons, hospitals ... and mental institutions.

In this case, of course, the joke was likely to be on the urban explorers themselves, not to mention all those gorehounds eagerly awaiting the next chapter in the hook-handed killer saga. Because as far as Adam understood it, the investigating detectives were increasingly interested in Gillian Howes' boyfriend and fellow trespasser, Nick Jessup. Oh yes, he'd been injured himself, found wandering and dazed several miles from here with head injuries, but it wasn't impossible that those had been self-inflicted after he'd realised that the fight with his girl had turned fatal.

Then a *snap* – like a branch breaking – echoed through the trees somewhere behind.

Adam spun around, ears pricked.

Nothing else followed.

Only silence, but it was an odd kind of silence, a hush – as if all the nocturnal creatures scurrying about their business out here had suddenly stopped what they were doing to listen.

He headed back along the entryway, treading as softly as possible. When he reached the road, he glanced left. Thirty yards off, the command post sat against the far verge, its pale bodywork dappled with moonlight. Its door stood ajar.

Adam felt a pang of unease.

He was sure that he hadn't left the door open, though on reflection there was no guarantee that he'd closed it firmly. It could have opened naturally, of its own accord. But in truth, that didn't seem very likely.

He hurried along the road, stopping once to listen. He'd have liked to have turned down that hiss of static on his radio, but he was so new to the job that he wasn't sure how to do that. He listened out anyway, but heard nothing else.

Most likely, that sound had been some heavy nightbird taking off from one of the boughs overhead, causing a ruckus among the twigs and what remained of the leaves.

He continued on, glancing past the crime scene tape as he did, trying to penetrate the depths of foliage but seeing nothing out of the ordinary, though now that he thought about it, it was eerie how that slivered moonlight out there between the trees caused vague, hallucinatory images.

Several were near human in their outline.

"Stupid," he muttered to himself. "Stupid."

As the command post loomed out at him, a dark form darted out of sight at the other end of it.

Adam stopped dead, the bristles on the back of his neck tingling. He licked his dry lips.

He knew it hadn't been a hallucination this time.

Quick as he could, he took stock of his position.

He was standing at the north-east corner of the caravan. He'd only glimpsed that dark form in his peripheral vision, but it had leaped out of sight around the south-east corner.

Adam's heart thudded. This was a nervy situation and no mistake, but it was also an opportunity.

Was he about to make his first arrest?

OK, he didn't know who this was, so he didn't want to jump the gun; but whoever it was, they quite clearly should *not* be sneaking around a crime scene like this.

They had to be collared. The question was: did he go right, and slide stealthily around the back of the caravan, or did he dash forward and charge around the corner where he'd just seen the interloper take cover, catching him out with sheer force and speed?

Before he made a decision, he drew the expandable baton from its pouch, and as he'd seen them do on the TV, snapped it open to its full length. About twenty inches, he reckoned. He wasn't sure what it was made of – some kind of lightweight steel, though when he'd practised with it earlier, it was strong and sturdy, and had delivered a terrific *thwack*.

A rustle of leafage sounded from somewhere ahead and to

the right; by the sounds of it, at roughly the opposite corner of the caravan from the one where he was currently lurking.

OK – that was all he needed to know.

Adam went forward quickly, but sidling rather than striding, his tall, rangy body flattened against the front wall of the caravan, passing its open door and approaching its south-east corner. There, he halted, holding his breath, before spinning around the corner at top speed, baton to his shoulder.

There was no one there.

Directly ahead, beyond the caravan's south-west corner, stood the wall of motionless undergrowth. Adam crept towards it like a cat. When he glanced around this next corner, he'd be peering down the full length of the vehicle. Given how close the bushes were, it would be a good place for someone to hide – but it was too late to pull back now.

He went for it again, though this time he gave the corner a wider berth, convinced that someone would be lying in wait for him.

But again, there was nobody there.

The very narrow gap between the caravan and the foliage led all the way to the far end, with no figure of any sort hovering there. He turned his Maglite on and thrust the bright beam forward, but it revealed nothing out of the ordinary. Frustrated, Adam fought his way along the passage, lashing angrily at the twigs and branches that groped his face. When he rounded the north-west corner, he'd circled the entire vehicle, and still he saw no one.

He held his ground.

Silence. Absolute stillness.

Was it possible he'd been mistaken? Could he have imagined that darting shape?

"No … I couldn't!" he said aloud, going hard for the north-east corner, the point where he'd first started. Adam was now angry. OK, this was his first night, but he was damned if some little hooligan was taking the piss out of him.

He flung himself around the corner, and the two people waiting there flew right at him, arms raised, as in unison they shouted: "*BOO!*"

Adam stood frozen, scalp prickling, baton locked overhead – as it gradually dawned on him that the unexpected twosome, both already reeling about the road, laughing and high-fiving each other, were also wearing police gear.

It was a man and a woman.

The man, who had red hair and a beard, had to knuckle at both eyes to remove tears of mirth. The woman shook her head, though her eyes were moist too.

Slowly, stiffly, Adam lowered his baton.

His cheeks burned as his lips crooked into a wry smile. He was humiliated, yes, but he was a policeman now, and this was the sort of nasty trick they played on each other. You had to go along with it. As he closed the weapon up and put it away, he noticed that about sixty yards along the road, a car with Battenberg flashes was parked in a patch of shadow.

"Put the wind up you, did we?" Red Beard chuckled.

Adam shrugged.

"Sorry, pal … just a joke." Red Beard still seemed amused by it but made an effort to get himself together. "Bit spooky out here tonight, eh?"

Adam surveyed them both. Red Beard was somewhere in his mid thirties, shortish and tubby. But the woman, who was a lot younger, not much more than twenty, was rather cute: slim and bright-eyed, with a nice smile, her lush brown hair tied at the back in a fetching bun.

"What can I say …?" Adam slotted his baton and Maglite back into their requisite pouches. "Yes."

Red Beard offered a gloved hand. "Tony Mulroony. Drive the area car on the East. This is Cassie Winters. You're the new lad on the West, I'm guessing?"

Adam nodded and shook hands with both of them.

"Do you want to go inside, Cass, love?" Mulroony told his sidekick. "Make us all a coffee?" He glanced at Adam, a mischievous twinkle in his eye. "Don't worry, pal, I'm not being sexist. Cass is new too … I'm puppy-walking her, so she has to do everything I tell her. No point having a probie and barking yourself, as they say."

PC Winters rolled her eyes as she stepped up into the caravan.

Adam said nothing. He was still trembling from the fright they'd given him.

"You OK?" Mulroony asked.

Adam shrugged again. "Sorry. It's my first night. Didn't know what to expect."

"Nights can be a shock to the system if you're not used to them. Who's your tutor con, anyway? Dave Ellis, is it?"

"*Erm*, yeah … Dave."

Mulroony nodded. "Dave usually has the new lads. Good bloke though, eh?"

"Yeah … great."

Winters stuck her head back outside, focusing on Adam. "You having a coffee too, love?"

"No, I've already had one, thanks."

"Bloody hell, son," Mulroony said, laughing. "You'll soon learn never to turn a brew down. Not on nights." He indicated the open door. "Come on … after you."

They entered the command post, which felt cramped with all three of them inside.

"Ohhh, yeees!" Mulroony plonked himself down in the chair. "Life doesn't get cosier than this, eh? Mind you … what a job to pull, sat in here all night. You sneaked your iPad out with you, or your phone … so you can watch a movie?"

Adam had just removed his helmet and didn't at first realise that he was the one being spoken to; he'd also been stealing crafty looks at PC Winters, who was busying herself around the kettle.

"Sorry, what … iPad?" He shook his head.

"You really are new," Mulroony said. "Still … I think the East are copping for this job tomorrow. Should free you up to do some proper bobbying."

Winters handed her tutor his drink, which he relished with smacking lips.

"When you're back on days, you'll get all the shoplifters and shit like that," she said, addressing Adam again. "I did for my first couple of months. They're easy jobs, but it'll get you up to speed."

Adam said nothing, hoping this would prove to be true.

Mulroony loudly slurped his coffee, proclaiming it "Nectar!" before glancing up, looking serious. "You've heard the new developments, I take it?"

Adam shrugged.

Mulroony leaned forward. "You know the Serious Crimes Division had this lad, Nick Jessup, in the frame? For the murder, I mean?"

Adam nodded.

"Well, now they're not so sure. Looks like Woodhatch have misplaced someone after all."

"Who?" Adam asked.

"Dunno. But, sounds like some loony escaped about two months back, and only now are they admitting to it. They were so sensitive, Woodhatch being *the* place and all, that they tried to find him on their own. Now they've had to put their hands up. Tell you, heads are going to roll. And not just this nut job's victims."

"And he's supposed to have attacked this urban explorer couple?" Adam said.

"Well, someone did, didn't they? Quite a coincidence if it wasn't him."

"Didn't they search the hospital immediately after the attack?" Winters said, sipping her coffee.

Mulroony shrugged. "Yeah, but I think they were just paying lip service to the old legend. Tomorrow, it'll be a bit more thorough."

"Tomorrow?" Adam asked.

"Yep …" Mulroony finished his drink with a swallow. "It's all going to kick off first thing in the morning. Massive search team coming. Everything."

Adam blew out an unsteady breath. "So … who am I looking out for tonight?"

"No clue. Just make sure there's no one hanging round here who shouldn't be. If there is, get on the blower."

Adam nodded, po-faced.

PC Winters giggled. "You've really cheered him up, Tony."

"Sorry, pal ..." Mulroony tossed his paper cup in the bin and stood up. "But someone had to tell you, eh? Give Dave Ellis a rocket in the backside for leaving you on your own in a place like this when you're so new. Anyway ... nice brew that, Cass. Ta muchly." Before he could say more, he looked around the tiny room, curious. "Is it me, or is there a funny smell in here?"

Adam sniffed the air but didn't detect anything. PC Winters did the same, but looked unsure.

Mulroony wrinkled his nostrils. "Like someone's been in here who hasn't washed in a while."

There was a brief silence while they absorbed this and its possible implications.

"For God's sake, Tony!" Winters blurted. "Haven't you scared this lad enough?"

"No, I'm serious ..." Mulroony made another show of sniffing. "For a minute, then ...?"

Adam shook his head. "I can't smell anything."

Winters shrugged. "I thought there was something at first, maybe ... but I've not got much of a sense of smell anyway. Is it not just the woods? Rotting vegetation, stagnant ponds ...?"

But Mulroony had now fixed Adam with a beady gaze. "You didn't leave this station unmanned for too long, did you?"

Adam felt his face redden. "I was just checking the crime scene."

"Yeah, but how long did it take you?"

"Couple of minutes."

"Nothing missing from in here, is there?"

"There's nothing to take," Adam said.

A second passed, before Mulroony relaxed. "You're probably right. Just me being daft."

"God's sake, Tony," Winters chided him again. "If it *was* this escaped bloke from Woodhatch, he's not going to still be hanging round here *now*, is he?"

"Well … if it's the only place he's ever known …"

The girl rolled her eyes towards Adam. "Don't let him bother you, love. Trust me, you're better off spending your first week of nights here with the badgers than wandering around some town centre, where every dickhead who's had a drink'll take a poke at you. Speaking of which …" She looked at him more closely. "You've cut your face."

Adam felt at his cheek, and when his fingertips came away, they were smeared red.

"Fighting your way through those bushes at the back, I'm guessing?" Winters said, directing this at Mulroony in a tone of rebuke.

"It was a joke," Mulroony said defensively. "And he's taken it well … which is all part of being a decent bobby, isn't it, pal?"

Adam forced a smile. He'd never liked being mocked, but he was sure he could get used to it if it was part and parcel of his new job.

"We're off, anyway," Mulroony said. "Oh … Sergeant Pennyworth will be popping round to see you."

"Who's that?" Adam asked.

"Our section sergeant," Winters said. "Known as Iron

Britches, she's such a tartar. So … be sure everything's shipshape."

"When can I expect her?"

"Can't help you there, pal." Mulroony stepped outside, but his voice carried back indoors. "Strictly speaking, it should be your own section sergeant, but Pennyworth's so bloody officious, she'll never miss a chance to chuck her weight around. She'll turn up when she feels like it. So like Cass says, be ready."

Winters went out next, Adam following her.

Mulroony sniffed the air again as he stood on the road. "You know … it's faint, but there *is* a funny smell round here."

"Give it a rest," Winters said. "This lad's got a difficult enough night as it is."

Adam couldn't help liking the way she referred to him as "a lad", even though he was probably older than she was by a good ten years. It gave her an air of strength and confidence, which he'd always found a challenge in women, but which he also admired. He couldn't be doing with weak-kneed screamers. And she'd called him "love" too, at least twice. He hadn't missed that, even if she'd meant it as a gesture of comradeship.

"And don't be worried about what Tony's just said, either," Winters added. "Remember, we're only a radio call away."

"Yeah, don't sweat it." Mulroony zipped up his anorak as he edged off along the road. "We're covering the whole of the East, and the area car's got some speed under its bonnet. We can be back here in two or three minutes."

It was reassuring to know that, Adam decided. But though this place was eerie and lonely, he didn't anticipate that he'd be calling them. It wasn't because he didn't believe the story about the hook-handed killer – even though he didn't – it was because he was a policeman, not a security guard. And tonight was very important in that regard. It was his first one, so he didn't want to come over as a weakling. He *had* to make a good impression.

Particularly on PC Winters, he told himself, as their patrol car pulled away, its tail lights vanishing amid the trees. He was working here now, admittedly on the West rather than the East, but as the two subdivisions abutted each other, he'd no doubt be seeing a lot more of her. He certainly didn't want her thinking he was the sort of bloke who'd call for help every time anything peculiar happened.

Which was probably why, some ten minutes later, at the sound of three loud metallic clangs – like someone hitting iron with a sledgehammer – from the direction of the hospital, his first reaction was not to get on his radio.

Adam was back inside the command post at the time, trying not to lounge again, when he heard it.

He all but jumped from the caravan, standing rigid on the road.

No further sounds followed, but again this entire stretch of woodland seemed to have fallen into an eerie, listening hush.

He stared towards the distant ruins. The caravan stood west of the hospital by several hundred yards, but Adam was certain that was the direction from which he'd heard the noises. He hadn't imagined it, so someone was definitely over there. In which case, it might be the correct thing to call for assistance. But suppose Adam managed to collar the miscreant all on his own: how cool would he appear in the eyes of PC Winters …

If nothing else, he knew that he ought to go over there and look.

It couldn't hurt. And it wasn't as if he didn't know his way. About two hundred yards north of here, well beyond the outer cordon, a path diverted from the road and wove through numerous trees and thickets, at some points almost hidden from view it was so deeply overhung by them, finally emerging alongside the hospital buildings. It was little known to outsiders, which meant there was a good chance, if you used it, that some non-local wouldn't even see you coming.

Adam pondered this, and then went back inside to collect his helmet. When he came out again, he closed the caravan door and walked north, passing the common entryway and, a few dozen yards after that, the outer cordon and POLICE VEHICLES ONLY sign. It was discomforting to be trekking further and further from the crime scene, but Adam's confidence grew that he was doing the right thing. He wondered how PC Winters would respond when she learned that he'd investigated the spooky old building all by himself.

He resisted the temptation to switch his Maglite on as he stepped off the road and onto the path, even though the ground was now rutted and mulchy and covered with clumps of treacherous fungi, because he didn't want to announce that he was coming. Thus, for long minutes he worked his way along the looping, meandering route, at times advancing through complete darkness, at others in moonlight again, albeit moonlight reduced to spectral gloom by the tangled vegetation. A more delicate soul would surely have been having second thoughts by now, but not Adam. He was fortunate, he supposed, in that bravery came naturally to him. At least, he assumed it did – he'd rarely ever felt what others called fear. One reason why he'd always thought that he'd make an excellent policeman.

Not that Springburn Special Hospital wouldn't test that belief.

On the best occasions, these old asylums had never *looked* good. They might have given themselves genial names as part of the pretence that they were normal medical facilities, but the barred windows would always be a giveaway. Ditto the high walls and the electrical fences encircling their grounds, while the immense soullessness of the buildings themselves, everything so functional, so uniform, added immeasurably to that aura. OK, they weren't Dracula's castle. But they were sufficiently bleak to imply that anyone entering here was going to have a cheerless time.

And yes, that was on the *best* occasions.

Now, in a state of utter ruin, only vaguely visible in the midnight darkness, Springburn Hospital was every inch the horror movie myth.

As Adam approached the end of the path, his progress was briefly blocked by a high mesh fence, which ran across in front. It was a safety precaution by the local authority, but no one had bothered maintaining it, and Adam already knew that, at this point, the two sections merely stood against each other and were not fastened. He pushed them apart and slid his body through, before progressing across open ground covered with dead but tussocky grass. As he did, the hospital emerged from the gloom, a silent, towering outline, like a phantom ship breaching the ocean fog.

All he saw of it at first were sheer, weather-worn bricks covered with ivy, and occasional yawning gaps where windows had once been. Some of these, mainly on the lower levels, were still barred, but many of the higher ones were nothing but rotting apertures. If you'd been prepared to climb up there, they'd have granted you easy access. Not that Adam was willing to go that far. He'd distinctly heard something over here, so he felt it his duty to check, but it would be a cursory check only. He wasn't taking his life in his hands.

He walked forward, and a few yards further on, ducked under a single strip of blue and white incident tape left over from the first search of the premises. Beyond this, he found another path – more overgrown than the one before but veering away between the buildings themselves. Adam followed it, still keeping his Maglite off, primarily because, now that he was out from under the trees and had the moonlight to steer by, he didn't need it.

Springburn Hospital might only have been closed for nine years, but an awful lot of dereliction had occurred in that time. Desolate brick structures now reared on either side of him, coated with ivy, their pipework hanging loose, more blind gaps where windows had once been. One thing he didn't see many of were exits and entrances, though with Springburn's high-security status that was understandable. On this subject, it was noticeable that quite a few of the ground-level windows were not so much barred as heavily grilled; an extra-strength security measure, no doubt, which meant that when everything else had rotted away, these still remained.

Adam's gaze roved across them as he strolled – before he halted abruptly.

For a split second, he'd thought he'd spotted someone looking out from behind one of those grilles. It was impossible to be sure, but he played it back through his head, and could have sworn that a white face had fleetingly peered out at him.

Adam was unmoved by the story about the hook-handed killer. He knew it was nonsense. But he also knew what he'd just seen. And that no one else should be here.

Realising there was no longer any point in trying to mask his presence, he switched his Maglite on, and waded through thorns until he reached the window in question. It might be at ground level, but the bottom of the frame was almost six feet in the air. Adam was tall, but even he had to stand on tiptoe to shine his light through. The powerful beam split, multiplied by the rusted grille-work, but it still revealed the drab room on the other side. He saw bare walls marked with faded graffiti, exposed floorboards.

And an internal door on the far side of the room – which stood wide open.

He struggled his way back through the thigh-deep vegetation and took the path again, now following it faster, more determinedly. If he was going to get this thing done, best to get it done quickly. He emerged into more open space, on the other side of which, perhaps forty or fifty yards away, the lowering hulks of further silent buildings stood half hidden amid the trees and darkness. Searching this whole place could take all night, but as it was only the building on his left where he thought he'd spotted someone, Adam turned that way first, walking along another path, finally coming to what had once been the building's main entrance. The two front doors had been boarded closed some time ago, but those boards had been torn away since, and the huge panels of floor-to-ceiling glass behind them smashed, leaving the place wide open.

He entered without hesitation, stepping into a world of rank shadows – and almost immediately thought he heard something again.

He swivelled where he stood, turning full circle.

As his eyes attuned, he saw that he was in a kind of lobby, though it was so dilapidated that few recognisable fixtures or fittings remained. There was space in front of him where a reception desk might once have been situated, but nothing sat there now except a pile of broken, rotted timbers. The wall behind that was bare plaster, still displaying a pattern of squarish pale marks where posters had formerly been attached.

He turned left, shining his Maglite down a long, broad corridor. The torch illuminated eighty or so yards of empty passageway, though almost inevitably, halfway along it there was an abandoned wheelchair. When he turned right, it was the same story, though this second passage was empty and puddled with green-tinted water.

"You shouldn't be in here!" he shouted. "I'm a policeman and you need to leave!"

His voice echoed back from the deepest recesses of the abandoned hospital.

Belatedly, he wondered if that had been made a mistake. If he might have alerted the hook-handed killer to his presence. But then he shook his head and forced a laugh.

Hardly.

There was no such thing as the hook-handed killer.

He opted for the left-hand corridor first, advancing down it, glancing behind him just to be on the safe side, and pushing the rickety old wheelchair out of his way. At the far end, he encountered a barred gate standing half open, and behind that, on the right, a stairway rising. Adam ascended. Again, he trod quietly, but his footfalls still resounded up the stairwell ahead of him. This created weird sound effects, at one point making it seem as if someone was hurrying down towards him, at another as though they were creeping up from behind. Brave as he liked to think he was, this set his nerves on edge, though he managed to steel himself and get to the first level without incident.

"I am *not* frightened of this place," he said tightly. "I am the last person to be scared here. OK, I saw someone, I heard them … but I *know* this is not the hook-handed killer. He isn't real. On top of that, I'm the law now. I can't just walk away. I *won't* walk away."

The first level comprised a small landing and the gated entrance to a passage. This gate was barred and rusted, too, but it also stood ajar. Beyond it, the passage dwindled off in a straight line, a succession of steel doors opening on the right, zebra-striping it with moonlight.

Adam warily jabbed his torchlight into each room as he passed.

It was always the same: dank, empty cells, their hollow window frames clustered with ivy, their floorboards damp, their walls marked with scrawls of pathetic writing. Largely this was names and dates, cryptic symbols or reams of incoherent gibberish, but there were also poems, prayers and pleas for help, even thumbnail autobiographies left by people who'd evidently expected that they'd never come out of here alive.

Halfway along the corridor he heard a sound again, and spun backwards. Fleetingly, he thought he saw a person framed in the door at the farthest end, the one near the top of the stairs. But if they'd ever actually been there, they vanished in the blink of an eye.

Another optical illusion. Or a ghost.

The latter would be easily understandable.

He moved on.

In the next room but one, there was less ivy around the window, which allowed him an unrestricted view through the trees outside. Thanks to their mostly being leafless, and to his elevated position, he found that he had good vantage over a significant distance, which was why, about half a mile to the south of here, on the very edge of Springburn Wood, he spied the lights of several large vehicles juddering back and forth. It was a small lorry park, he recalled. On a cold, clear night like this, it was possible that the noises he'd heard had emanated from way over there, the crashes and bangs of shunting wagons echoing through the frigid air.

The more Adam thought about that explanation, the more sense it made. It didn't explain the face he'd seen below, but perhaps that had simply been another ghost.

He was now almost at the far end of the passage. In the last room, there was a mattress and what looked like bedclothes improvised out of broadsheet newspapers and pieces of cardboard.

Adam stepped into the room, but then heard another sound, this one undeniably originating from *inside* the building. He stiffened and listened, and heard it again.

A shuddering and grating – like heavy steel being shoved across stone.

It was coming from downstairs, and yet was so loud that it reverberated through the entire structure. He moved out into the corridor and listened again. The sound fell silent, and the place was suddenly deathly quiet. He walked on to the end of the passage. Again, there was a barred gate standing open. On the other side, a stairway led both up and down.

Still, there was no further sound, but Adam knew that he hadn't been mistaken.

He descended. At the bottom, beyond a brick archway, was what looked as if it had once been a dining room; all across it his Maglite detected the corroded nubs of screws protruding up from the concrete floor, where tables had once been secured. Movement caught his eye, and he twirled around, driving his wedge of torchlight leftward.

A bottle was rolling. Not of its own accord, but as if someone had clouted it with a foot while they were passing. Adam advanced into the room, shining his light into every corner. There was evidence all over the place that vandals had once been here: more bottles, beer cans, black stains against the walls where fires had been lit. A used condom lay curled like a flattened worm. Not quite so terrifying a reputation after all, then, this place. It wouldn't have been safe for anyone to hide out here – until these last few weeks, of course.

More movement.

Adam spun, zooming in on another door at the far side of the room. A single door this time, again made from scabby steel, but a figure had just flitted past the other side of it.

He flicked his light off as he approached, taking cover by the wall next to the door.

Tense moments passed, during which he heard no sound from the next room. Whoever it was, were they listening right back at him – or were they already running, moving silently and swiftly away through the darkened building?

If it was the latter, it proved that they were up to no good. And how would that sit at the police station, especially with the likes of PC Winters? That he'd done all the hard work, detecting the offender when no one else could and sneaking up on him, only to blow the whole thing at the last second?

Adam swung himself around, ramming the heavy steel door with his shoulder, and having to exert considerable strength to screech it all the way open.

It wasn't clear what the room was on the other side. It was spacious and dark, but he couldn't see anyone in there until, with a metallic click, he himself was bathed in a blinding light. He stood stock-still, helpless, shielding his eyes with his left arm, the other hand groping for his baton, which he realised he ought to already have drawn.

"As you can see … I'm a policeman," he stuttered.

"Really?" came an unimpressed female voice.

The beam of light was lowered to the floor, and Adam was finally able to see the person behind it. Initially, it was vague, as he was still half dazzled. Though when his eyes adjusted, the first thing he saw was another police uniform. She came towards him with short, quick steps, as if she was marching. A far cry from Cassie Winters, she was short, sturdy, and wore her iron-grey hair cropped severely, her policewoman hat sitting on top of it in neat, non-fussy fashion.

Adam flicked his own Maglite back on but aimed it at the floor. The extra light it created was sufficient to show him the woman's face, which was pinched and pale, and etched with a deep, disapproving frown. It also reflected off the sergeant's stripes on her epaulettes.

"PC Carver, I presume?" she said.

"*Erm* … yes."

"I'm Sergeant Pennyworth."

"Oh …" Adam wasn't sure whether to feel relieved by that, or disappointed.

Her face remained locked in a frown. "What are you doing away from your post?"

"I … *erm*, I thought I heard something in here …"

"You thought you heard something in here, *Sergeant*. Use the correct terminology when addressing the supervisory ranks, if you don't mind."

"Yes, Sergeant … *erm*, sorry." And he threw up a clumsy salute.

She rolled her eyes. "And you don't salute sergeants."

"Oh, sorry …"

"You ought to have been told that by now."

"Yes … I, *erm* … I forgot."

She assessed him with thinly veiled disdain. "PC Carver … you have one job tonight. And one job only. That is to maintain the security of the crime scene."

"I thought that's what I was doing … *erm*, Sergeant."

She waggled her torch around, its blob of light bouncing from one decayed wall to the next. "This old ruin is *not* part of the crime scene."

Her domineering tone was irritating him now. Surely she could see that he'd only done what any copper would? Or maybe what any copper wouldn't? Wasn't she at least impressed with the bravery he'd demonstrated?

"This crime scene's … *erm*, a few weeks old," he offered, "and I wondered if …"

Sergeant Pennyworth arched an eyebrow. "You wondered if there was any truth in that stupid story about the hook-handed killer?"

"Oh, no …" Adam was almost insulted.

"You thought you'd be the one to catch him? Make your name in the job while you were still on probation?"

"Not at all, I …"

"Not at all … *what?*"

"Not at all … *erm*, Sergeant."

"PC Carver … if you were to investigate every odd sound you heard in the middle of this forest, where would that take you?"

"I, *erm* …"

"These woods go on for miles. These old buildings go on several hundred yards west of here. If you started checking them all, you'd be a long way from your post in no time, wouldn't you?"

Adam's cheeks were now aflame. "Yes, Sergeant."

"In fact, you've checked one so far, and you're already a long way from your post … aren't you?"

"Yes, Sergeant."

She shook her head dispiritedly, as if she couldn't believe the standard of recruits they were attracting these days. "Well, there's no point in us wasting more taxpayers' money doing things we're not supposed to be." She turned on her heel. "Come along, please. Now!"

She vacated the building by a broken-open fire door in the next room, Adam plodding behind her like a chastened child. Outside, they took another narrow, overgrown path leading between the shells of the buildings. Adam was tall and long-legged, but he struggled to keep up with his supervisor, she walked so fast.

"And what did you do to your face?" she asked. "It's cut."

"I think I did that shaving, Sergeant."

"What did you use, a lawnmower?"

"Sergeant?"

"It's hardly the professional image, is it? It's a good job you're not dealing with members of the public tonight. Though you *might* have been. There'd be nothing to stop someone coming and knocking on the command post door, perhaps with information. What kind of impression would you make then, eh? Mind you, you wouldn't be there, would you? You'd be too busy gallivanting around these ruins. Then a vital lead could be lost to us."

Adam felt like replying tersely, demanding to know what would have been said if he'd ignored those noises he'd thought he'd heard. But from Sergeant Pennyworth's manner, he knew that he'd get short shrift no matter how reasonable he was. There was one dynamic here. She was in charge and he wasn't, and he had to take whatever grief she gave him.

They passed through the gap in the fence and proceeded along the path, the hospital's gaunt outline falling behind them. Adam had thought that only people as familiar with Springburn Wood as he was knew this route, but clearly he could add Sergeant Pennyworth to that number. Within a very short time, it seemed, they were back on the road, approaching the command post.

"No one else has been around, I take it?" Pennyworth asked.

"*Erm*, PCs ... Mulroony and Winters."

"I see." Her tone stiffened again. "No doubt they stopped for a brew. Well ... so long as they didn't dawdle too long." They arrived at the door to the caravan. "I take it you logged them?"

Adam tried not to look as nonplussed as this question made him feel. "I'm ... I'm sorry?"

Yet again, she looked exasperated. "PC Carver ... you were surely told that you are supposed to log everyone who visits this crime scene, both when they come in and when they go out?"

Her withering tone left him abashed but also angry. He hadn't really done anything wrong, and yet she was making him out to be a complete idiot.

"They didn't go onto the actual crime scene," he said.

Her eyes widened. "I should think they damn well didn't! But they were still inside the outer cordon. Look, PC Carver ... this is basic stuff. Everyone who comes here, you need to document." She chopped the air with her gloved right hand, adding emphasis. "You can't make mistakes like that! I say again, it's about being professional. That's what you're *supposed* to be, at least ... a professional. Not some civilian who likes playing at uniform."

Sighing exaggeratedly, she went inside the caravan.

She was really enjoying this, Adam realised. As she no doubt always did; it was like a cat with a mouse – she had a smaller creature in her grasp and was determined to gain as much power and satisfaction as possible from the torment she inflicted.

Frustrated that this seemed to be the story of his entire life – even now, as a copper – he trooped in after her, taking off his helmet.

Inside the caravan, Pennyworth took down a small booklet from the shelf above the coffee-making things and tossed it onto the desk.

Then she sniffed. "Curious smell, isn't there?"

"It's the woods, I think … Sergeant. Dankness and that."

She glanced at Adam sidelong, as if implying that it was somehow more likely to be *his* fault, before turning and picking up the empty kettle. While she did, he took the opportunity to grab the booklet and leaf through it. It was official GMP issue, its lined, headed pages filled in chronological order with the scribbled names of visitors to the crime scene, plus the dates and times of their arrival and departure.

While Pennyworth took a fresh bottle of water from the fridge, to refill the kettle, Adam dug a pen from his pocket, paused to think – he was pretty sure the full names of the two officers who'd visited earlier were PCs *Tony* Mulroony and *Cassie* Winters – and began writing.

"What on earth are you doing?" came Pennyworth's sharp voice.

He glanced round at her, puzzled. "I'm making the record you asked for."

She snatched the booklet off him and saw that he'd timed the entry to thirty minutes ago and had already half-filled in Tony Mulroony's details. Previously, she'd been irritated and condescending, putting on a kind of "it's understandable that you're thick, but it's still annoying" act. But now she seemed genuinely angry.

"Were you planning to forge *both* their signatures?" she asked tautly.

"I … oh." Adam was immediately furious at how dumb he must look. It was down to the visitors to sign *themselves* in and out, whereas *his* role – now that he looked at the booklet more closely – was clearly to countersign, in other words to witness it. "Oh …"

"For Christ's sake!" she hissed.

"It's … it's only paperwork."

"Paperwork matters in the police, PC Carver! On which subject, you've given the time of their arrival as 2.50 a.m. Is that correct, or have you just guessed? I mean, suppose they were doing another job at the time? That would put them in two places at once …"

Adam was tongue-tied, not least because as well as being embarrassed, he felt increasingly enraged. She was being totally unfair; he was new to the job, and she should understand that. She ought to be telling him things, not shouting. He needed guidance rather than a bollocking. But maybe that was beyond her? They called her "Iron Britches", after all.

He held out his hand, and somewhat bemusedly, she gave the booklet back to him. Half smiling, he ripped out the page, crumpled it into a ball and tossed it into the bin.

"Problem solved," he said.

She stared at him aghast.

Adam was bewildered. Hadn't he just fixed it? What nonsense was this?

"You bloody, bloody fool!" she whispered harshly. "These pages are audited!"

She snatched the book back and indicated the header on the next page; in its top right-hand corner, a coded number had been stencilled.

"If one of these pages goes missing, someone – perhaps even the SIO – will wonder why." She leaned so far forward that she invaded Adam's personal space. Her eyes were steel pins as they bored into him. "And even if he doesn't, we could still have a problem. Suppose someone gets charged with murder based on evidence not yet recovered from the scene, and the defence finds out that a page in the visitor log is missing. That will mean someone was here, on the scene, who's not been accounted for. I surely don't need to tell you what will happen then?"

Adam's cheeks burned at the full realisation of what he'd done.

Hurriedly, he rooted in the bin, digging out the scrunched page. He made a brave effort to flatten it out on the desktop, but his hands were quivering too much.

"This is a great start to your new career!" Pennyworth said acidly. "Attempting to destroy a legal document! For Christ's sake, find some Sellotape and stick that page back in the book. I'll contact Mulroony and Winters and get them back here to give us their signatures and the exact time. In the meantime, who's your own section sergeant?"

"I, *erm* ... I haven't met my own section sergeant yet, Sergeant."

"You haven't met your own section sergeant?" Pennyworth looked as if she couldn't quite believe this. "Are you telling me this is your very first shift?"

He nodded.

"Well… who's your tutor constable?"

"Dave Ellis."

"Dave Ellis. And where is he?"

Adam shrugged. "I don't know."

She shook her head. "Things always this cack-handed on the West?" Before he could answer, she glanced again around the interior, distracted and visibly disgusted. "And I ask again … what in heaven's name *is* that smell?"

"I don't—"

"You don't know. Yes, I get it. Bit of a pattern developing, isn't there?" She paused for a moment, her eyes narrowing. "Is it possible, is it remotely possible, that you left this post earlier for any reason, again for longer than you should have … and perhaps allowed one of your new colleagues to sneak in and secrete something here while you were out? A rotten fish perhaps? Or a dead rat?"

"I …" Adam was lost for words. Something as horrible as that had never even occurred to him. Though he still couldn't smell anything out of the ordinary.

"Yet again, you don't know." One by one, Sergeant Pennyworth forcibly yanked out drawers. "Good God, you've got a lot to learn."

"Look," he tried to say, "look— Sergeant, I just— I just want to be a policeman."

"What in God's name!" Pennyworth wasn't even listening as she stepped back and pulled what at first looked like a mass of dirty, ragged cloth from the bottom drawer, though when she shook it out, it soon assumed a recognisable shape. "Has someone left their old pyjamas in here, or something?"

Adam was briefly stricken speechless by the sight of the odiously stained jacket and trousers, but not for too long. He had to get back on track, and quickly.

"I thought I'd made an OK start?" he said.

She said nothing, sniffing gingerly at the bundle of rags.

"I'm sorry if I've made mistakes. I know I can do better."

"What?" She was now busy looking round the room for something else, opening yet more drawers and cupboards. "Look, it's not all your fault that you're next to useless, PC ...?"

"Bellwood."

"Must be a roll of bin-liners somewhere. We should never have closed the training colleges. I mean, they weren't brilliant, but at least you'd find yourself on the streets with some kind of idea." Something struck her, and she glanced round at him. "Bellwood ...?"

"Oh, sorry ... my mistake."

"Another one?"

"I used to be Bellwood. But I changed my name."

Pennyworth shook her head again at the sheer ridiculousness of this guy, before opening the next cupboard – out of which a nude body tumbled.

It landed with dead-wood impact on the command post floor, a mass of bruised and twisted limbs, a face brutalised beyond recognition by repeated, savage blows.

It was several seconds before even Sergeant Pennyworth could react. The breath trapped in her throat, and then she threw herself down onto her knees to check for vital signs. The victim was male – she could see that much immediately. And perhaps the cause of death would also be plain to her, had she not been so stunned; the horrible blotch of bruising on the dead guy's throat could only mean one thing.

"What the hell …" Pennyworth stammered. "What … is this, some kind of …"

"Mainly because of *him*," Adam said, thinking aloud.

She glanced up at him, perplexed. *Good Christ, who is this?*

"PC Carver. The old PC Carver." Adam shrugged. "I'm the new one."

Pennyworth rose slowly, unsteadily to her feet.

"Most of the stuff I've learned so far, I've learned from him," Adam explained, pointing upward. "And others like him."

Pennyworth glanced overhead – and saw the open skylight.

"It's amazing what you can pick up over a few nights," Adam said. "Listening to people chatting, listening to radio exchanges, listening to phone conversations …"

She grabbed for her radio, but Adam was quicker, sweeping the baton from behind his back, catching her with such an impact across her knuckles that she dropped the device, and then swiping it back, thwacking the side of her jaw with bone-cracking force.

Pennyworth spun as she fell, but Adam caught her from behind. The next thing the dazed woman knew, an inflexible steel bar was compressing the front of her throat. Her assailant gripped it at either end, and now exerted tremendous force as he lugged it backwards, his knee jammed firmly into the nape of her neck.

"Imagine me up there!" he said. "All that time, and none of you *professionals* noticing."

Pennyworth couldn't reply; her face was already turning purple.

"But you know," he hissed, "there was no need for any of this. I was for real! I was *genuine*! I wanted to make a new start. I was trying so hard … doing everything I could. I wanted to be on the other side for a change. And I thought I'd learned enough. But people like you never let it happen, do you! Pushy loud-mouth pissant busybodies … always shouting, giving orders. Always saying what people like me can and can't do, how useless we are. How useless *I* am. Didn't you say that, you bitch? That I'm useless. Even though you know nothing about me. You criticise my shaving, but how would you do with broken glass? You criticise my smell, but how would you smell with no bath?"

Pennyworth's face was almost black, her chin and cheeks slathered with blood and froth. But she still managed an incoherent gurgle.

Adam leaned down to her ear. "What's that, Sergeant? You might have got it wrong about me? Might've made a mistake?" He giggled. "Seems to me that you lot make nothing but mistakes. Still thinking it's Nick Jessup? How about the hook-handed killer? Jesus, that's so much bollocks. Killing with a hook, with one fucking hand. Take it from someone who knows …" With a crunch, her windpipe gave way. "It's much easier with two."

THE
RECIPE

LOUISE JENSEN

The ground is as cold and solid as the knot of grief weighted in my stomach. The song thrush abandons his futile search for worms and rises, hovering against the flat, grey sky before coming to rest on the bird table with a happy chirp, head bobbing as he pecks at my half-eaten toast. It's stupid, but I open my mouth to call your name – birdwatching was your passion – before I remember the reason my appetite has vanished. I rest my forehead against the window as the knot in my stomach tightens. I am incredulous; daffodils are poking their yellow heads from muddy slumber, bluebells pushing through the tangle of weeds. Spring is supposed to signal new life, isn't it, and it's torturous that time is still marching on. It's only been two weeks since you've gone but winter suited my sense of loss, all mutinous clouds and lashing rain. Now the trees are beginning to don their new green overcoats and colour pops in every border.

Gardening was always your domain. "Keep the coffee and fruitcake coming, Cleo," you'd say. "A man needs his fuel." And I'd stand in the kitchen, an apron wrapped around my age-thickened waist, the way my mum used to all those years ago while she'd fashion the mince Dad hadn't sold in his butcher's shop at the end of the day into burgers, chilli, lasagne. Meat in various disguises until I grew sick of the texture, the taste, the congealed white fat that formed on the surface of the leftovers. I inherited her cookbook after she died but I never used it. Baking. I was always baking; cakes, biscuits, pastries, and you never tired of telling me how much you loved them. How much you loved me. Ridiculously, yesterday I had gathered ingredients on the worktop, shaken flour into the bowl on the scales and had got as far as cracking an egg before I realised you weren't here to eat a just-out-the-oven warm cookie any more, and I swept the whole lot into the bin with an anguished cry. It's hard to focus on anything. The coffee table is littered with half-finished crosswords; the pages of the adult colouring book I'd bought remain a stark white.

My thoughts rush towards me like the sparrowhawk that swoops headlong at the thrush before veering to the side at the last minute as his target takes cover in the clutch of brambles by the fence. The bird trapped inside my chest flutters, flutters, flutters with panic. Calm. I need to stay calm. I've never lived alone, married at eighteen, but I'm forty-five. I *can* do this. I *am* doing this. Mum managed for twenty years without Dad until cancer claimed her. And it's not like I'm completely alone, is it? Belinda, my younger sister, will be here later. After dinner she's going to help me pack away your things, just like we did with Mum and Dad's possessions all those years ago, although they still sit in the garage in cardboard boxes, slowly rotting through time along with my memories and the dead insects with stiff legs and brittle wings.

I'm not ready.

Still not ready.

I'll have to donate everything to the charity shop. I suppose

I'll have to sell up soon anyway. The house is too big for one, with its four bedrooms and a study we'd always earmarked for a playroom. It was too big for us, really, but we never stopped wishing for the children we longed for, did we? The happy laughter and after-school chatter we hoped would transform this redbrick new build into a home.

My fingers pick at the skin around my nails until it is raw and bleeding. The garden catches my eye again, the buddleia trailing neglect, the rosebush straggling against the fence at the end of the garden. We planted it when we got married. "It will blossom like our love," you'd said and I'd rolled my eyes, but inside it warmed me that you were such a romantic. My mind hops. I've no idea what I'll cook for dinner. It seems too soon to be sitting around the table for a family meal, it won't be the same without you, but Belinda insisted. "The sooner you're back in a routine the better you'll feel," she said, but still, I'll be half-expecting you to join us. Perhaps she's right. I should make a start before she arrives.

My oldest jeans hang low on my hips; stress is shrinking me. I pull down a T-shirt to cover ribs that protrude and think perhaps one day I'll vanish entirely, and I find that thought comforting. The garage is a mess; it stinks. As I step inside I am overwhelmed by the volume of boxes, the half-empty paint tins – sunflower for the kitchen and cornflower blue for the lounge – your gardening tools suspended from hooks in the brickwork. The air is thick with memories and all of a sudden I can't breathe. I push my way back outside, sucking in air as the bird in my chest battles to be free. It takes a while to compose myself. I fetch the spade, wrapping my hands around the wooden handle, touching the places you touched. The ground around the rosebush is firmer than I thought it would be, and as I drive my spade into the earth, tiny rockets of pain shoot through my wrists, up into my shoulders. Tears spring to my eyes and I tell myself it's frustration, pain, anything but this horrible sense of missing you. I drop to my knees, the coldness seeping through my jeans, and I burrow at the soil with gloved fingers, but it's as solid as the gold band I still wear on my wedding finger. It's fruitless. I hardly make an indent and the weeds throw back their thorny heads and laugh and laugh.

I drag the back of my hand across my eyes, furiously wiping away the tears that spill, and remind myself that all is not lost. Belinda will be bringing Sophie later, my niece. She's only three and too young, I hope, to feel the raw sense of loss I feel, but Belinda said she'd explained to Sophie you are gone and Sophie had cried.

"Sophie will miss him," Belinda said. "We all will." Grief shimmered in her eyes. She adored you, as did Sophie, and you were so good with her. Every visit, I caught a glimpse of the father you could have been and a painful lump rose in my chest.

Sometimes I'd pretend Sophie was ours. She has the same colouring as you. You'd stretch in front of the open fire, her cradled in your lap, reading stories about big bad wolves and too-hot porridge, heads bent, blonde hair glimmering as the flames crackled and hissed. She could almost have been ours, I thought, as I toasted pink marshmallows brown. Almost.

Except she isn't ours.

She *is* yours though.

I still remember the heart-wrenching pain when you'd told me you were leaving me for my sister. All those birdwatching trips you took – it was a different kind of bird you were watching, wasn't it? I still remember the weight of the iron in my hand. The sizzle as it hit your face. The sickening crack as your head hit the flagstone floor. I hoped the blood didn't leave a stain.

It hasn't. Scrubbed away as though it was never there at all.

I'd told everyone you'd run off with your secretary. I almost felt sorry for my poor sister as I watched confusion, disappointment, anger slide across her perfect, perfect face. She believed me. Why wouldn't she? After all, I'm not the liar here and once a cheat, always a cheat. Isn't that what they say?

I discard the spade. It's no good. I can't dig a hole big enough to bury you in. No matter.

In the garage again, I rummage through the boxes, reading fading labels until I find the one I want. Dad's old industrial mincer. Glancing at your body, draped in tarpaulin in the corner, I'm not convinced it's up to the job – I'd hefted you out of the chest freezer last night but I'm not sure you're fully defrosted – but what choice do I have? I lift the chainsaw from your workbench and plug it in, my teeth grating with vibrations. I wonder if you're looking down? Or most likely looking up. I like to think you are.

It's six hours later when my deceitful sister chimes the bell.

She air kisses hello. Fake. Everything about her is fake.

I hug my niece tightly before she wriggles out of my grasp and pelts into the lounge. There's a clatter and I know Sophie's upended the small plastic tub of toys we keep for her here.

Belinda trails me into the kitchen. "My God," she exclaims as she stares out the window. "It looks like a Hitchcock film out there." The lawn is shrouded under a mass of beating wings. Jackdaws, magpies and crows swing from the home-made fat balls I'd strung from the garage, trees and bushes, satisfaction glistening in their beady eyes as they peck-peck-peck. Red kites swoop for the slivers of flesh I'd scooped out of the mincer.

"Hope you're as hungry as they are …" I pull plates from the cupboard.

"Starving. Something smells good."

"Burgers."

"Like Mum used to make?" She smiles.

"Exactly like Mum used to make." And as I say this I think about the way Dad left suddenly when I was fifteen. We never saw him again. It's a slow, sickening dawning. I fight to keep the revulsion out of my voice as I say, "It's the traditional family recipe."

You'll be joining us at the table after all, darling.

ABOUT
THE AUTHORS

JEFFERY DEAVER is an international number one best-selling author. His novels have appeared on best-seller lists around the world. His books are sold in 150 countries and have been translated into twenty-five languages. He is currently the president of the Mystery Writers of America. The author of forty novels, three collections of short stories and a non-fiction law book, and the lyricist of a country-and-western album, he has received or been shortlisted for dozens of awards. His *The Bodies Left Behind* was named Novel of the Year by the International Thriller Writers association, and his Lincoln Rhyme thriller *The Broken Window* and a stand-alone, *Edge*, were also nominated for that prize. *The Garden of Beasts* won the Steel Dagger from the Crime Writers Association in England. He's been nominated for eight Edgar Awards.

Deaver has been honoured with the Lifetime Achievement Award by the Bouchercon World Mystery Convention, *Strand Magazine*'s Lifetime Achievement Award and the Raymond Chandler Lifetime Achievement Award in Italy.

His book *A Maiden's Grave* was made into an HBO movie starring James Garner and Marlee Matlin, and his novel *The Bone Collector* was a feature release from Universal Pictures, starring Denzel Washington and Angelina Jolie. Lifetime aired an adaptation of his *The Devil's Teardrop*.

FIONA CUMMINS is an award-winning journalist and writer. *Rattle*, her best-selling debut novel, was described by *The Times* as being "up there with the best of them", while David Baldacci hailed its sequel, *The Collector*, "a crime novel of the very first order". Her third novel, *The Neighbour*, was published in April 2019. Fiona's books have been published in more than ten languages. She is a graduate of the Faber Academy's 'Writing a Novel' course and lives in Essex with her family.

MARK BILLINGHAM is one of the UK's most acclaimed and popular crime writers. His series of novels featuring DI Tom Thorne has twice won him the Theakston Old Peculier Crime Novel of the Year award, and his debut novel, *Sleepyhead*, was chosen by the *Sunday Times* as one of the 100 books that shaped the decade. His latest novel is *The Killing Habit*. A television series based on the Thorne novels starred David Morrissey as Tom Thorne, and a series based on *In the Dark* and *Time of Death* was broadcast on the BBC in 2017.

Mark lives in London with his wife and two children. When he is not living out rock-star fantasies as a member of the Fun Lovin' Crime Writers, he is hard at what is laughably called "work", writing his next novel. Website: markbillingham.com Twitter: @MarkBillingham

JOHN CONNOLLY was born in Dublin in 1968. He is the author of almost thirty books, including the Charlie Parker mystery series, *The Book of Lost Things*, and *he*. He divides his time between Dublin and Maine, and is mostly kind to animals, old people and small children.

SARAH HILARY'S debut, *Someone Else's Skin*, won the Theakston Old Peculier Crime Novel of the Year award in 2015 and was a World Book Night selection for 2016. The *Observer's* Book of the Month ("superbly disturbing") and a Richard & Judy Book Club best-seller, it has been published worldwide. *No Other Darkness*, the second book in the series, was shortlisted for a Barry Award in the US. *Come and Find Me* is the latest in the Marnie Rome series. www.sarahhilary.com

MARTYN WAITES was born in Newcastle upon Tyne. Before becoming a writer he was an actor. His fourth novel, *Born Under Punches*, won the Grand Prix du Roman Noir Étranger and *The White Room* was a *Guardian* book of the year. In addition to the books under his own name, he has written eight internationally best-selling thrillers under the name Tania Carver and was chosen to write the official sequel to Susan Hill's *The Woman in Black*, *Angel of Death*. He was also responsible (along with Mark Billingham, David Quantick and Stav Sherez) for *Great Lost Albums*, the "funniest book about music ever written". He's now back under his own name with the Tom Killgannon series, the first of which was *The Old Religion*. *Cage City*, the second in the series, is forthcoming.

DENNIS LEHANE grew up in Boston, Massachusetts. Since his first novel, *A Drink Before the War*, won the Shamus Award, he has published twelve more novels, which have been translated into more than thirty languages and become international best-sellers: *Darkness, Take My Hand*; *Sacred*; *Gone, Baby, Gone*; *Prayers for Rain*; *Mystic River*; *Shutter Island*; *The Given Day*; *Moonlight Mile*; *Live By Night*; and *World Gone By*. His most recent work is a stand-alone novel, *Since We Fell*.

Four of his novels – *Live By Night*; *Mystic River*; *Gone, Baby, Gone* and *Shutter Island* – have been adapted into films. A fifth, *The Drop*, was adapted by Lehane himself into a film starring Tom Hardy, Noomi Rapace and James Gandolfini in his final role. Lehane was a staff writer on the acclaimed HBO series *The Wire* and also worked as a writer-producer on HBO's *Boardwalk Empire* and the Netflix series, *Bloodline*. Lehane currently is a writer and producer on the television adaptation of Stephen King's *Mr Mercedes*.

Lehane was born and raised in Dorchester, Massachusetts. Before becoming a full-time writer, he worked as a counsellor with mentally handicapped and abused children, waited tables, parked cars, drove limos, worked in bookstores and loaded tractor-trailers. Lehane and his family live in California.

ALEX GRAY was born and educated in Glasgow. After studying English and Philosophy at the University of Strathclyde, she worked as a visiting officer for the Department of Health and Social Security, a time she looks upon as postgraduate education since it proved a rich source of character studies.

She then trained as a secondary school English teacher. Alex began writing professionally in 1992 and had immediate success with short stories, articles and commissions for BBC radio programmes. She has been awarded the Scottish Association of Writers' Constable and Pitlochry trophies for her crime writing. A regular on the Scottish best-seller lists, her previous novels include *Five Ways to Kill a Man*, *Glasgow Kiss*, *Pitch Black*, *The Riverman*, *Never Somewhere Else*, *The Swedish Girl* and *Keep the Midnight Out*. She is the co-founder of the international Scottish crime writing festival, Bloody Scotland, which had its inaugural year in 2012.

LEE CHILD was born in 1954 in Coventry, England, but spent his formative years in the nearby city of Birmingham. By coincidence he won a scholarship to the same high school that J.R.R. Tolkien had attended. He went to law school in Sheffield, and after part-time work in the theatre he joined Granada Television in Manchester for what turned out to be an eighteen-year career as a presentation director during British television's golden age. During his tenure his company made *Brideshead Revisited*, *The Jewel in the Crown*, *Prime Suspect* and *Cracker*. But he was fired in 1995 at the age of forty as a result of corporate restructuring. Always a voracious reader, he decided to see an opportunity where others might have seen a crisis and bought six dollars' worth of paper and pencils and sat down to write a book, *Killing Floor*, the first in the Jack Reacher series. There are now twenty-three Jack Reacher novels, all *New York Times* best-sellers, with foreign rights sold in 101 territories. *Forbes* calls it "the strongest brand in publishing".

His series hero, Jack Reacher, besides being fictional, is a kind-hearted soul who allows Lee lots of spare time for reading, listening to music, the Yankees and Aston Villa. He is married with a grown-up daughter. Visit www.leechild.com for info about the novels, short stories, the "Jack Reacher" movies and more – or find Lee on: Facebook.com/LeeChildOfficial, Twitter.com/LeeChildReacher and YouTube.com/leechildjackreacher

VAL MCDERMID is a number one best-seller whose novels have been translated into more than thirty languages and have sold over fifteen million copies. She has won many international awards, including the CWA Gold Dagger for best crime novel of the year and the *LA Times* Book of the Year Award. She was inducted into the ITV3 Crime Thriller Awards Hall of Fame in 2009, was the recipient of the Crime Writers' Association Cartier Diamond Dagger in 2010 and received the Lambda Literary Foundation Pioneer Award in 2011. In 2016 she received the Outstanding Contribution to Crime Fiction award at the Theakston Old Peculier Crime Writing Festival and was elected a Fellow of the Royal Society of Literature. In 2017 she received the DIVA Literary Prize for Crime. She writes full time and divides her time between Cheshire and Edinburgh.

STEPH BROADRIBB has an MA in Creative Writing (Crime Fiction) and trained as a bounty hunter in California. Her debut thriller *Deep Down Dead* (Orenda Books) featuring single mom bounty hunter, Lori Anderson, was shortlisted for the eDunnit eBook of the year award, the International Thriller Writers Best First Novel, and the Dead Good Reader Awards for Fearless Female Character and Most Exceptional Debut. The third book in the series, *Deep Dirty Truth*, was published in January 2019. Under her pseudonym Stephanie Marland she also writes the Starke/Bell psychological police procedural series (Trapeze – Orion). She blogs about all things crime fiction at www.crimethrillergirl.com and is a writing coach at www.crimefictioncoach.com

CHRISTOPHER FOWLER is the multi-award-winning author of forty-five novels and story collections, and the author of the Bryant & May mysteries. His novels include *Roofworld*, *Spanky*, *Psychoville*, *The Sand Men* and two volumes of memoirs, the award-winning *Paperboy* and *Film Freak*. In 2015 he won the Crime Writers' Association Dagger in the Library for his body of work. His latest novel is *Bryant & May: The Lonely Hour*.

When he was a senior in college, DEAN KOONTZ won an *Atlantic Monthly* fiction competition and has been writing ever since. His books are published in thirty-eight languages and he has sold over 500 million copies to date. Fourteen of his novels have risen to number one on the *New York Times* hardcover best-seller list (*One Door Away From Heaven*, *From the Corner of His Eye*, *Midnight*, *Cold Fire*, *The Bad Place*, *Hideaway*, *Dragon Tears*, *Intensity*, *Sole Survivor*, *The Husband*, *Odd*

Hours, Relentless, What the Night Knows and *77 Shadow Street*), making him one of only a dozen writers ever to have achieved that milestone. Sixteen of his books have risen to the number one position in paperback. His books have also been major best-sellers in countries as diverse as Japan and Sweden.

The New York Times has called his writing "psychologically complex, masterly and satisfying": *The New Orleans Times-Picayune* said Koontz is "at times lyrical without ever being naive or romantic. [He creates] a grotesque world, much like that of Flannery O'Conner or Walker Percy ... scary, worthwhile reading"; and *Rolling Stone* has hailed him as "America's most popular suspense novelist".

Dean Koontz was born and raised in Pennsylvania. He graduated from Shippensburg State College (now Shippensburg University), and his first job after graduation was with the Appalachian Poverty Program, where he was expected to counsel and tutor underprivileged children on a one-to-one basis. His first day on the job, he discovered that the previous occupier of his position had been beaten up by the very kids he had been trying to help and had landed in the hospital for several weeks. The following year was filled with challenge but also tension, and Koontz was more highly motivated than ever to build a career as a writer. He wrote nights and weekends, which he continued to do after leaving the Poverty Program and going to work as an English teacher in a suburban school district outside Harrisburg. After a year and a half in that position, his wife, Gerda, made him an offer he couldn't refuse: "I'll support you for five years," she said, "and if you can't make it as a writer in that time, you'll never make it." By the end of those five years, Gerda had quit her job to run the business end of her husband's writing career.

Dean Koontz lives in southern California with Gerda, their golden retriever, Elsa, and the enduring spirit of their goldens, Trixie and Anna.

Formerly a punk-cabaret singer and composer, **A.K. BENEDICT** is now "one of the new stars of crime with a supernatural twist" (*Sunday Express*). Her debut novel, *The Beauty of Murder*, was shortlisted for the eDunnit award and is in development for a major eight-part TV series. Her poetry and short stories have appeared in *Best British Short Stories*, *Magma*, *Great British Horror*, *New Fears*, *Phantoms* and *Best British Horror Stories*; her audio drama includes episodes of *Doctor Who* and *Torchwood*. Her second novel, *The Evidence of Ghosts*, published by Orion, explores her obsession with haunted London. She is Royal Literary Fellow for the University of Kent, Medway and Deputy Programme Director for the Crime Thriller MA at City, University of London. She lives in Rochester with writer Guy Adams and their dog, Dame Margaret Rutherford.

JAMES OSWALD is the author of the *Sunday Times* best-selling Inspector McLean series of crime novels, as well as the first in the new Constance Fairchild series, *No Time To Cry*. As J. D. Oswald he has written the epic fantasy series *The Ballad of Sir Benfro*. In his spare time James runs a 350-acre livestock farm in Fife, where he raises pedigree Highland cattle and New Zealand Romney sheep.

JOE R. LANSDALE is the author of forty-five novels and four hundred shorter works, including stories, essays, reviews, film and television scripts, introductions and magazine articles. His work has been made into films – *Bubba Hotep*, *Cold in July* – as well as the acclaimed US TV show *Hap and Leonard*. He has also had works adapted for *Masters of Horror*, on Showtime, and wrote scripts for *Batman: The Animated Series* and *Superman: The Animated Series*. He scripted a special Jonah Hex animated short, as well as the animated Batman film, *Son of Batman*. He has also written scripts for John Irvin, John Wells and Ridley Scott, as well as the Sundance TV show based on his work, *Hap and Leonard*. His works have been optioned for film multiple times, and many continue to be under option at the moment.

He has received numerous recognitions for his work. Among them the Edgar, for his crime novel *The Bottoms*, the Spur, for his historical western *Paradise Sky*, as well as ten Bram Stokers for his horror works. He has also received the Grandmaster Award and the Lifetime Achievement Award from the Horror Writers Association. He has been recognised for his contributions to comics with the Inkpot Life Achievement Award, and he has also received the British Fantasy Award and has had two *New York Times* Notable Books. He has been honoured with the Italian Grinzane Cavour Prize, the Sugar Pulp Prize for Fiction and the Raymond Chandler Lifetime Achievement Award. *The Edge of Dark Water* was listed by *Booklist* as an Editor's Choice, and the American Library Association chose *The Thicket* for Adult Books for Young Adults. *Library Journal* voted *The*

Thicket as one of the Best Historical Novels of the Year.

He has also received an American Mystery Award, the Horror Critics Award, and the Shot in the Dark International Crime Writer's Award. He was recognised for his contributions to the legacy of Edgar Rice Burroughs with the Golden Lion Award. He is a member of the Texas Institute of Literature and has been inducted into the Texas Literary Hall of Fame and is Writer in Residence at Stephen F. Austin State University.

His work has also been nominated multiple times for the World Fantasy Award and numerous times for Bram Stoker Awards, the Macavity Award, as well as the Dashiell Hammett Award, and others. He has been inducted into the International Martial Arts Hall of Fame, as well as the United States Martial Arts Hall of Fame, and is the founder of the Shen Chuan martial arts system.

His books and stories have been translated into a number of languages. He lives in Nacogdoches, Texas with his wife Karen, a pit bull and a cranky cat.

PAUL FINCH is a former cop and journalist now turned best-selling crime and thriller writer, and is the author of the very popular DS Mark "Heck" Heckenburg and DC Lucy Clayburn novels. Paul first cut his literary teeth penning episodes of the British TV crime drama *The Bill*, and has written extensively in horror, fantasy and science fiction, including for *Doctor Who*. However, he is probably best known for his crime/thriller novels, specifically the Heckenburg police-actioners, of which there are seven to date, and the Clayburn procedurals, of which there are two. The first three books in the Heck line achieved official best-seller status, the second being the fastest pre-ordered title in HarperCollins history, while the first Lucy Clayburn novel made the *Sunday Times* Top 10 list. The Heck series alone has accrued over 2,000 five-star reviews on Amazon.

Paul is a native of Wigan, Lancashire, where he still lives with his wife and business partner, Cathy.

LOUISE JENSEN is the author of international number one best-sellers *The Sister*, *The Gift*, *The Surrogate* and *The Date*. Her novels have sold in excess of a million English language copies and been published in twenty languages, while *The Gift* has been optioned for a film. Louise was nominated for the Goodreads Debut Author Award in 2016 and is a best-selling author of *USA Today* and the *Wall Street Journal*.

ABOUT
THE EDITORS

PAUL B. KANE is an award-winning author and editor who has worked in the fields of science fiction and dark fantasy (most notably the best-selling *Arrowhead* trilogy, a post-apocalyptic reworking of Robin Hood – as Paul Kane – gathered together in the sell-out *Hooded Man* omnibus) and the young adult market (*The Rainbow Man*, as P.B. Kane). He penned the well-received Sherlock Holmes stories "The Greatest Mystery" and "The Case of the Lost Soul", and the critically acclaimed full-length mass-market novel, *Sherlock Holmes and the Servants of Hell* (which appeared on several "Best of 2016" listings and won a Skadi Award). Paul is also the author of the serial killer chiller, *The Gemini Factor*, the number one Amazon best-seller *Pain Cages*, *The PI's Tale* and he has a collection of crime/psychological stories out now called *Nailbiters*.

His other co-edited anthologies include *Beyond Rue Morgue* – all new stories revolving around Poe's detective C. Auguste Dupin – *Hellbound Hearts* and *A Carnivàle of Horror*, while others in the past have featured the likes of Michael Marshall (*Intruders*), Richard Matheson (*Duel*) and Robert Bloch (*Psycho*). He has been a guest at many events and conventions, and his work has been optioned for film and television (including Lions Gate/NBC, who adapted one of his stories for US primetime network TV). Several of his stories have been turned into short films, he is currently adapting his novel *Lunar* into a movie for a UK production company, and Loose Canon Films are turning his story "Men of the Cloth" into a feature. His website www.shadow-writer.co.uk has featured guest writers such as Thomas Harris, Mo Hayder, Stuart MacBride, Ian Rankin, Kathy Reichs and Stephen King.

MARIE O'REGAN is a three-time British Fantasy Award-nominated author and editor. Based in Derbyshire, she is the author of three collections of short stories – *Mirror Mere*, *In Times of Want* and *The Last Ghost and Other Stories* – as well as the novellas *Bury Them Deep* and *Resurrection Blues*. Her short fiction has appeared in a number of genre magazines and anthologies in the UK, US, Canada, Italy and Germany, including *Best British Horror 2014*, *Great British Horror: Dark Satanic Mills* (2017) and *The Mammoth Book of Halloween Stories* (2018). She was shortlisted for the British Fantasy Society Award for Best Short Story in 2006, and Best Anthology in 2010 (*Hellbound Hearts*) and 2012 (*Mammoth Book of Ghost Stories by Women*). Her genre journalism has appeared in magazines such as *The Dark Side*, *Rue Morgue* and *Fortean Times*, and her interview book with prominent figures from the horror genre, *Voices in the Dark*, was released in 2011. An essay, "The Changeling", was published in PS Publishing's *Cinema Macabre*, edited by Mark Morris and introduced by Jonathan Ross. She is co-editor of the best-selling *Hellbound Hearts*, *Mammoth Book of Body Horror* and *A Carnivàle of Horror – Dark Tales from the Fairground*, plus editor of the best-selling *The Mammoth Book of Ghost Stories by Women* and *Phantoms*.

Marie is co-chair of the UK chapter of the Horror Writers Association, and is currently organising StokerCon UK, which will take place in Scarborough in April 2020. She is represented by Jamie Cowen of the Ampersand Agency. www.marieoregan.net

ACKNOWLEDGEMENTS

Time for some thank-yous. To begin with our heartfelt thanks to all the authors who kindly contributed to this anthology – and especially John Connolly for all his help throughout. Our thanks also to Miranda Jewess for taking on this project, Joanna Harwood for all her hard work on it, and the whole team at Titan Books. Thanks to Jamie Cowen and, as always, our family for all their help and support in bringing *Exit Wounds* into being.

COPYRIGHT AND FIRST PUBLICATION INFORMATION

For more fantastic fiction, author events,
competitions, limited editions and more

Visit our website
titanbooks.com

Like us on Facebook
facebook.com/titanbooks

Follow us on Twitter
@TitanBooks

Email us
readerfeedback@titanemail.com